ADRENALINE SHOCKED HER BODY. HER MUSCLES TENSED.

She smelled the earth. She could not scream. She smelled sweat and felt the fear rising in her throat. She tried to see; the bushes scratched at her eyes. She twisted her head violently. Somehow, he had pulled her back on top of him, then rolled on top of her without removing his hand from her mouth. He smelled of gasoline. She wanted to scream. Then she saw the knife . . .

PUBLIC MURDERS

BILL GRANGER

A JOVE BOOK

PUBLIC MURDERS

First Jove edition published February 1980

10 9 8 7 6 5 4 3 2 1

Printed in the United States of America

Jove books are published by Jove Publications, Inc., 200 Madison Avenue, New York, NY 10016

For Ted O'Connor, a good homicide detective and a friend from our South Side days

Author's Note

Realism presents a problem in this book.

The novel is set in Chicago. Chicago is portrayed as it really is and the novel incorporates some names of streets, parks, restaurants and bars, newspapers, famous or landmark buildings—and real job titles—because to do otherwise would destroy the illusion of reality sought.

To further heighten this illusion, I have scrupulously attempted to have my characters follow actual police and courtroom procedures during the unfolding of this story.

Nevertheless, the story is fiction. It did not happen. The characters are creatures of the author's imagination. I know many policemen—and never met policemen with the names used in this book. I know many attorneys and never met prosecutors or defenders with the names given to the characters in this book. To further the sense of fiction, the policemen in this book work out of a special squad of Area One Homicide in police headquarters. At this writing, while there is a Homicide Review Section in headquarters, all Area One Homicide operations are located on the South Side.

I realize that using common Chicago ethnic names— O'Connor and DeVito and Ranallo and Flynn and Kovac and all the rest—might result in a coincidence in which a real policeman or prosecutor with one of those names might exist. But they are not the characters of this novel; the characters portrayed herein do not and are not intended to bear a resemblance to any person living or dead.

Bill Granger

"*There is no such thing as justice—in or out of court.*"

—*Clarence Darrow in Chicago, 1936*

1. THE MAN ON THE MOVIE SCREEN WAS RECLINING ON A BROWN
LEATHER COUCH. HE HAD BLOND HAIR AND DULL BLUE EYES. HE
was naked. He smiled now at the blond woman who came
into view on the screen; she, too, was naked except for dark
stockings fastened to a thin black garter belt. For a moment
she stood awkwardly in front of the man until he made a
gesture. Slowly she sank to her knees on the carpet in front of
him. He reached for her.

It was nine fourteen A.M.

Outside the shabby theater the streets of Chicago's Loop
were rapidly filling with people. It was Tuesday and for the
thirteenth straight day the weather bureau had predicted that
the temperature would rise above ninety degrees Fahrenheit.
In an hour a half-million workers would have completed their
daily treks to the Loop and closeted themselves in the dry
coolness of a hundred air-conditioned buildings clustered
within and around the mile-square confines of the looping
elevated tracks which gave the district its name. It had been
hot for so long this June that the sidewalks never lost their heat
and the pavement seemed to steam. The overuse of
air-conditioners had caused a brownout the day before.

The woman on the screen looked reluctant, even frightened, as she bent forward toward the man's lap. She began to perform fellatio; the dull eyes of the actor now seemed to glisten. He touched her hair. The sexual act portrayed continued for several minutes.

None of the men in the theater spoke or seemed in any way to react to the scene depicted on the screen.

The woman on the screen moaned once.

Outside the theater a policeman wearing the white cap of the traffic division paused to wipe a long bead of sweat from his forehead. He looked at the billboard on the theater which said: "The Finest in Adult Films." He heard an auto honk and turned away and began to cross Washington Street. His name was James McGarrity; he was assigned to direct traffic at the intersection of Washington and Dearborn streets just east of the old City Hall. He was now a half block further east of that intersection.

He walked to the middle of the street and motioned furiously to several drivers sitting in cars waiting to enter a nine-story parking lot. "Double it up, for Christ's sake," he shouted, and the cars, slowly and almost reluctantly, formed a double line of autos at the parking-lot entrance. In forming the lines, they blocked nearly half of the traffic on crowded Washington Street. Patrolman McGarrity received one hundred fifty dollars a month from the owners of the parking garage for facilitating entry into it during the rush hours. Which is why McGarrity was in the wrong place at nine twenty-one A.M. on this hot June morning in 1973.

On the movie screen the scene had shifted. Now a black woman was on the rug by the same leather couch, and a white woman with black hair was crouched over her. The white woman opened her mouth and placed it on one breast of the woman beneath her.

One of the nine men in the theater got up from his seat. He turned away from the screen and started up the dimly lit aisle to the neon exit sign which buzzed above the door. He pushed open the door to the small lobby without turning back to the screen.

McGarrity removed his white cap and wiped his bald forehead again. As he did this, he glanced across Washington

Street and saw the man leave the theater. For a moment McGarrity thought the man looked at him briefly and then shuffled nervously east to State Street. McGarrity replaced his cap and smiled. Pulling his wang at nine in the goddamn morning, he thought. Feels guilty. The man shuffled away and McGarrity noticed he had a gimpy leg. Waves of heat shimmered up from the street and strips of tar patching the sidewalks softened in the early intense sunlight.

Several women had caught their shoe heels in the tar strips that morning.

McGarrity swung around and turned his attention back to the double lane of cars waiting at the garage entrance.

McGarrity noticed the blond then.

She was pretty, he decided. McGarrity was no longer married, but he had a girlfriend he kept in an apartment in Elmwood Park. She was a dark-haired woman of forty-five who worked as a waitress in a west suburban restaurant. McGarrity noticed the blond because she stopped on the sidewalk and consulted a small map.

McGarrity hitched up his gun belt and sauntered from the middle of the street to the sidewalk where the blond stood.

"Need help, honey?" he asked and smiled.

She looked up at him, annoyed. "No." There was a trace of an accent.

"You from outta town?"

"Yes." Clipped.

McGarrity thought she was an unfriendly bitch. He looked at her breasts.

"Where ya going? I can help ya find it."

She shrugged to him and started to walk rapidly away. McGarrity smiled after her. Nice ass too, he commented to himself.

It was the last he would ever see of Maj Kirsten. Months later, it would occur to him who she was. But by then, of course, it would be too late.

McGarrity turned back to his double line of cars.

Maj Kirsten was a Swedish schoolteacher on her third independent tour of the United States. She had decided to fly home tomorrow night on an SAS flight from O'Hare Airport

3

to Kastrup Airport at Copenhagen. From there she had already arranged to take the early morning ferry across the Sound to her native Malmö. She had also decided it would be good to be home.

The tour had gone badly. An unusual heat wave in the eastern part of the United States helped defeat her plans to travel more extensively. She hated the sultry, lingering heat; it drove everyone from the streets, day and night; it created an apathy in her and in the country she was visiting. The heat pervaded everything.

Maj Kirsten was twenty-seven and an independent woman.

This was her first visit to Chicago. On the two previous tours she had gone to New York, San Francisco, Los Angeles, and New Orleans. She had even spent a week on a ranch in Wyoming.

In Chicago she went to Old Town and rented a room at a cheap hotel near the section which was often used by foreign visitors. The night before she met a man in Butch McGuire's bar on Division Street. The bar was a meeting place for young, single people, and Maj Kirsten had felt oddly lonely that night. After several drinks she had agreed to go with him to his apartment; he was not unattractive. Her hotel on Rush Street might have frowned on his company; Americans were difficult to understand in this area, swinging erratically from official puritanism to public lasciviousness.

He had a small, messy, expensive apartment. They drank wine and then made love. He told her he was an accountant in the Loop. In the morning, after they had eaten breakfast together at a restaurant near his apartment, he had driven her to her hotel on his way to work. At first she had wanted to sleep and then decided against it. She took a long shower instead and then dressed; she took her map and purse and walked the short distance from the near North Side to the Loop.

Everything was dirty, she thought. The streets were littered with newspapers and broken bottles. The walls were covered with graffiti. The dirtiness of the city offended her and excited her. She could not explain why.

4

The young man had suggested that they meet again that evening. She decided she did not want to see him again.

She turned down Washington Street, going east, toward the Art Institute; the guidebook had recommended it as a very good museum.

Near State Street she stopped for a moment to get her bearings. Then she noticed a policeman coming across the street toward her. She instinctively did not like policemen; policemen in Chicago were like policemen in Malmö, she had decided. They were venal, and they practiced their petty tyranny on the young and poor.

The policeman smiled at her and asked to help her in a crude accent. The people of New York and Chicago—even those in places of authority—spoke English so badly. She answered him in monosyllables and walked quickly away from him. She was aware that he was watching her.

The Art Institute was on Michigan Avenue, according to the guidebook. Maj Kirsten always made it a point in her travels to America to visit the cultural attractions of each city; on her first visit she had even found a Picasso and a Renoir in a small museum in southern Ohio.

Maj Kirsten taught English in Malmö, and she was probably an Americanophile.

At the corner of Michigan Avenue and Monroe Street she paused again. Two blocks further south she saw the bulk of the Art Institute with its great stone lions guarding the entrance. The sun was halfway to the top of the sky. Maj Kirsten felt tired and hot.

A noxious-smelling bus belched at the curb in front of her. She was nauseated. The traffic light turned green, and she crossed the street, away from the heat of the buildings, to the grass and shrubs of Grant Park.

Like those around her, she developed the habit of walking with her eyes focused straight ahead on some middle distance, ignoring the flotsam of religious salesmen and Hare Krishna dancers and the black men in three-piece suits selling *Muhammed Speaks* and the giggling Puerto Rican boys and—

Her white blouse was stained with perspiration, and beneath her cotton skirt her nylon panties felt damp and uncomfortable. The elastic edges chafed her bare legs.

Suddenly she detoured away from the sidewalk which led to the museum and began to walk on the cool grass of the park. She smelled the lake on a sudden cool breeze.

Her map marked a little harbor just over the railroad bridge, across the park. She hesitated again but then she smelled the breeze a second time and decided to cross the park to the lakefront to refresh herself with the sight of water and boats.

She had eight minutes left to live.

She took her shoes off on the grass and carried them in her right hand, holding her purse in her left. She felt her bare feet sink deeply into the carpet of grass which still carried a trace of the morning's dew. The bead of sweat forming across her forehead was blown away by a steady new wind from the lake. She felt much better now; it had been so hot in the Loop's prison of buildings.

For a third time Maj Kirsten paused.

She had a sudden, overwhelming need to urinate. It had been this way—the sudden urge—since her long infection six years before. She glanced around; she had crossed the railroad bridge over the Illinois Central commuter tracks and now stood next to a broad field. The neat geometry of the field was fringed with thin trees and bushes and the center of grass was sectioned into four softball diamonds. About a quarter mile diagonally across the field she saw a wooden lavatory; a sign reading "Women" pointed toward it. As she started across the field, she saw a group of black children playing softball on one of the diamonds.

The city noise churned on beyond the trees.

She thought about these things as she walked: her boyfriend, Sig Mansson, would not know what ferry she had decided to return on. The traffic from Kastrup to the old harbor could be very slow in the morning in the narrow streets of Copenhagen. If she were lucky, she could catch the nine o'clock ferry and be in her apartment by eleven. They could have lunch together if she did not feel too tired. Sig was a teacher too. He had broad shoulders, the broadest she had ever felt. When she returned, it would be cool in Malmö. It

6

would be a relief to speak Swedish again. Sig would come to see her right away, after she called him. Then...

The hand pulled her backward.

She landed heavily in the bushes at the door of the lavatory.

She clutched her shoes in her right hand and still held her bag tightly in her left.

She was startled. Adrenaline shocked her body awake; her muscles tensed. She smelled the earth around her. She could not scream. She smelled sweat and felt the fear rising in her throat.

She couldn't see clearly. The bushes scratched at her eyes. She twisted her head violently.

He had pulled her back on top of him and then rolled on top of her, all without removing his hand from her mouth.

His hand smelled of gasoline.

She wanted to scream, and then she wanted to vomit.

That was when she saw the knife.

It was an ordinary butcher knife. The kind her mother cut bread with when they had all lived in Gothenburg before Malmö and before—

He seemed angry and muttered to her; but his words weren't English or Swedish.

She forced herself to become calm.

It was familiar to her, like the sound of her own voice, like a dream before waking.

He pushed her skirt above her waist, tearing the zipper.

She felt him pull at her blue panties. She thought her eyes were open, but she could not see. There was only light and flashing of the sun.

She smelled many things: bread, coal, earth, a glass of Scotch whiskey she had first drunk when she was sixteen at a party in Helsingborg. Scotch whiskey like smoke.

She did not struggle against him. She lay on her back and tried to count. He forced her legs open. She smelled his sweat. It would be over soon. He was very heavy on her. When he penetrated her, roughly, the pain arched down in her legs, across her back. She stretched her back.

Soon it would be over.

Now she could see. There was the knife only. She could see

7

her own terrified eye reflected in the blade. She watched her own eye staring at her.

When he pushed the blade of the knife into the side of her neck, severing the jugular, it did not surprise her. She was very calm. And then the spurt of blood foamed over her eyes and blinded her again in redness. The calmness surprised her.

Again he slashed down and plunged the blade to its length above the left breast, pulling it down through the skin, muscles, veins, and arteries, scraping against the ribs and then cracking them, ripping her heart.

Maj Kirsten was dead then.

"Who found her?"

"Kid." It was Sid Margolies.

"Kid? What kid?"

"Kid over there with Jackson. We already talked to him. Kid named Wallace Washington. He says he was playing softball with a bunch of other kids, by that diamond over there. He had to pee, he says, and he came across her. That's when he found her. He says he went back to the other kids and they split. So he called the poh-leese."

"Public spirited." Matthew Schmidt, the tall, cadaverous lieutenant of homicide, looked at the black kid; the boy was staring at the covered body. The lieutenant spat then on the dry, hard ground. The grass around the body was bloody.

"Who talked to him?" asked Schmidt.

Margolies took out his little notebook. "I did."

"You happen to ask him if he could read?"

"No," said Margolies, scanning his notes. He was imperturbable, even in the face of Lieutenant Schmidt's frequent sarcasm.

"Why do you suppose he wanted to take a leak at a women's lav? The men's room is over there."

"Oh." Margolies studied his notebook. "I did ask him that. I just didn't know what you meant by reading. He said he was going in the bushes."

"Bullshit," said Matthew Schmidt. He wore a blue suit despite the heat, and a light straw hat. The brim shaded his dark blue eyes.

Schmidt turned away from Margolies to the plainclothes

sergeant near the body.

"Who was she?"

"You're not going to like this."

"I don't like it already. I don't like people being killed in broad daylight in Grant Park. It's enough to ruin my week."

Terry Flynn consulted the notebook. It was smaller than Margolies's notebook, and the handwriting in it was not as neat. "I can't pronounce this first name. Looks like Madge or something. Her last name is Kirsten. K as in Kitty, I Ida, R Robert, S Sam, T Thomas, E Edward, N Nellie. I got her name out of her passport. She was carrying it. A Swedish passport, Matt."

"So she was a tourist, right?"

"It looks that way. There were some letters in her purse, also in some foreign language that looks like the stuff in the passport. Little dots above some of the letters—you know. I guess it must be Swedish. I saw 'Sverige' on the passport, that's Swedish, I think. She lived in—wait. M-A-L-M-O."

"Malmö," Schmidt repeated. "It's across this bay from Copenhagen. I was there once. Three years ago when Gert and I went to Europe."

"Yeah."

"Well, let's look at her."

Matthew Schmidt had been in homicide for nineteen years, and he hated dead bodies. The sight of them always startled him. He avoided wakes as well. And he did not like the smell of flowers.

He pulled back the rubber cloth covering her head. Her eyes were open. There was dried blood on her face, and her neck and her blouse was still wet with soaked blood. Her face was white.

"It looks like he raped her too," said Terry Flynn slowly. "Her panties were torn off. He must have been huge. There are bruises around her pussy."

Matthew Schmidt pulled the rubber open, revealing the lower part of the body. The moment of panic at the sight of her—it was always the same for him and he was ashamed of it—was past. He looked carefully at her torn and bloody sexual organ.

After a little time during which they said nothing, Matthew

Schmidt pulled the cloth carefully back over the face of Maj Kirsten and stood up. His knees crackled.

"Flynn. Call First District and ask for Dalby himself. Tell him I would appreciate it if he could send a couple more uniformed men over here. I want to find that knife or whatever it was. The blood on her blouse is still wet. I want to search the park, thoroughly, *now*. He might still be around. I want one sweep starting at the Field Museum on the south end and working north on both sides of the Outer Drive. Get a second sweep working south from the parking lot. Include the west side of the park, on the other side of the IC tracks, all the way to Michigan Avenue. Flush all the bushes—winos, lovers, muggers, everyone. Take the obvious ones over to First District, but get the names of the others. Tell Captain Dalby this is priority, Flynn. If Dalby doesn't respond to your usual pleasant approach, tell him he will talk to the superintendent this afternoon. This is not a cheap murder, and his help is not open to negotiation."

Flynn was writing it all down; Schmidt spoke in a purposely flat voice that seemed to carry a shrieking edge. Four years before he had been operated on for lung cancer. One more year and he could say his body had been free of cancer for five years. The doctor assured him that his chances for survival were very good. But it frightened him all the time to think of the death that had been in his body and might still be there, waiting to fool him. Almost as a reaction to it, to the fragility of life, he had become quiet, slow to speak, introspective. Or perhaps he had always been that way and was now aware of it and exaggerated those traits. Of course, he did not smoke anymore. Once in a while, when the shrieking edge threatened to overwhelm the calm, he sat at home alone and consumed a bottle of bourbon. Those were the times when he was very frightened.

Flynn folded his notebook and shoved it into his sweat-stained shirt pocket. "I'll tell him, Matt. He'll know what you mean." Flynn turned and walked to his car parked on the grass behind the wooden public lavatory. The sun was almost directly overhead, and because he did not want to sit on the hot vinyl seat, Flynn reached through the open car window and took his radio microphone in hand.

Terry Flynn was glad to be working with Schmidt again. He liked the older man. They had met when Flynn was just a uniformed tactical cop working out of Area Two on the South Side. Normally a lieutenant did not direct a murder investigation—let alone a sergeant; but a murder in Grant Park—any murder so public, so fraught with ramifications beyond mere life and death—called for investigators with clout inside the department. Flynn called First District on the radio.

Matthew Schmidt strolled over to the coroner; like everything else, the coroner's office had changed its designation in recent years to the more technical sounding "medical examiner's office." But the same red-faced coroner's man who had examined the body on Schmidt's first murder case was waiting with the two policemen who would remove the body in the squadrol to the county morgue on West Monroe Street.

"You got everything, Mattie?" asked the coroner whose name was Watson.

"Yeah, Doc." Schmidt looked back at the rubber-covered body. "Must have been a butcher knife."

"Or a bayonet. But something big," agreed Watson.

"About noon?"

"Oh, Christ, I don't know. Noon. Eleven. Even ten o'clock. The colored kid told Margolies he found the body at twelve fifteen. Precise little bastard. I'd say eleven or thereabouts off the top of my head."

Schmidt bit his lower lip. Everything had been taken care of, but he was reluctant to close up a "scene," as the homicide detectives called it. They had an almost magical faith in the scene of the crime and its power to extract an emotional confession from the killer then and there. But there was no one to question except one young boy, and it was indecent to leave the remains of this young woman in the sun, covered by a rubber bag.

"You got all your photographs?" said Schmidt.

One of the young policemen volunteered that the police photographer was already back at Area One Homicide with his roll of film.

He nodded. "All right. You can have her."

"Thanks, Mattie," said the old coroner. "I'll see you down at the morgue later."

But Schmidt had turned away, back to the small crowd of spectators standing a few feet from the body, held in check by a surly traffic patrolman. Schmidt looked at the faces of the curious. Did any of you kill her? The faces told him nothing. Then he spotted the young reporter from the *Chicago Daily News*.

"What do you want here?"

"Can you tell me who was she? What happened? We got on the radio that she was shot down—"

Schmidt glanced at the name he had copied from the passport.

"Her name was Maj Kirsten," he said. He spelled it. "Twenty-seven. She was stabbed at least once in the neck, several times in the breast."

He waited while the reporter copied down his words. Unlike some of his colleagues, Schmidt talked to reporters. Along with his mystical faith in the power of "the scene" was a belief in the ancient practice of raising the hue and cry: a murderer is at large among us.

"She was from Sweden. Correction. She carried a Swedish passport and we assume now she was a visitor in the city. It appears there was a possibility of rape. Her clothes were in disarray, but they had not been removed from her body."

"Were her panties torn off?"

Schmidt looked at the reporter. He guessed he was about twenty-two. "Yes." He made a face. "They had been torn off."

"Got the murder weapon?"

"No."

"Any motive?"

"Of course. But we don't know what it was. Some money may have been taken from her purse, but there's a ring on her finger. Also her wristwatch was left."

"Can you give me a description?"

"Not very well beyond her age. She was blond." He felt sick to his stomach, and the old wound across his chest flared. "She had blue eyes." They had stared at him.

"Any suspects?"

"We're following several leads."

"Did—"

"No more now." Schmidt spoke quietly. "Except you can put out that this was a very bloody crime. Whoever killed her had blood on his clothes. A lot of blood. Someone had to see the blood. You can put that out."

"Thanks, Lieutenant. I got your last name right?" He showed him his painful scrawl. The name was wrong. Schmidt did not bother to correct it.

"Hiya, Matt. I got Dalby."

Schmidt turned and saw Sergeant Flynn cross the grass toward him. Schmidt waved him away from the reporter.

"It's set. Couple of uniforms'll be here in a few minutes. He wasn't very happy about it, but he couldn't resist my honeyed words."

Schmidt smiled. He felt terrible. He wanted a cigarette. "The hell with Dalby."

"What now?"

"Oh, the usual thing. You run the sweeps, Flynn, and then hit some of the joints where our old colleagues congregate. Get the word out. This guy is a real creep, but it might be one of our old, familiar creeps moving up to the big leagues. Take a look at the people you find in the park—don't leave it to the uniforms. Or get Margolies to go over them at the district. If we get any good-looking suspects, let's call up Donovan and see how the state's attorney wants to handle this thing. I don't like public murders like this, there's too much heat. You haven't had one like this before, have you, Flynn?"

"Don't you remember? I was in uniform on tac when I was with you down at Area Two. When that broad started trash-compacting her kids."

"Oh yeah." The trouble was, Matthew Schmidt could always remember the bodies. "That was public, wasn't it?"

"Yeah," said Flynn. "But not like this." He watched Schmidt like a bright student who studies a teacher's face to learn the tricks and find the truth revealed in little gestures.

"The papers'll go crazy this afternoon and the TV tonight. I'll take the heat on it, Flynn, as much as I can so you and Margolies can get the damned thing cleared. If we can clear it. I'll talk to the superintendent this afternoon and the same with Ranallo."

Flynn nodded. Leonard Ranallo was chief of homicide.

"Did you or Margolies find a hotel key in her purse?"

"No."

Schmidt sighed heavily. "There's still the kid to talk to. He didn't come all the way across the field to take a piss. He saw something."

"That's what Margolies thought." Flynn was defending Sid Margolies to Schmidt in case Schmidt thought Margolies had fallen down on the interview.

"Then he should have asked him about it." Schmidt stared at Flynn for a moment. He was glad the sergeant had defended Margolies; Flynn, he thought, came on like an aggressive and unthinking loudmouth, but there might be more there.

"We don't have another man. See if you can get one of the smarter-looking uniforms to do the hotel check. She might have been in the Hilton, down at this end of the Loop."

Flynn wrote it down. There wasn't anything more to say. The doors of the blue-and-white squadrol, which was nothing more than a small truck, slammed shut. Inside, on a bench that usually carried prisoners to the county jail complex and drunks to the district lockup, lay the body of Maj Kirsten. It was one fifty-three P.M., and the temperature was now ninety-six degrees.

Because he did not own a car, Jack Donovan usually hitched a ride to the Loop from Dominic Lestrada, an assistant state's attorney in the criminal division who lived rather ostentatiously in one of the Marina City towers. The arrangement suited them both. Because Lestrada was ambitious and aggressive, he saw the ride to the Loop from the West Side Criminal Courts building as a chance to propound his legal theories to the boss. Donovan, as chief of the criminal division, did not appreciate Lestrada's rather banal ideas but did appreciate the ride from the courts. So, on most nights, he endured twenty minutes of Lestrada on the Law to save himself forty-five minutes on public transportation.

Tonight, as usual, Lestrada pulled to the curb at the corner of Wacker and State, and Donovan got out and waved goodnight. He walked a block south down State Street, under the brilliant marquee of the Chicago Theater to the subway-el entrance. It was a little past seven o'clock P.M. and the city was still bathed in smoky, humid light.

As usual he bought the first editions of the morning newspapers at the corner and went down the steps to the subway. He brushed past a sinister figure insistently selling an underground weekly paper in a doom-laden voice. The salesman cursed him as he passed. Donovan continued down in the manner of those around him—as though in a trance. He pushed through the turnstiles, went down the escalator, and waited on the platform for the roaring whoosh of the northbound A train. When it screamed into the station, he pushed with the others through the doors, found a place to stand and brace himself, and opened the papers. He began to read about the murder of Maj Kirsten.

Both of the morning newspapers—the *Sun-Times* and the *Tribune*—had played the story on page one. This, in itself, might seem unusual in a city that counted nearly nine hundred murders in one year. But this was a public murder and not mundane. A man had not killed his wife. A black teen gang had not murdered a grocer on the South Side. This murder involved a white woman, butchered (as they put it) in daylight in Grant Park, between the hulking Loop skyline and picturesque Monroe Street Harbor. Further, as the papers pointed out sternly, she was a tourist, a guest of the city. She had also been "brutally raped," and the newspapers understood that such a thrilling murder was of more interest to their readers than bloodshed in Southeast Asia or even the new wage-and-price guidelines. Jack Donovan had understood this as well when Matt Schmidt phoned him that afternoon.

Two years before, Jack Donovan had been appointed chief of the criminal division for the state's attorney's office of Cook County. He did not understand then why the new state's attorney, Thomas P. Halligan, had given him the job. Though he did not especially desire the job, he did not reject it. Some people saw his passive acceptance of events in recent years as strength; Donovan knew that was wrong.

It had turned out all right.

"Bud" Halligan was a buffoon in many ways but a shrewd buffoon. He had largely left the handling of the sprawling criminal division to Donovan—except for the interference from time to time of Leland Horowitz.

Horowitz had been Halligan's campaign manager in his successful bid for office. So Halligan had made Horowitz his first assistant.

At first Horowitz had tried to pack the clerical staff with party patronage workers, and Jack Donovan had resisted. There had been a showdown in Halligan's office. Though Halligan had compromised on some of the people Donovan wanted to keep, he had sided mainly with Horowitz. Jack Donovan had nearly quit then, but his entrenched passivity led him to do nothing. A few months later Horowitz again made personnel selections, this time in the ranks of the lawyers—the assistants who prepared and tried cases. Again Donovan went to Halligan, and this time Halligan had sided with Donovan against Horowitz. Donovan now thought he knew where Halligan stood; he also decided he could live with it.

The El suddenly bolted out of the subway tunnel and climbed effortlessly to the tracks thirty-five feet above the street as it rumbled into the North Side. Sunlight flashed across the thousand rooftops of the old three-story flat buildings. Donovan sighed and folded his newspapers. Two teen-agers pushed to the doorway of the train next to him. Both were smoking beneath the defaced "No Spitting, No Smoking" sign. Donovan turned from them and stared out the window.

The train slowed into rickety, wooden Fullerton Avenue

Station, and Donovan pushed out through the doors onto the wooden platform, down the steps, through the grimy turnstile, and onto the sidewalk. The trance was broken. He paused, rubbed his hands across his mouth, and decided he wanted a drink; it had become a usual decision in the past year. Quickly he walked two blocks east to Halsted Street.

He pushed the door into the Seminary Restaurant and walked through to the cocktail lounge in the back. It looked like a lot of other bars, but he had gotten used to it; some ex-cops drank there and so did a few priests and students from nearby DePaul University. He sat down and rested his hands on the plastic cushion that edged the bar top. His shirt was wet from the heat; he had long since loosened his tie. The bar was very cold, and he thought he heard the air-conditioning system thump and hum from somewhere behind him. He looked around and didn't find anyone he knew. He realized he was disappointed.

"Vodka and tonic. No lime," he said and pushed a five-dollar bill across the bar top.

He drank the first very quickly. The second only a little more slowly.

The third felt better. Someone was saying the Cubs were going to win the pennant this year. It was the same talk every June. Jack Donovan was raised on the South Side, and when he had been interested in baseball, was a White Sox fan. He didn't think they would win the pennant either.

The man next to him started to talk to him about the murder of Maj Kirsten, and Jack Donovan realized he would get drunk if he stayed. He did not want to talk about the murder. He took his change from the last drink, shoved it in his pocket, and got up.

The heat outside hit him like the opening of a furnace. He sucked in his breath and turned down the block. He lived in a one-bedroom apartment carved out in an old four-story building on Cleveland Street. He had lived in the neighborhood for six years, ever since he had given up the kids to Rita. He had seen the old families of the neighborhood move out and watched the real-estate speculators move in and renovate the old, post-Fire of 1871 houses into apartments for the young and affluent. The neighborhood made him feel like a stranger now.

In the vestibule of the building he opened his mailbox and found the usual bills, then unlocked the hall door and went up the stairs to his apartment on the third floor.

There were two locks on his door.

He pushed it open at last and felt the welcome rush of cold air from the air-conditioning units in the living room and bedroom. He shut the door behind him and dropped the bills and newspapers and keys on a little table in the vestibule.

The telephone rang.

He shuddered. No one called him, and he preferred it that way. This call might be more about the murder or about some trial gone to jury. Or—or it might be Rita.

He let the phone ring three times and then went to the kitchen and picked it up.

"Hello? Jack?"

He listened to her voice. He felt cold. Maybe the air-conditioning was on too high.

"Jack?"

"Hello."

"I wanted to catch you when you came in from work."

"You caught me."

"I called you before. You weren't home."

It *was* cold. In their first apartment he slept with Rita's body cupped in his, belly to back, under the old comforter. Did she still have the comforter? Everything got lost eventually.

"Jack? It's about the boy." She always called Brian that. "The boy's got into trouble again at school. They sent him home. I have to go down tomorrow to get him back in. Father McCauley says he was stealing."

Jack Donovan waited, frozen in his own passivity, in the dark coldness of the apartment. Rita didn't want him to speak except to scream, to say he couldn't stand it or that he didn't give a damn. He waited.

"I just wanted to let you know about the boy."

"What do you want to do?" he said quietly.

"It wasn't that much money. Maybe it wasn't even the boy

at all. They just blame things on him."

"Then why send him to a Catholic school anyway?"

She laughed. But the laugh held no amusement. "Because we promised to raise him a good Catholic. Remember, Jack?"

He remembered that when they heard the children stir in sleep, he would uncouple himself from the warmth of Rita beneath the comforter and tread across the cold floors to the back bedroom and see his children in the dim half-light of the hallway. There would not be a sound beyond the window but that of the wind or of the El rumbling past.

She laughed again. "Don't worry. That's why I called you, Jack. I promised I'd call you about the kids. Because you wanted me to, so I'm calling you."

Sometimes, not very often, Rita went down to the tavern on Ninety-fifth Street and got a little drunk and called him from the telephone booth. But he had not heard the operator break in, and he decided she was probably at home. Not that Rita drank often or called often. Just enough.

"All right, Rita," he said.

"I'm going down to school tomorrow and take care of it, Jack, just like I always do." St. Rita the Martyr. He waited.

"Oh, Jack, sometimes I just think the boy needs someone else." St. Rita the Good. St. Rita the Mother of Us All. Holy Mother of God, pray for us.

He waited.

"Jack, what should I do?"

"I don't know." And he didn't. Leave me alone, Rita.

"Well, I just wanted to let you know. Are you all right, Jack?"

"Yes."

"Isn't it hot?"

"Yes."

"But I'll bet it's cool there on the lake where you are."

"Yes."

"You don't sound right, Jack."

"I'm all right."

It came to an end, finally, after another minute or an hour; he couldn't be sure. When he heard silence, he replaced the receiver on the cradle. He stood for a moment in the coldness of the apartment and slowly began to remove his clothes. He carried them into the bathroom and carefully sorted them. Then he took a long shower, scrubbing his thin red hair with bar soap. He got out of the shower and looked at his narrow face and green eyes. He stared at his image for a long time.

When he went back to the living room, he prepared a giant vodka and tonic for himself. He sat down in his towel and turned on the television. He was not hungry; he would go out later and have a sandwich at the Seminary and a few drinks and look for a familiar face.

He awoke much later.

The television set was still on, but programming had ceased. There was a buzzing of white noise coming from the set. Why had he awakened?

The telephone was ringing.

The phone. He groped toward a lamp and turned it on. He was very cold. He shivered in the towel and went to the kitchen and picked up the receiver.

"This is Goldberg. I'm on felony review down at Area One."

"Who?"

"Goldberg. Down at Area One."

An assistant. Working night duty on review at Area One.

"Yeah?"

"I'm sorry to bother you at home, but I thought I should call you."

"What time is it?"

"Three."

"Three." He repeated the time, but it didn't seem to mean anything.

"That Kirsten murder this morning."

"Kirsten?"

"Kirsten. In the park. A woman, a tourist."

"Yeah?"

"The cops just got someone."

"Who?"

"A wino, some guy they found in the park—"

Jack Donovan was awake now and alert. "Bull. They can't pull that crap on me."

"Well, that's who they got, and I figured you'd want to know."

"Who picked this guy up?"

"Arresting officer is a motorcycle cop named Delancey."

"What kind of crap is this?" He shook his head. "Who's running the case right now out of homicide?"

"Lieutenant Schmidt."

Yes, that was right. He had talked to Matt.

"This is bullshit, Goldberg. Did you talk to the cop?"

"Yeah. The creep's name is Norman Frank. He's a hillbilly, I think, but we didn't get anything from him, he's so damned drunk. Like I say, he looks like a bum."

"And where'd they find him?"

"This three-wheeler cop named Delancey found him about one A.M. In the park. He had a lot of blood on his shirt when they brought him in, and he was bruised up a little. So we took his shirt and we're gonna send it down to the lab. But it isn't open right now. I had to ask the assistant super to get someone."

"What did the guy say?"

Goldberg misunderstood. "He said something about overtime."

"Not the superintendent. The suspect."

"Norman Frank. He told Delancey he cut himself. That's why there's blood on his shirt."

"Did he?"

"No. No cuts on him at all. Just some bruises. Fairly good bruises. And a little cut above his right eye."

"So there was a cut."

"No, Mr. Donovan. This was a little cut. And his shirt was soaked with blood."

"What does it look like to you?"

There was a pause. Donovan realized that Goldberg was going to be very careful. Goldberg, being new in the state's attorney's office, was assigned to the dreary chore of felony review. He was one of the men who waited in the area offices and tried to evaluate arrests from the legal standpoint at the moment they took place. The program had been started with federal funds. Naturally the police detectives resented the young lawyers telling them the worth of their cases and arrests.

"Well, there is blood. Lots of it. And if the blood can match with this Kirsten woman...oh, they didn't find a weapon."

"This really sounds like crap, Goldberg. A wino. Is Schmidt there?"

"No. They called him at home, but the regular guys on night homicide are handling it."

"Get me Schmidt's number."

"Well, they called him twenty minutes ago and he said he was coming down, so I figure he must be on his way."

"Goldberg. Tell the super you talked to me. Who's on tonight?"

"Hills."

"Tell Hills you talked to me and that we'd appreciate it if he could get someone in the lab. I'm coming down. Don't let anyone charge anyone until I get there."

"They haven't made a move. Delancey wanted to, but the homicide guys said they wanted to check out the area where he found this Norman Frank guy."

"Good. I'm coming right now."

"Sorry I had to wake you up."

"It's all right. These fucking motorcycle cops. Sitting on those motorcycles fucks their brains up."

"It seemed important enough to wake you."

"It's important," said Donovan. "More important is not to let us get our collective tit caught in the wringer."

"Yeah. Us and the cops."

"Fuck the cops. Mainly us."

Donovan replaced the receiver gently and stood in the kitchen scratching his head. He felt a little sick, and it was hard to think. The kitchen clock said three-thirty A.M. Beyond the coolness of the dark apartment, the hot black night waited in stillness.

Donovan opened the refrigerator and took out a can of Old Style. He popped the top and went to the window and squinted out at the quiet street, illuminated by a dull orange glow from the high-intensity, anticrime lamps. There was no breeze.

2. JACK DONOVAN ENTERED THE SMALL ROOM WITH GREEN-PAINTED WALLS. THERE WERE TWO WOODEN DESKS BUTTED against each other on one wall; above the desks was a calendar from the Federation of Police. A small electric clock next to the calendar said it was four thirty-two A.M.

Matthew Schmidt was leaning against a green filing cabinet next to a window; the window was dirty. From below the window came the familiar grunt of a bus pulling away from the curb down State Street.

"Where's Goldberg?" asked Jack Donovan, nodding to Schmidt.

"Down the hall. Taking a leak. I got here myself about fifteen minutes ago. Unfortunately the arresting officer has already talked to the kid from *Chicago Today* because I just got a call from downstairs about it. The *Daily News* has sent a man over." Schmidt, despite the hour, was dressed and shaved and looked awake. He wore a blue suit, one of several that he owned.

"Where did they find him?" Donovan asked.

"He was sleeping it off under a clump of bushes right where Columbus Drive butts into Monroe Street. He was wearing a white shirt. Soaked with blood. Some of the blood was stained on the skin of his forearms and chest. Unfortunately they couldn't rouse anyone for the lab until seven A.M. so I suppose we'll have to wait. In the meantime we're holding him on a disorderly."

Donovan continued to stare at his shoes. He wondered when he had shined them last. "Who is he?"

"A wino. Name of Norman Frank. A shitkicker."

"Where's his flop?"

"He wouldn't say. Or couldn't at the time."

"Oh."

"Delancey," said Lieutenant Schmidt. "Delancey is the motorcycle cop who found him. The guy had no papers. There was an empty bottle of muskie next to him."

"Anything on the knife or whatever?"

"Nothing."

"Delancey made the call to homicide?"

"Yes. Relatively quickly. He brought Frank in first. He said he tried to question him. He said he tried to find out where the guy flopped. But Delancey's persuasion was not sufficient. Or our wino was too drunk."

"So now Delancey has called the paper boys to protect his collar."

Schmidt shrugged. He couldn't blame Delancey for his ambition, but he had no wish to antagonize Jack Donovan either. For a lawyer Donovan wasn't a bad sort; he had once been a cop. Schmidt stared at the record on his desk. No one spoke when Maurice Goldberg entered the little room.

"Hi, Mr. Donovan," said Goldberg. He smiled.

Everyone waited. Finally Goldberg began his recitation. Donovan finally held up his hand. "Well, what do you think, Goldberg?"

Goldberg blushed. He was flattered by Donovan's deference.

"I don't know. I think we have to wait until we get a lab report on the blood."

"And the trousers?"

"No." Goldberg looked startled. "I don't—"

Donovan turned to Schmidt. "One of these guys looked at the trousers? . . ."

"I don't know," said Schmidt.

"Christ." Donovan turned away from Schmidt. He had no wish to embarrass him by staring at him. "Tell someone to get the trousers. And shorts if he's wearing any."

"I'm not sure—" began Goldberg.

"Matt," said Jack Donovan.

But the old lieutenant was already on the phone. "Hello? Hello? Is this Holloway? This is Matt Schmidt up in homicide. Your lockup boy—Norman Frank?—get him a pair of pants to wear and take his for the lab. And the underpants. Right. Right. Label them and send them down."

Jack Donovan did not say anything more. Matt Schmidt was a good enough man. It had not been his fault.

Donovan finally said: "I don't think we should do anything until we can interview him and until we get the lab report. Will you talk to him, Matt?"

"Sure. I'll get Terry Flynn or Margolies with me. Or both of them."

Donovan turned back to Goldberg. "I want to tell you why I don't like any of this." He paused. "We got a wino, first of all. Generally winos do not rape or kill young women. It isn't their style." Donovan looked at Schmidt, but the old, lined face was impassive. "They don't have the energy, for one thing. But now we apparently have a wino found with a bloody shirt. If the lab reports that the stains on the shirt match blood from, from"—he glanced at the report on the desk—"from Maj Kirsten, we merely have confirmation of an unusual coincidence."

He went to the door of the little room and looked out. The fluorescent lights in the corridor buzzed coolly. "Is there semen on his trousers?" Donovan continued. "Or his shorts? That would be a second confirmation of circumstantial evidence, but it would probably be enough. But what I am trying to tell you is that I don't like this goddamn suspect one bit. I've never heard of a wino involved in a random daylight rape-murder and—"

Goldberg interrupted: "But the blood. It was there."

"Maybe he stole the shirt. Maybe he stuck a chicken. Maybe he cut another wino."

"And he was found less than a mile from the murder scene," continued Goldberg. "Do that many bums sleep in Grant Park?"

"Who knows where bums sleep?" said Donovan. "God. On a hot night."

"I see," said Goldberg.

Schmidt did not say anything. He took out a toothpick from his shirt pocket and began to pick between his molars. Despite his crisp appearance he felt very tired.

No one spoke for a few minutes. It was as though each of them was intent on absorbing the stillness of the summer night and the empty corridor and the buzzing of the overhead lights. Schmidt looked at the calendar. When he had thought he was going to die from cancer, he had put a calendar in his bedroom and stared at it and tried to calculate the days he would be alive.

Donovan sat down suddenly in an empty chair. "Don't do a thing, Goldberg. Not until you get the reports from the lab on both the semen, if any, and the bloodstains—and until Matt here has talked to this guy, Frank. I mean nothing." He waited for Goldberg to speak, but Goldberg was studying the end of Matt Schmidt's toothpick. It bobbed and weaved in his mouth.

"There's not a lot we can do about Delancey calling the papers now," said Donovan. "But Matt can duck them. That's up to him and the rest. But don't you do anything. When the day man comes on felony review, tell him you're handling this case for me. I might as well stay up and get something to eat. I got to go to Twenty-sixth and California. I expect I will hear from you before court time. Then we can figure out what to do."

Schmidt spat out the toothpick and missed the wastebasket. He bent down and picked up the sliver of wood and placed it in the basket. "I'll make sure on the lab, Donovan. We should have it by nine. I'll let Mr. Norman Frank sleep it off until eight in the morning. Do you want Goldberg there?"

"I'd prefer it. But whatever you want to do, Matt."

Schmidt nodded. He appreciated the courtesy from the state's attorney's office. "I'll have him there."

"Don't let Delancey near Frank again, Matt. That could screw it if this guy is for real."

"I know. I'll tell him we'll give him the credit but to keep his yap shut."

"Good."

After another silence Goldberg said, "Is there anything else?"

"Don't call Bud Halligan, whatever you do. Until we have something more."

They agreed that would be best.

The killer awoke.

He knew he was awake, but he did not open his eyes. He lay very quietly, listening to his own breath. It was slow and regular. Other times, when he woke up, he could hear his heart beating very fast, and he was afraid then that he would have a heart attack. A bank of pain would spread across his chest beneath the breastbone, extending under his arms and around his back.

But there was no pain this morning.

He kept his eyes closed so that he could see the blond woman again. At first she was walking across the grass. Her breasts swayed beneath the white blouse. Then he became confused again: he thought she wore nylon stockings, but her legs were bare.

The slut had even spread her legs, inviting him into her. Slut.

Now he could hear his heart. It was beating loudly and rapidly. He was remembering. The girl had worn her first pair of nylon stockings at the age of fourteen when she was going to a party. He only found out about it afterward. When he saw the stockings hanging in her room.

Why did he remember that?

He tried to call up the image of the blond woman again, as she was, walking across the grass, but the other image, the later one, the one of the face covered with blood, blocked his memory.

He listened to the old woman snoring.

She had not made a sound when he stabbed her, but she had opened her eyes wide, as though surprised. Then her blood stained his shirt. He had not believed that would happen. He had not really believed any of it would happen. She had not worn nylon stockings. Why did he think she had?

He heard the clock ticking next to the bed. He listened to the ticks and then to the beat of his heart. The blood pounded in him. There. The pain again.

It began to spread slowly across his chest. Now he knew he would not sleep.

He opened his eyes and waited.

It was shortly after nine in the morning when Jack Donovan pushed through the massive door at the entrance of the Criminal Courts building. The two black security men waved him through while other security men patted down the steady stream of visitors and lawyers and criminals and relatives of criminals and victims and jurors and all the others who came to the old stone court building every morning.

Jack Donovan noticed none of these things; they were too familiar. Lost in his own thoughts, he ran up the stairs to the second-floor offices of the state's attorney's criminal division.

Mrs. Farrell was in the outer office before him. She usually was. Donovan glanced at the wall clock as he pushed into the retreat of his own office. Because the ceilings in the old Criminal Courts building at Twenty-sixth Street and California Avenue were very high, they made the rooms look small and dark. There was no rug on the floor of his office and, in fact, there was little to distinguish it from anyone else's office in the rabbit warren of storerooms and conference rooms and offices. On one faded wall was a picture of Thomas P. Halligan, the state's attorney. Someone had placed it on the wall automatically after his election. Jack Donovan did not mind it very much. On a second wall there was a large calendar from the county clerk's office.

And that was all.

Donovan had walked from police headquarters to Grant Park and the murder scene in the hour before dawn. He had first gone to the wooden lavatory building where the body of

28

Maj Kirsten had been found and then had traced the route to the place where Norman Frank was found in the bushes and arrested. He didn't know what he was looking for.

After awhile he had taken the Madison Street bus west into the early morning black ghetto where the county morgue building was located, on Monroe Street. There he went into the basement to look at Maj Kirsten's body.

He stared at her face. It was now composed. Her eyes were closed.

From the morgue he took another bus to Twenty-sixth and California and managed to drink a cup of coffee at the little restaurant across the street from the courts. He was very tired and felt depressed by the hour, by the silent city, and by the composed face he had seen in the basement of the morgue.

He sat at his desk and pushed the intercom. "Mrs. Farrell—"

"Mr. Halligan wants you to call him," she interrupted.

"I'm not here yet."

"He said to say he wanted to talk about the arrest in the papers this morning."

"Bring me some coffee, please. Then send in Mario."

"All right. As soon as I can," she said. Her voice reminded him of sour milk.

Mrs. Farrell would not be put off. "There was also a call already from Mr. Horowitz." Leland Horowitz, the first assistant and chief political meddler in the office. Of course he would call.

"Thank you."

"Do you want me to get Mr. Horowitz?" Mrs. Farrell persisted. She conducted intercom conversations like a guerrilla fighter.

"No. Not now." He looked at his watch. It was time for Matt Schmidt's call. He glanced at the headline on the final edition of the *Tribune* on his desk. Delancey had protected his collar very thoroughly. Norman Frank was ready to be hanged.

He rose, stretched and yawned, and walked to the dirty window that cast a long, gloomy light into the office. There was nothing to see. It was an air shaft, a penitentiary of light that formed a small square down through the building to let in air and light and a promise of sunshine.

He put his fingers on the window.

Beyond the building, on the other side of the courtyard in the back, was the rambling Cook County Jail building, one of the largest county jails in the nation, serving the largest single criminal courts division in the country. Waiting in the tiers of the jail were thousands of men and women: some were still to go to trial and were technically not guilty of any crime; others were serving sentences. All were treated the same.

Mario DeVito entered the office without knocking and flopped down at one end of the leather couch.

"Hello, Jack."

Donovan did not turn around. He tried to look up through the air shaft. The day was cloudy.

"Close the door, Mario."

Mario groaned and, reaching with his foot, kicked the door closed.

Donovan thought: the office was air-conditioned and the overhead light was sufficient. Really, there was no need for an old-fashioned air shaft anymore. It reminded him only of how closed in the office really was.

Jack Donovan turned. Mario DeVito had placed his feet up on the chair next to the couch. Donovan leaned against the window ledge and gripped it with both hands.

"As you can see, we have a suspect in the killing of that Swedish girl whether we want one or not," he began quietly. "Personally, I don't. He's a wino, a hillbilly, and some goddamn motorcycle cop found him down in Grant Park this morning wearing a bloodstained shirt. They didn't find a knife. That would be too much. So the arresting officer lets the newspapers know all about it. Technically, unless someone has screwed up, the guy is still a disorderly conduct until I hear from Matt Schmidt and from the crime lab."

"How bloody?"

"Bloody enough."

"And so Bud Halligan already knows."

"You're better than Jeanne Dixon."

"And Horowitz called you already."

"Keep it up. We'll get you an astrology column."

Mario smiled his wide broad-toothed grin. "Little bit of heat, eh, Jackie?" Donovan tried to smile in return. "So when is Matt Schmidt going to call you to tie this guy up?"

"Before court. Any time now."

Mario DeVito did not say anything; there was no need. Jack and Mario had been friends for a long time. They had gone to DePaul Law School at nights together, and Mario had helped him when Rita had gone insane. A long time before.

Mario said, "I never heard of a wino raping no one. They can't get it up. It's a scientific fact."

"I know. Goldberg called me at three thirty this morning from Area One Homicide. Goldberg did the right thing. He's a bright boy. Maybe we ought to bring him out here."

"I know him." Mario made a face. "Leave him where he is. He'll be out soon enough. He'll have my job in a year and yours in two."

"As long as he can take Halligan and Horowitz."

"The Gold Dust Twins," said Mario. "If Goldberg wasn't a Jew, they could elect him state's attorney."

But Donovan was following another thread of conversation. "Think about Goldberg. I like him. Anyway, I went down to Area One and Matt came in. He looked like hell."

"You look like hell yourself at four in the morning," said Mario. "But I know what you mean. I saw him testify last week in the Washington-Lee trial."

"Yeah. Well, I don't think Matt cared for the bust either, so I told him to talk to this guy Norman Frank and call us—"

Mrs. Farrell buzzed his office. It was Matt Schmidt on line one. Donovan picked up the telephone and punched the appropriate button.

"Yes, Matt?"

"He's ours for now."

Donovan felt sick.

"Why, Matt?"

"Type A on the shirt. She was type A. He's O. He's still a little shaky about last night. I interviewed him with Goldberg and Margolies. He said he got drunk with a friend of his and ran out of money. So he mooched a bit down in the Loop and then decided to flop in Grant Park. He said he got enough for a bottle of muscatel and then went over to the park. He said he usually lived over at the Red Lion Hotel."

"That's on Clark near Oak Street?"

"Yeah. Flop heaven. I'll send a man over there to look it over. So I asked him to tell me about Maj Kirsten. He said he never heard of her."

There was a pause. Jack Donovan looked across the desk at Mario and shook his head.

"We talked about his problems. He's got problems. He came up here from Lynchburg, Tennessee, six years ago and said his wife died and his children went back to Tennessee to live with relatives. He said he lost his job a year ago. He used to be a truck driver. I listened to him, and then I brought up Maj Kirsten again. Then Margolies started on him hard and I cooled him, but he wouldn't say anything. Then he said he really wasn't sure."

"What?"

"He said he wasn't sure."

"What does that mean?"

"I don't know. He says he sometimes blacks out. I asked him where he kept his knife, but he said he didn't know."

Matt Schmidt's voice was low and flat, as though he were reading from a notebook. Which he probably was.

Mrs. Farrell came into the office. She carried two paper cups of coffee and put them on the edge of the desk and quickly turned away so that she did not have to acknowledge Mario DeVito's little wave of thanks.

"Go ahead."

"Norman said he kept an old army bayonet knife for protection, but he didn't know where it was now. He said he was robbed once when he flopped in a crib in one of those chicken-wire rooms they got at the New Era Hotel on Skid Row. So he said he had a knife but he didn't know where it was. He didn't even know where his gear was. Norman is a careless boy."

"What about the bloody shirt?"

"Norman seemed amazed. He said he must have bled when Delancey roughed him up."

"Is he roughed up?"

"A little. I don't think Delancey really did very much. He must have got his nose bloody and there's a little bit of swelling above the left eye. He could have got that falling down."

"Delancey has the mentality to keep him on three-wheelers for the rest of his life."

Schmidt did not respond.

"The lab checked the trousers," he finally continued. "He wasn't wearing any underwear. The trousers have traces of everything from catsup to dried wine, but there's no semen."

"Did he use his prick for a spoon?"

"He's thirty-eight years old, and when we checked with the feds, they said he served two years for auto theft in Tennessee in 1963."

"Truck driver," said Donovan sarcastically.

"He killed someone."

Donovan closed his eyes for a moment and tried to see Matt Schmidt, to catch the tone of voice and connect it with a phantom face. "Are you sure?"

"He killed someone or he knew someone who killed someone. He's trying to get something out to us but he won't let himself."

"Did he kill Maj Kirsten?" Donovan asked quietly.

"I don't know."

Another pause.

"Hold him. Talk to him some more, Matt. I'll call you back."

"All right."

They broke the connection. Donovan picked up his coffee and sipped it. It scalded his tongue.

"You got a customer?" Mario inquired mildly.

"It seems he may be forced down our throats."

"What's it all about?"

Donovan began to explain, quietly, slowly, the facts of the matter and his own reservations about Norman Frank. He realized he was not presenting substantial objections, but he valued Mario's opinion and he knew that Mario could grasp the nuances of all that Donovan could not even say aloud.

As he spoke the clocks in the old building passed ten A.M.

Now the vast, bumbling juggernaut of bureaucracy stumbled again into motion in the sprawling, incoherent system of courts and jail of Cook County. It had started again: the crimes of passion committed during the long, hot, windless night were now exposed and picked over like bleaching bones laid out in the cloudy daylight of justice. Judges entered their imposing oak-paneled courtrooms from their chambers in the rear; bailiffs stood around with beefy arms folded; clerks called the courts to attention; lawyers in three-piece suits crowded forward with briefs and pleas and writs while clerks dickered with lawyers for appearance times set in the future, and judges attempted to fill in the court calendar in the long, losing race against merely staying even with the swelling sea of cases. All the while prisoners taunted one another in the dirty lockups behind the courtrooms while more bailiffs watched outside the cages, regarding the prisoners as though they were strange animals captured for a zoo.

And in the long corridors outside the stifling courtrooms they waited and smoked and talked to each other in low voices and ate sandwiches and drank coffee and laughed— the deputies, bailiffs, state police troopers in Boy Scout hats, Chicago policemen and suburban cops and men from homicide, general assignment, robbery, vice, tactical, narcotics, and gambling; undercover policemen from the Illinois Bureau of Investigation and the Chicago police red squad; gang members and their relatives, petty thieves out on bail; rapists, murderers, Mafia killers, armed robbers, political activists, and assistant prosecutors. All of them were actors on the dozens of stages of the bureaucracy of crime and justice. Their performances spilled from courtrooms in the old Criminal Courts building on the West Side to the new family court house; to the Civic Center courts in the Loop across from City Hall; out to the suburban branch courts of the Cook County circuit court system which encircled the city like a stolen necklace; to police courts in the six police areas of the city; to courts in police headquarters like the gun court and women's court full of strutting pimps and tired whores; to courts in the old warehouse building on South Michigan Avenue, including violence court, as though violence were a thing apart from crime; to courtrooms secreted in the massive red-brick traffic court building on the banks of the Chicago River north of the Loop.

Every day it came alive, enmeshing thousands of lives, a monster of a thousand heads reborn with the morning court call.

Quietly Jack Donovan finished his explanation of the case involving the rape and murder of a Swedish tourist named Maj Kirsten. Mario DeVito finished his cup of coffee and contemplated the dregs. He looked up at Jack Donovan who was still leaning on the windowsill. He liked Jack very much and sometimes he felt sorry for him.

"Well," Mario said. "Hang it on him."

"I can't explain it, Mario. I just can't believe he did it. It doesn't work. Not that it's so neat—I can understand that. But it still doesn't make sense. The guy is a stewbum."

"Well, you can't let him go."

"I wish I had the weapon."

"Yeah. And I wish I had a name for every gun in the Chicago River."

Jack Donovan was silent, but Mario was agitated now. He got up and began to pace.

"Look it, Jack. Matt Schmidt isn't a rookie. He's got his feeling about it too. And he thinks Norman did it. You ain't even talked to this creep."

"You're right."

"So why stick your neck out on this? You got the papers, you got Halligan, you got the cops. What's the percentage for you to hold the process of justice up?"

Mario spread his hands; Donovan smiled. "I've got to tell Matt something. I wish I had a little more time."

"So does Maj Kirsten," said Mario.

"Cheap shot," said Donovan. "We're not in court now."

"I'm sorry."

Donovan considered. Was this instinct of his only further evidence of his inability to act and to make a decision? Or was it a valid feeling? Why the hell wait anyway?

He pushed himself up from the sill and went to the intercom on the desk.

"Get me Maurice Goldberg. He's at Area One felony review."

A moment later Mrs. Farrell said, "He's on line two."

"Hello, Goldberg. Tired?"

"Hello. No, not really. I sat in on the questioning, but I figured you wanted to hear it from Lieutenant Schmidt." Donovan smiled at Goldberg's clever self-deprecation.

"What do you think, Goldberg?"

"I think we've got enough for a charge."

"What, for instance?"

Goldberg sounded confused. "Murder? Rape?"

"You want to do it?"

There was hesitation. "Uh. Mr. Donovan. This is a major charge. I don't mind going ahead, but is that the way you want it handled?"

"Why not?"

"Well, Mr. Halligan was calling over here. He talked to Margolies who didn't really seem to tell him anything. And the newspaper guys are all over the place. We got the first edition of the *Daily News* here, and it says the cops got the killer of Maj Kirsten and that he's been charged with murder."

Donovan smiled at Mario.

"Okay, Goldberg. We'll go along with the *Daily News*. Get him booked through on murder and rape and stay out of the rest of it—Matt Schmidt can handle it. Ranallo at homicide will probably want his piece of the credit, and I'll talk to Halligan later. Tell Matt we really have to have a weapon to go to the grand jury with."

"I'll tell him. What about the newspapers?"

"Fuck the papers. Let Lee Horowitz handle that shit. I don't want to see quotes in the papers, okay, Goldberg?" His voice was not friendly anymore; his tongue had been scalded by coffee and his stomach hurt. "That's not your concern, Goldberg. Go home." He hung up.

Mario was smiling. "Didja scare Sammy Glick?"

"I don't know. He wears on me a little. But he's young. I still think you ought to bring him out, Mario, and see what he can do."

"You're the boss," said Mario. "Feel better?"

"No. Now I have to call Uncle Bud Halligan."

"Suffering is good for the soul, Jack. It makes you a better man." Mario grinned. Then, he said:

"Well, I've got to go upstairs and see Judge Frankenheimer this morning, so I better go. Did I tell you he's thrown out three gang cases this week, including one murder? Remember that grocery murder? Son of a bitch. All insufficient evidence. Little prick. I wish one of our little black brothers would carve him some night. Maybe his heart would stop bleeding then."

"What does he want with you?"

"Conference. He wants to talk about the declining quality of prosecution."

Mario DeVito was in charge of trial work.

Jack Donovan sighed and sat down behind his desk. There were little pieces of paper scattered on it, all messages. "It is, isn't it?"

"Declining? Sure. We want to keep up with the times. We should only prosecute when we've got fourteen witnesses and the arrest is made by Jack Webb."

"Delancey," Donovan said suddenly.

"Who?"

"That goddamn motorcycle cop."

Mario was annoyed; Donovan was not listening. "Frankenheimer let off fucking Geoffrey Tucker last week, de big hit man of de Black Gaylords."

"You told me," said Donovan. "Do you want me to go up with you?"

"Fuck, no. I'll handle the little Kraut bastard."

"Take it easy, Mario."

"Yeah." He finally threw the empty coffee cup in the wastebasket. "Two points. You know, Davis had really prepped that case. We even had three witnesses—"

"And they all scattered—"

"Because de big judge, he granted de big lawyer, Rev. Peebles, six fucking continuances." "Rev. Peebles" was Mario's name for Thomas Peebles, a prominent defense lawyer who specialized in criminal gang cases. Geoffrey Tucker was his client.

"Don't worry about it, Mario," Donovan said softly. He

reached for one of the slips of paper on his desk and began to dial a number. Without another word Mario DeVito left the office.

Justice moved swiftly in the case of Norman Frank, thirty-eight, unemployed, of no fixed address.

He was charged with murder (one count), rape (one count), unlawful use of a weapon (one count), and assault with a deadly weapon (one count).

He was taken in a squadrol to the Criminal Courts building on the West Side. The trip took thirty minutes in the late-morning traffic, and Norman Frank slept on the soiled back seat of the locked van. The squadrol pulled into the courtyard behind the building where Frank was taken out and to the elevator used for prisoners.

A Chicago policeman and a deputy sheriff escorted him to the fourth-floor courtroom of Judge Thomas Mulroy. Mulroy waited in the chambers until the public defender and prosecutor were ready. The clerk told him there were four reporters in the court as well.

Mulroy entered the courtroom quickly, mounted the bench, and looked down at the forlorn countenance of Norman Frank. Then he looked out at the reporters. He beckoned the public defender forward and told him to confer with his client.

At one A.M. Norman Frank was taken to court. His hands shook. The public defender asked that bail be set at ten-thousand dollars. It was a formality. Mulroy denied bail, and the prisoner was taken through a back door to the lockup and then down in the elevator to the long tunnel that connected the building with Cook County Jail. He was being held for the grand jury on a murder charge.

3. THE HEAT WAVE BROKE FINALLY IN THE AFTERNOON DURING STATE'S ATTORNEY THOMAS P. HALLIGAN'S PRESS CONference.

Jack Donovan had finally phoned Halligan at ten twenty-three A.M. after deciding to go ahead with the prosecution of Norman Frank. Once Halligan got the news of Frank's imminent arraignment, he ran down the carpeted hall in the Civic Center building to Leland Horowitz's office. That office had two doors. Halligan went in quietly through the back one.

Horowitz, a small man with neatly plastered gray hair and wide, incredulous eyes, sat at his desk reading a newspaper.

Secretly Halligan felt envious of Horowitz's desk. It was the largest in the entire state's attorney's office, including Halligan's own.

Halligan told his political mentor almost everything about the arrest of Norman Frank except Donovan's own misgivings. Horowitz told Halligan he would call a press conference as soon as the arraignment was complete and before the police superintendent called his own press conference. They set the time for one o'clock which, it turned out, was technically three minutes before Norman Frank even appeared in court.

The conference was held in a little white-walled room off the main corridor of the downtown office. Halligan entered and stood behind the lectern inscribed with the seal of Cook County. He waited for the television crews to finish setting up.

Channel Five was late and that delayed the conference further. Meanwhile the reporter from the *Chicago Daily News*—pressing his last deadline—got Halligan to release a brief statement to him while the TV crews finished their work. This annoyed the *Chicago Tribune* reporter, who reminded Halligan he was the only Democrat on the county ticket supported by his paper in the previous election. When they were all ready to go, Halligan began:

"Today, I am pleased to announce the arrest and arraignment of Norman Frank for the brutal rape and murder of a Swedish visitor to our city, Miss . . . er . . . Maj Kirsten, whose body was found yesterday in Grant Park. Thanks to quick work by Chicago police led by Commander Leonard Ranallo, chief of homicide, and his men, and our own office, led by Assistant Maurice Goldberg and John J. Donovan of the criminal division, we believe we have tracked down the man responsible for this brutal slaying. Justice delayed is justice denied, and in this case we believe we have acted swiftly and responsibly to bring the guilty to our court of law as quickly as possible consonant with the rights of the accused."

After the statement there were the usual questions, and Halligan began to field them as the clouds finally broke with rain. The rain fell in winding sheets that slashed at the city from the southwest, blowing rain against the open windows on the fourth-floor cellblock of the massive county jail where Norman Frank was now held.

The rain washed at the grime on the tall gloomy window in Jack Donovan's office where he sat eating the remains of a bologna sandwich he had purchased in the cramped lunchroom. The rain danced across the plaza in front of the

Civic Center and washed down the rusty sweeping sides of the huge Picasso statue in the center of the plaza.

On the streets of the Loop office workers out for a breath of air on their lunch hours were caught suddenly by the rain. Some of them dashed for their offices down slippery sidewalks, and others walked calmly with newspapers shielding their heads from the rain. Within a few minutes the streets were empty of pedestrians, but cars and buses and cabs continued to course their way along the wet, glistening streets.

The rain caught everyone unawares.

Including Angela Falicci.

She was a student at the Art Institute school. She had gone to the Monroe Street Harbor at noon to paint a picture which would bear no resemblance to the small boats moored there. She worked with acrylics, and angry dashes of red and orange were splashed on her canvas though the predominant colors of the harbor at that moment were blue and green and gray.

When the rain began, she found brief refuge in the entrance of the Chicago Yacht Club. At one-forty P.M. the storm let up briefly, and she ran from the entrance up the winding road to the Outer Drive and then darted across the drive with the lights in her favor. At that instant the storm renewed its force, and lightning flashed in the western sky over the towers of the Loop. New clouds came up, gray and green and menacing.

Angela Falicci was frightened by the rain. She had always been afraid of the noises of a storm.

She ran along the line of trees that led to Columbus Drive, usually called the Inner Drive.

A sudden clap of thunder startled her, and she dropped her acrylic paints. There was a second thunderclap, and the sky was lit furiously by a third lightning bolt that danced on the television antennae atop the Hancock building.

She bent to pick up the paints. She felt frustrated and angry with herself. Her painting was ruined.

The action saved her life.

The form—was it a man?—passed very close to her. She smelled his breath.

Thunder rolled. She turned and screamed. Then she saw

the flash of a knife. Another wave of thunder rolled over the embankment of buildings that fringed the park.

She screamed again.

Was it a man? She thought she heard footsteps behind her as she ran.

No one. No one. But she ran across the open field, and the rain pelted her in large drops. If she looked behind her, she would die. She ran until the breath in her lungs ached.

The trees and bushes were blurs, and she was sure of the sound of steps behind her, splashing in the mud, gaining on her.

Once she slipped and fell, but she scrambled up quickly and ran on.

She screamed again. Why wasn't there anyone to hear her?

She stumbled across the railroad bridge, fell, got up, and ran on. There, ahead on Michigan Avenue, were people bent against the rain, holding umbrellas and briefcases; there cabs cruised the streets and the great green buses muscled their ways along the road.

Safe.

On the stone steps of the Institute, she slipped again and fell hard on her knee. Blood trickled from the cut.

Angela Falicci sat down on the steps, crying, and that was how the guard found her.

At the same moment a puzzled patrolman from the First District station sat talking to Angela Falicci in a waiting room inside the Art Institute, Sergeant Terrence Flynn of Area One Homicide was on his way to the Red Lion Hotel on Clark Street.

Flynn pushed open the doors of the flophouse and knew he had smelled worse. Not that it didn't smell bad. But then Flynn had worked a long time in the ghetto slums of the South Side before he was transferred up to Loop homicide. Because he liked to consider himself a limited man, Flynn's goal in life was to work homicide on the Northwest Side of the city in Area Five, where murders were few. And where the buildings did not smell bad.

He went to the little niche under the worn stairs that served as a front desk. There was a big iron safe behind the desk. A thin man with a gray complexion sat in the cubicle, reading the Daily Racing Form.

"Hiya." Flynn did not pull out his star. It was usually unnecessary. The only people with clean shirts who went into places like this were cops.

The man with the racing form did not look up but managed a grunt.

"I want to know about one of your guests, Norman Frank."

Without looking up, the thin man pushed the register toward him. Flynn shoved it back across the counter so violently that it struck the clerk in his chest.

"Hey, what the—?" The man looked up. "What the hell're you doing? Ya hurt my chest."

"Don't play games with me, shithead." Flynn reached across the counter and tore the racing sheet from the clerk's hand, then threw it on the stained carpet.

"Hey. Whaddaya want? We got no beef here. You got no right."

"I asked you a question."

"You got no right to talk to me like that. I know Captain Nelson at the district."

"And I know Jesus Christ. Listen, you dumb son of a bitch. I ain't from East Chicago Avenue station, I'm from homicide, and I ain't on nobody's pad, and this ain't a game. So answer me when I talk to you, or we're going bye-bye."

Flynn realized that Lieutenant Schmidt would say he was turning on his charm.

"Awright, will ya? I didn't know who you are." The gray man lit the end of a new cigarette with the smoldering remains of an old one in a tin ashtray. "What's the guy's name again?"

"Norman Frank."

"He ain't here."

"I know he ain't here. Tell me about him. Where's his room?"

"He ain't been here for a month. Look in the book."

"If I got to play with that book again, I'll shove it up your ass."

The clerk reached for the book and gave Flynn a hard look.

He flipped to a page marked "May." He turned the book around carefully. "See, he ain't been here for nearly a month. He was here about two months and then he got into some trouble with one of the guests and he split."

Flynn waited.

"I ain't seen him around. Ask around the corner at the tavern. I don't know about the guy."

"Where's his gear?"

"He didn't leave nothing here."

"Who's the guy he had trouble with?"

"I don't remember."

"Sure you do."

"You shouldn't treat people like that. You got no right to treat white men like that."

"When's this place been inspected last?"

"What?"

"You know guys, I know guys. My cousin works at the fire inspection office."

"Come on, buddy. We had to pay off the building department just last month."

"Tough."

"Guy was named Shorty, I think. Honest to Christ, I don't know."

"What kinda trouble they have?"

"Hell, I don't interfere with the guests."

"Shit, there isn't anything you don't know about these stewbums. What kinda trouble?"

"I don't know."

"Norman Frank carry a shiv?"

"He had a bayonet, I think."

"Where is it?"

"Musta took it with him."

"Where's his gear?"

"Took it with him. He was paid up, so I didn't hold nothing. This ain't the goddamn Greyhound depot, you know."

Flynn stared at him, and the gray man squirmed under the gaze. "I'm tellin' you on the square."

"Listen. What's your name?"

"Frankie."

"Listen, Frankie. This isn't for fun." He pulled out a color Polaroid picture from his notebook. He held it up. It was a picture of Maj Kirsten, dead.

"Who's that?"

"You tell me."

"Looks like a hooker."

"Someone you knew around here?"

"Listen, all we get are nigger hookers and fags around here. And the stewbums. Shit, you go out on the corner of Bughouse Square at night and those fag whores practically rape you driving through."

"You go that way, Frankie?"

"Fuck no. I ain't no fag. And I don't let no fags in this joint neither. This is strictly a residential hotel."

Flynn nodded and wanted to smile. "You seen this woman though."

The gray man named Frankie studied the picture. "I can't say I did. But you never know. They all look alike, all got blond hair. She sleeping?"

"Dead."

"Norman Frank do it?"

"Did he do those things?"

"How do I know?"

"Look, Frankie. I don't want trouble for you. I just want to know about Norman Frank."

"I don't know anything more'n I told you. The guy just split. And took his shit. But if I see him, I'll call you."

"Sure. But you won't be seeing Norman Frank for a while."

"Got him, huh?"

"What about the bayonet?"

"I don't know, I told you. Listen, I ain't gonna fuck around with a murder beef. Why didn't you tell me it was murder when you came in?"

"You didn't ask." Flynn replaced the picture in his notebook almost with tenderness. He dropped a card on Frankie's desk, turned, and walked out.

When Flynn was out the door, Frankie threw the card in the wastebasket, leaned over the desk, and picked up the scattered racing form.

Outside it was still raining and very dark for the middle of the afternoon. Flynn looked at the heavy sky and decided he might as well hit the tavern, too, while he was there. Besides, his father, a patrolman for years, had once told him, "A good copper never gets wet." Flynn edged along the building to the tavern door fifty feet away.

The bar was permeated with the odor of stale beer and a bad basement. Flynn moved down to the end and leaned against the bar top. He knew he smelled like a cop to them but that was all right. Sometimes a fleabag bar like this had old-timers who didn't hate cops but lived quietly on their meager Social Security checks in bad hotels and spent their afternoons trying to forget everyone had forgotten them.

As he waited for the bartender to come over, he noticed two customers quickly downing their shots and walking out.

"You wanna beer?" asked the bartender.

"Make it J and B and water," said Flynn who was trying to lose weight. He knew he looked like a beer drinker.

The bartender brought the drink in a short glass.

Flynn sipped at it. The bartender waited. Flynn had not paid him.

"You know a guy comes in here named Norman Frank?"

"Lotta guys come in here."

"Good. I'm glad business is so fine. This was a southern guy with a long face and real white skin."

"We get a lot of hillbillies in here from the flophouse around the corner. I don't know all their names or maybe I know only their street names. Those guys all got street names. Maybe the night man knows. He comes in at six."

"This guy Norman Frank was staying around the corner. I wanna know some more about him. You wanna take a look at a picture of him?"

"You from the district? We got no trouble in here. We're okay. Call Sergeant Fogarty over in the district, he'll let you know."

Flynn waited. When he trusted his voice, he said, "I'm not from the district and this doesn't have anything to do with this joint. I just want some information about this guy Norman Frank. He must've come in here. I wanna know who his pals were."

"I dunno anything about the guy."

"You wanna look at a picture?"

"I got no time for pictures. I got customers."

Flynn finished his drink and set it down. The little bartender stood waiting to be paid.

"I'm from homicide. This guy Norman Frank is involved in murder, and if you're obstructing, you're involved too."

"Fifty cents for the drink."

"Hard case, huh?" Flynn pulled a bill out of his pocket. The bartender cranked a register, made change, and threw it on the bar.

"What's your name?"

"Krause. What's yours?"

"This is all you gotta see, Krause." Flynn flashed his star and replaced it in his pocket.

"Okay, Captain," said Krause with sarcasm. "If you were to head over to Top's joint on LaSalle, you might find out a little more about your buddy."

"Top's?"

"Just down on LaSalle Street. I remember maybe this guy Norman. He came in here awhile, but I had to eighty-six him."

"Why?"

"He had a hard-on for this steady customer came in here. So one night I got to call the cops on him, and he spent the night in the lockup. So he comes in the next day and I said, 'out' and I eighty-sixed him."

"Who was the guy?"

"What guy?"

"Guy he fought with."

"I don't want no trouble for him."

"You don't want no trouble for yourself, Krause."

"Hey, don't come on like Kojak. I'm okay. I got friends, too, and you wanna lean, lean and you'll fall flat on your fat Irish face."

Flynn pushed suddenly away from the bar and pulled his pistol.

"Okay, clear the goddamn bar. Everyone out. Police."

He stared down the line of drinkers.

"This joint is closing early. Everyone out now."

The drinkers stared.

"Police, you goddamn rummies. Get the fuck out of this joint. We're closing up early. Come on, come on, move it, move it—" His voice seemed to break the spell. The customers awoke from their afternoon stupor and began moving toward the door. Krause started for the telephone in the middle of the bar.

"Who you calling, Krause?"

"I'm calling the cops, you goddamn crazy man."

"I am the cops, asshole," said Flynn. The last patrons stumbled out into the rainy half-light of the afternoon.

"You bastard, you bastard," Krause screamed. His face went purple, and his eyes seemed to bulge.

"You're under arrest for obstruction of justice, you son of a bitch. Play with me, you little shit, you little Kraut bastard, you'll eat turd pie before I get done with you."

"You drove my customers out," Krause yelled.

"Get your fucking raincoat, you heinie son of a bitch."

Suddenly it was over. Krause went to the back bar and took down a bottle of J&B Scotch and brought it to Flynn. He poured the light Scotch in the glass.

Flynn put the pistol back on his belt and closed his suit coat. He picked up the glass and smelled it. "Water," he said.

Krause splashed water on the Scotch and waited.

Flynn sipped the drink.

"Let me see the picture."

Flynn passed across the picture of Norman Frank, front view and profile.

"Yeah."

"Who did he have trouble with?"

"Guy named Shorty."

Flynn waited.

"Shorty. Always comes in here." The voice of the bartender sounded dull and drained. "Shorty what, I don't know. But Shorty. He don't work too steady, but he comes in here two, three times a week. A hillbilly like Norman What's-his-name. I guess they're both from the same burg or something. Small world, huh?"

Flynn put down the drink and shoved the remaining coins across the bar. Krause didn't move.

They waited for a moment.

"I'll bet you find Shorty over at Top's now. Always goes over there in the afternoon. He'll be there for sure. Shorty. Little short guy with a moustache, one of those real thin moustaches like William Powell wears in the late late show. Looks like William Powell, in fact, if he was short. Hey. Maybe he was."

"Where's Shorty flop?"

"He did flop 'round the corner at the Red Lion, but I don't think he's been there awhile. I dunno where. But go over by Top's. You'll find him there. Specially on a crummy day like this. Jesus Christ, look at this joint. You drove all my customers out."

One week after her murder the body of Maj Kirsten was placed in a metal shipping coffin. Her father, Gunnar Kirsten, of Malmö, had asked that the body be shipped back to Sweden. All the tests had been completed at the morgue, and there was no longer a reason to keep the remains.

The papers were all signed and delivered with the body to the Simplon Funeral Home on East Ohio Street. There it was embalmed, packed into a coffin, and transported to O'Hare Airport. At eight P.M. it was placed aboard the S.A.S. flight to Copenhagen.

The story of the body's departure was movingly recounted by a columnist for *Chicago Today*, and there were other stories of the crime and of the arrest and jailing of her accused killer, Norman Frank. But the community outrage was satisfied by the arrest, and the story held the front page of the four papers for only three days.

Ten days after Norman Frank's arrest a story appeared in the *Tribune* on page twenty-four reporting that he had petitioned the court for reduced bail because he had been beaten by fellow inmates in the jail. In fact, Norman Frank had been beaten when he attempted to resist the sexual advances of a powerful inmate named Thurgood who had the run of the fourth tier. Frank's objection to his rape had been futile in any case and the story in the *Tribune* only lasted one edition. Five days later another story buried even further in the paper said that Norman Frank had been indicted on all charges by the June grand jury and that he had appeared pale and nervous at his formal arraignment in felony court later that day. A third request for a lower bond was denied.

After that the story disappeared from the public consciousness.

But the search for evidence continued even though the sense of urgency that had first surrounded the case was gone. Jack Donovan, chief of the criminal division, asked Mario DeVito to handle the preparations for trial. Norman Frank had pleaded not guilty at his arraignment.

At first DeVito called Lieutenant Matthew Schmidt of Area One Homicide at least once a week on the case. Later he only talked with Sergeant Flynn. But there was nothing new. Shorty was gone, seemingly disappeared, and so was Norman Frank's gear, including the bayonet. No one could shed further light on its whereabouts.

Nearly four weeks after the murder a certified public accountant went to Area One Homicide and was interviewed by Investigator Sid Margolies. He had dated Maj Kirsten the night before her death and had been afraid to come forward. He made a statement and signed it. It added nothing to what they knew about her last day.

In July Norman Frank was moved to the jail infirmary after a second beating while imprisoned on the fourth tier of the jail. Jack Donovan called the superintendent of Corrections after a private plea from Norman Frank's public defender. Donovan told the superintendent that he did not want Norman Frank to die before trial. For his own protection Frank was to be isolated in a deadlock cell after he was returned to jail. Donovan then called the sheriff of Cook County who had charge over the jail and repeated that Norman Frank had been raped twice by inmates in the jail and that the superintendent of corrections made vague promises about his safety. The sheriff made a remark about Norman Frank getting what he gave the Swedish woman. Finally the sheriff said he would telephone the superintendent and explain the seriousness of the matter.

Naturally the family of Norman Frank had been notified

of his incarceration and indictment on charges of rape and murder. The family—in the person of his uncle, Alvin Frank—said Norman Frank had always been trash and no one would have expected more of him.

The brief report on the alleged attack of Angela Falicci in Grant Park on the afternoon after Maj Kirsten's murder was written and filed with the First District. A copy of the report was routinely circulated to the vice squad.

On the morning of July 18, when the temperature had again risen to ninety-seven degrees Fahrenheit, Mr. and Mrs. Omar Dalrymple of Duluth, Minnesota, decided to take the Wendella lake cruise from the foot of Michigan Avenue.

The Wendella craft was docked in the Chicago River, and the green sluggish water slapped at the hull as the Dalrymples and the others got aboard.

Omar Dalrymple, fifty-seven, was a pharmacist attending the Midwest convention of the American Pharmaceutical Association. He and Mrs. Dalrymple had decided—with a certain spirit of mischief usually foreign to their natures—to skip attendance at the annual breakfast installation held in the grand ballroom of the Conrad Hilton Hotel. Instead they decided to take the boat tour which their friends assured them was a treat. Omar Dalrymple had been to Chicago only once before in his life, after he was mustered out of the navy at Great Lakes in 1946.

"We'll just treat ourselves this time," he said to his wife, and that was why they were the first ones aboard the Wendella that morning and why they chose the airy front seats in the prow.

And that was why Omar Dalrymple was the first man to see the body in the river.

Omar Dalrymple looked over the side and saw the white, bloated remains and said, "My God." When his wife leaned over to look at the sight, he said, "Look away, Martha. There's a body in the river."

Of course, Mrs. Dalrymple turned to look at it more thoroughly.

The skin on the hands was gone so that the bones were visible. Because the corpse was facedown in the water, Mrs. Dalyrymple did not feel as sick as she thought she would. They stared for a moment, and then Omar Dalrymple made his way to the middle of the boat where a thick-necked sailor stood taking tickets. The sailor thought the man wanted his money back.

"Captain, there's a body in the river."

The sailor, Peter Stephenowicz, went to the side of the boat with the frail-looking pharmacist and stared down at the bundle of rags and swollen skin bobbing in the gentle river current. It looked like the body was snagged on a piling on the north side of the river.

"I better call the cops," he said to no one. But Mrs. Dalrymple nodded and then turned to stare at the body. Other passengers joined them at the rail.

Stephenowicz jumped off the boat with a light step that did not seem suitable for his thick body. He pumped a dime into the pay telephone on the bright dock.

"There's a body in the river right at Michigan Avenue," he said.

Now, it is a peculiarity of the Chicago police districts and area commands that the river divides them. On the north side of the river begins the East Chicago Avenue police district and Area Six Homicide; on the south side begins the First (Loop) police district and Area One Homicide. So the police dispatcher on the phone asked Stephenowicz: "Which side of the river is it in?"

"Right in the river," said the sailor.

"If it's on the north side, I call one district, and if it's on the south side, I call another," the police dispatcher explained. It was absurd, of course, but the young patrolman had been impressed by a superior who once told him the hoary story about the man who jumped into the river from the Michigan Avenue Bridge. When his body surfaced, it floated towards the First District side but the police there, who did not want to handle the matter, got a long pole and pushed the body to the other side of the river.

"It's on the north side of the river," the sailor said at last. "I think it's snagged on a piling."

"Can I have your name, sir."

"Fuck no." The sailor hung up and walked to the ticket shed and told them what had happened. The captain came down the steps and decided the boat could pull out without disturbing the corpse in the water.

Several people wanted their money back, but most of the rest wanted to go for their lake cruise.

As the ship pulled away, the police from the Eighteenth District arrived at the pier, but, since the fire department boat was near the scene, neither police district actually pulled the body from the water. It was taken to the morgue.

There was a further oddity: the firemen on the boat, as they wrapped the wet body in a rubber body bag, discovered something tangled in the clothing. It was a knife, and apparently it had been stuck into the body and never dislodged sufficiently to float away from it.

It was an army bayonet.

Four days after the discovery of the body in the river a teletype message from the Federal Bureau of Investigation in Washington identified the body from a thumbprint sent to the FBI by the Cook County coroner's office. The dead man was Albert C. Rogers, thirty-nine, born in Red Earth, Alabama. He had been in the army for two years and had received an honorable discharge.

The coroner in turn routinely sent the identification to the Area Six Homicide unit on the North Side, which was handling the case. Three days later a detective in Area Six alerted—by interpolice mail—the other five homicide units. The police now knew Albert C. Rogers's name but nothing else—they did not know where he had been murdered, or why, or by whom.

Matthew Schmidt entered Michael Reese Hospital on Saturday morning for tests. There was a lingering inflammation of the bronchial tubes leading to his right lung. His only lung.

On Monday Norman Frank—who had finally been placed in protective deadlock but was therefore not allowed to move outside his locked cell—was due to appear in felony court. His lawyer was seeking a continuance of the case.

4. ON SATURDAY MORNING JACK DONOVAN APPEARED AT THE
HOME OF HIS FATHER-IN-LAW, ARTHUR O'CONNOR.

For a moment he stood on the concrete stoop and looked
around him at the neat block of brick houses on Ninety-fourth
Street in the southwest suburb of Oak Lawn. He rang the bell.
Every house was alike, for they had all been built in the same
year right after World War II, yet each house had individual
touches. This house had green aluminum shutters, that one
had a statue of the Virgin Mary on the front lawn, and another
had blue roofing tile. Arthur O'Connor's house was the largest
on the block (by dint of two additions), but it was the only one
that bore no sign of identity.

It was his visiting day, and Jack Donovan made the long
trip to the South Side almost from duty.

Except for his daughter.

His son, Brian, was fifteen and incomprehensible. Jack
Donovan did not like him very much now. But Kathleen, his
daughter, was thirteen, and in her way she seemed to like his
company. He thought he was very fond of her. And though

Jack Donovan did not enjoy the implied formality of these visits, there was not much he could do about that—not without making an even worse mess than there already was.

Arthur O'Connor opened the aluminum outer door. He was nearly eighty and still carried the suspicious look of an Irish farmer. Which was what his own father had been.

"Hello, Jack. You're early."

Jack Donovan only nodded and followed his father-in-law into the house. He realized he was tensing; usuallly Rita did not wait around for him on visiting day but sometimes she did, and this uncertainty always cast gloom over the anticipation of the visit.

There was plastic sheeting on the white sofa and a statue of the Blessed Virgin on the oak sideboard in the hall. Last Easter's palms were behind the crucifix on the wall, and next to the cross was a picture of Rita O'Connor, taken when she was eighteen. Rita smiled in the picture. Sometimes, while he waited for the children to come down, Jack Donovan would look at the picture and try to find the madness in the smile.

"Where's Rita?"

He sat down without asking permission. His father-in-law remained standing. "She had to go shopping."

The mahogany German clock ticked loudly on the soft beige wall.

"Where's Kathleen?"

"I said you was early."

He fell silent. His father-in-law shuffled to the kitchen at the back of the house. When he returned, he carried a can of Schlitz beer. Jack Donovan did not like the brand, but he accepted the can and took a sip. It was shortly before eleven o'clock, and his father-in-law watched him like a bemused cat.

They had gotten married sixteen years ago, after Jack Donovan got out of the army and took the police-department examination. There was no doubt that Jack Donovan would become a policeman or that he would marry Rita O'Connor. Life did not admit doubts. All their lives they had lived two blocks from each other—Jack and his parents on Peoria Street and the O'Connors on Carpenter—and they had been in the same grades at Visitation Grammar School.

When high school came, the O'Connors moved to Oak Lawn to escape the black tide of the ghetto which was gradually encircling the Irish-Catholic neighborhood where they had grown up. Arthur O'Connor was a cop, a watch commander, and a well-off man as a result. There was always plenty of money for the watch commander from the district bagman, and if that was corruption, then it was also a way of life.

Jack Donovan's father worked for the rapid-transit lines. After high school Jack had gone to college for three years and then let himself be drafted into the army. He was bored with college and with living at home and with his father.

He went to Korea for thirteen months during his tour of duty. He wrote to Rita O'Connor, and when he came home on leave, they dated every night. On their last night together she let him make love to her.

Then, after Commander O'Connor used his clout to get Jack Donovan a good start on the police ladder, they got married. Sixteen years ago.

Jack Donovan put down the can of beer on the coaster next to the chair.

O'Connor said, "I see your name was in the paper so I cut it out and gave it to Rita Kathleen." His father-in-law always used both of Rita's names.

"Oh."

His stomach hurt again. He wondered if there was something wrong with him. He did not want to go to a doctor. He thought of Matthew Schmidt in his room at Michael Reese Hospital.

"I saw your father yesterday."

Jack Donovan sipped his beer. There was nothing to say. He rarely saw his mother or father. They were old, of course, and they were living in Ireland in their memories now, young lovers again in County Clare before taking the boat to America. He did not like to intrude on them. They sometimes thought he was a stranger. His sister had suggested putting them in a home, but Donovan had dissuaded her. They still lived in the city, in an apartment in the Beverly area. He called them every week and did not like to think he did it to see if they were still alive.

"Your father says to me, he says you don't come by."

There was nothing to say.

"He wanted to ride so I give him a ride and he comes by and visited with Brian John."

The old man watched him. Jack Donovan thought he must have been a hard cop in his time. "The two of them got on famous. They went off and had a chat, they did. But your mother don't look well."

The old man got up and shuffled around the room, arranging elaborate ashtrays. Jack Donovan did not smoke and neither did the old man, but Rita had always smoked, from grammar school days. She would cough in the night and when she woke up. Her breath tasted stale in the morning when they made love. He had bought her a lighter on one of her birthdays. Or Christmas. A silver lighter.

"Ah, he's quite the one for the basketball."

"My father?"

"Ach. Of course not. Your son, Brian."

"Oh."

"Very good at the game, he is."

"I'm glad."

Rita had stopped smoking in the hospital, but she had started again during the time with the lawyers.

Brian had been born a year after their marriage, and then there was the first miscarriage. And then Kathleen was born, and the marriage seemed stable. Jack Donovan started going to night school to take a law degree. Juggling his job, school, and married life was very difficult at first, and he couldn't talk it over with Rita. And then he often had to leave her alone with the two little babies and her own thoughts. She was pregnant again, for the fourth time in four years. She had wanted it that way. When she had been a little girl—when he had first teased her on the playground in first grade, when he had first loved her—she had said, "I'm gonna have lots of babies when I grow up."

And then the fourth pregnancy ended in miscarriage, and the doctor warned her about further attempts.

He prescribed the pill and she took it for almost a year, but she finally quit. She said it was a sin against God. Jack

Donovan tried to get one of the priests to talk to her, but the only one he reached said that Rita was absolutely right, that taking birth-control pills was against the laws of God.

With her fifth pregnancy she nearly died.

In his guilt Jack Donovan began to withdraw from her. They didn't speak to each other even as little as they had; something had been altered by her brush with death. Jack Donovan was afraid for Rita, and Rita was afraid for herself. And then she ran away for the first time.

The front door opened, and Jack's thoughts were jolted back to the present by the sight of his daughter. Kathleen was tall, perhaps too tall for her age. She had awkward legs which she hid in blue jeans. She was very thin, with a child's figure, and her lack of development worried her. She had even confided in him about that once.

"Sorry I'm late, Dad," she said, and he accepted her motherly kiss on his forehead. She went and sat down across from him on the plastic-covered sofa and folded her hands between her knees.

"You're not late, Kathleen. Your father is early, is all." Again the hard edge to the voice, the voice still carrying a trace of the West Country accent after nearly a century away from Ireland.

"Where do you want to go?" Jack Donovan asked his daughter.

But the old man interrupted. "Ah, you don't have to go anywhere. You can visit here, and if it's me in your way, I can go up to my bedroom."

He always said the same thing and they always made the same reply.

"No. I'm going to take Kate out for a hamburger. Okay, Kate?"

"Sure," she said, getting up. She always wanted something to eat. There was no junk food in Arthur O'Connor's house.

Kathleen had green eyes like her mother and father and dark hair from somewhere in their black Irish past.

"I'll take you home again, Kathleen," he said to her. It was one of their little jokes, and the fact that it annoyed Arthur O'Connor made it that much better.

"I'll see you, Mr. O'Connor," Jack Donovan said, and he got up and shook hands with the old man. That was part of the ritual too, like the single can of beer and the offer to go hide in the bedroom.

"Brian'll be home this afternoon when you come back. I'll tell him to stay in the house," said Arthur O'Connor.

"There's no need," said Donovan. "If he's here, I'd like to see him."

Tiny Preston was showing *Sex Slavery* again, but no one seemed to notice or care that the theater had shown it just six weeks before.

When he had decided to return it to the distributor in June, he had read that the distributor had been arrested by postal authorities on charges involving unsolicited lewd mailings. So Tiny Preston, after consulting the theater owners, decided to keep *Sex Slavery* and recycle it.

"Like recycled garbage," he had laughed.

Now he stood in the back of the theater and watched the dull, familiar scene flickering on the screen. He weighed four hundred twelve pounds, and if every human being has an identifiable odor, Tiny Preston smelled of French fries.

It was late in the afternoon, and Tiny Preston had been annoyed for some time by the man sitting in the back row.

He was a middle-aged man, as they all were, but he sat as though with grim fascination, afraid to move.

He annoyed Tiny Preston because he had purchased his ticket when the theater opened at nine A.M. He had now seen *Sex Slavery* and the accompanying feature four times. Tiny continued to glare at him for several minutes, but the man seemed lost in a trance. Finally Tiny shrugged and heaved his bulk into the small lobby.

"Fuckin' guy's been sittin' in there since we opened up," he said to the girl in the ticket booth. Gloria Miska nodded absently. She stared at the street in front of her and the people passing by. She'd be off in five hours, and her right foot hurt.

Tiny Preston looked down at Gloria. She wore slacks, and Tiny Preston let his eyes focus on her thighs and tried to imagine himself between them. He realized that Gloria Miska found him repulsive, but because he employed her, he felt a certain sense of power over her.

"Been here since morning, the prick," he said.

Still she did not respond.

Tiny Preston felt hungry again and said he was going out. Gloria Miska did not answer.

When he had first given her the job, he had tried to grab her in the office. He had touched her breast. She had said she'd get him killed if he ever did that again, and that had scared him.

Tiny Preston pushed open the glass door to the street and went out into the steamy Saturday afternoon.

If he had waited ten minutes, he would have seen his customer of the morning finally leave the theater. The man had gray hair at the temples and wore a plain gray work shirt. His hair was cut short and his eyebrows were thick and nearly joined above his long, broad nose. He carried a rolled-up newspaper in one hand and looked like a man coming back from a day's work. He had a slight limp.

Gloria Miska barely glanced at him, but she thought she smelled something strange above the stench of the popcorn machine.

Like gasoline.

By a bizarre coincidence motorcycle officer Clarence Delancey found the second body in the park.

It was Monday and Delancey had just spent an enjoyable hour racing his three-wheeler up and down the grassy embankments south of Monroe Street Harbor along the lakefront. He was ostensibly looking for vagrants, winos, and lovers using the early morning park for illegal purposes. Clarence Delancey was the scourge of them all.

His discovery of a wino named Norman Frank sleeping in the park six weeks before had resulted in a departmental commendation and an unwritten promise of transfer to the day shift on a permanent basis.

There were few winos who sought refuge in the downtown park in daylight, but the job still had its satisfactions. Unlike most policemen assigned to the motorcycle detail, Delancey simply loved it. He would parade on his cycle for the young art students from the Institute who came to the park during the day to sketch. And there were always hippies to roust, especially in the summer.

Delancey was incorruptible. His mission was to drive everyone from the park who did not belong there. And he was very strict in his ideas about who belonged. His three-wheeler was like the horse of a Western cowboy. He might even acknowledge to himself that he felt like a sheriff of the Old West.

And that was why the overweight and faintly comic figure of the policeman could be seen at nine-sixteen A.M. on the sidewalk which stretched to the north end of Monroe Street Harbor. He would never be guilty of dereliction of duty. As he cruised slowly down the pedestrian way, he looked from right to left, satisfied at the order on his beat.

Until he saw something.

Something that didn't belong there. Something under a thick clump of bushes near the roadway.

He stopped the cycle and dismounted. He hitched his belt and placed the butt of his personal pistol—a .45-caliber Colt automatic—within reach of his gloved hand.

He started up the grassy knoll to the bushes, pushing away a branch that scratched at his face.

She was lying on her back, naked. Her throat had been pierced, and there was dried blood on her neck, her jaw, and her cheek. It appeared that her back had arched sharply in death. One leg seemed unnaturally bent, and there was blood on her sex organ. It appeared that a second wound had torn across her left breast, down through her belly to the genitals, but there was so much blood that he could not be sure.

Delancey stared at the blood and the bits of exposed bone and muscle. He blinked, holding the branch away from his face. Then he turned and retched.

When he called in from the radio on his cycle, he said he thought the woman was about twenty. In fact, she was twenty-two.

5. AT THE MOMENT MOTORCYCLE OFFICER DELANCEY FOUND THE BODY IN THE PARK, COUNTY JAIL GUARDS AND COURT BAILIFFS were moving Norman Frank and nine other prisoners through the gloomy passageway which connects the jail with the Criminal Courts building. All were scheduled to make courtroom appearances that morning and all wore civilian clothes. Three of the prisoners were white and seven were black. Some of the men were scheduled for bond hearings; others were due to begin trial or were seeking continuances. None of them spoke.

The group waited at the elevator and finally began to talk. The guards ignored them.

Other groups of prisoners were also on the move, and some were already in the cages behind the courtrooms of the old building.

The elevator took Norman Frank and the others to the lockup on the fourth floor. Norman Frank's lockup was already crowded with twenty-two other prisoners. There was a stale smell of sweat and cigarette smoke in the room. Norman Frank sat down and waited.

When the Criminal Courts building was constructed nearly fifty years before, the architect planned a lockup behind each courtroom. The system was considered very modern and secure. The separate facility would mean prisoners would not have to be taken into court along public passages. When a prisoner was due in court, his name was read aloud in the lockup, and the prisoner shuffled out, showing his identifying tag to the guard. He was brought to a separate entrance behind the bench and led into court. When a prisoner was sent back to the jail, he moved again through the secure passage behind the courtroom.

By nine forty-two A.M. there were several dozen men in the lockup on the fourth floor. One of them was Norman Frank, who stood in a corner alone, cupping the glow of a cigarette in the hollow of his right hand. He was even thinner than when he had been arrested six weeks before for the rape and murder of Maj Kirsten in Grant Park.

Sergeant Terrence Flynn handed his identification to the guard in the foyer of the courts building and opened his coat to display his pistol. The guard nodded Flynn through. He crossed the lobby and saw Mario DeVito on the steps leading to the high second floor.

It was a little after ten.

"Hiya Terry," said Mario. He had a manila folder under his right arm and started up the steps. To his surprise Flynn puffed up after him.

"Whaddaya want, Terry?"

"I'm in training."

"I got no time to talk. I'm late for court."

"You got time for this." They reached the second floor and paused. Flynn was breathing heavily. He took DeVito's arm and pulled him aside by the elevator bank.

"You wanna make out?" adked Mario DeVito. He was in a good mood.

"Norman Frank goes to bat today, right?"

"Yeah. We're going to press for a trial date."

"I don't think you're gonna prosecute our boy."

"Why not?"

64

"I just got the word. Remember Delancey?"

"The cop who found Maj Kirsten. Sure. We've interviewed him. He's our star."

"He was on patrol this morning in Grant Park, and it sounds crazy, but he found another one. About an hour ago."

Mario smiled. "Another wino? Tell him we already got one."

"He found another body in the park. Not too far from where they found Maj Kirsten."

Mario stared at him.

"I don't know anything yet. They knew I was coming over this morning on the Frank hearing, and they had me call in. Sid Margolies is over in the park, and I gotta go back. White woman. Only this time she didn't have no clothes on."

"What the fuck are you telling me, Terry?"

Flynn looked at him. "Body. White female. In the park. She was cut pretty bad is the way I get it and was probably raped. I got to go back to the scene. Matt's in the hospital, you know, so I'm running it. At least until Ranallo butts in with his two cents worth."

"You're not saying that Norman didn't do it? The Kirsten murder?" But Mario knew that was exactly what Flynn was implying. "Listen, you can't leave until you talk to Jack Donovan."

"Shit, Mario, I ain't got time for this. I got to get over by the park. I just had to let you know so that you wouldn't look like shit when the newspaper guys start kicking your door down in an hour or two."

But Mario wouldn't let his arm go. "Your partner can handle it for now. You got to talk to Donovan. Shit. Shit and double shit."

Terry Flynn let himself be led through the double doors of the state's attorney's office, past the guard, through the second door, and down the narrow corridor to Donovan's office.

Mrs. Farrell was behind her desk, but they rushed past her and into Donovan's open office. DeVito slammed the door and flopped down heavily on the leather couch. Terry Flynn found a chair.

Jack Donovan looked up from the legal pad in front of

him. It was covered with numbers. He was making out a work schedule and realizing again that there weren't enough people. He put down his pencil.

"You know Terry Flynn?" began Mario, gesturing toward the red-faced detective.

"You're with Matt Schmidt," Donovan replied.

"Yeah. He's in the hospital."

"Jack, they just found another body in Grant Park," Mario DeVito said.

Donovan stared at him.

"Raped and murdered. Stabbed. Multiple wounds, right?"

Flynn nodded and picked it up. "Same cop that found Norman Frank found this one. White female, about twenty years old. Naked and pretty messy."

Jack Donovan waited. He picked up his pencil and then put it down again. There was nothing to write.

"Norman Frank goes up to get his trial date this morning," Mario said.

The pencil, Donovan noted, read "Eagle Mirado 174." He tried to remember what Maj Kirsten had looked like on the slab in the morgue, her face peaceful and still.

"What should we do now about Norman Frank?" Mario DeVito asked.

"We have a lot of circumstantial evidence."

"So what?"

Donovan looked at Flynn. "Were you at the scene?"

"Not yet. Margolies is there. I was going over. I wanted to let you know because I knew Norman Frank was going to bat this morning."

"No clothes?"

"That's the way they told me when I called Area One. They might have got it garbled. I didn't talk to Margolies direct. He was at the scene. I was on my way here from home, I didn't even go into Area One this morning. It was supposed to be my day off."

"Maj Kirsten was clothed."

"I was supposed to talk to the public defender about Frank," Mario said. "He wants to deal."

"How is Matt?"

Flynn looked at Donovan. "He's supposed to know

something this morning. They ran some tests Saturday and then again this morning."

"I don't know if I could go through that," said Donovan.

"You never know," said Terry Flynn.

"What do you think we ought to do, Mario?" Donovan asked at last.

"Play it on the square, I suppose, and go to bat."

"Yes." Donovan put the tips of his fingers together and looked first at Flynn and then at Mario. "What do you think, Flynn?"

"I don't know."

"Matt Schmidt told me that he was sure Norman Frank killed someone."

Flynn didn't look at Donovan. He scratched at a spot on the sleeve of his sport coat. "Matt has been at it a long time," he said.

"We got some evidence, Jack, circumstantial or not," Mario said. "We got his goofy statement and we got his bloody shirt and the blood types match. So maybe this new victim wasn't even connected with Maj Kirsten. There's the thing about her clothes. It might be coincidence."

"You mean, both of them being killed in Grant Park? But by different guys?"

"Something like that," said Mario. "It doesn't sound so good, does it?"

Donovan shook his head. "Well, Flynn, I'd appreciate a call as soon as you can. We'll figure out something about Mr. Norman Frank for now, but I'd sure like to hear from you."

Flynn got up. "Yeah, sure. I'll call you this afternoon."

He left the office.

Mario said, "Bud Halligan will crap in his pants."

"Fuck Halligan," said Donovan. He was now lining up the pencil at a right angle to the edge of his legal pad.

"What time is it?"

Mario glanced at his wrist; Donovan did not wear a watch. "Three minutes to eleven."

"Well, what are we going to do?"

"Play it straight," said Mario. "It's not as though Norman Frank isn't guilty of something."

"It'd be bad if it turned out he was only trespassing in the park after dark. Two homosexual rapes in the joint is a pretty stiff sentence."

DeVito shrugged. The two men got up without another word and left the office. "I'm going to the courtroom." Mrs. Farrell wrote it down.

They took the elevator to the fourth floor and pushed through the crowded hallway. Inside the old courtroom nearly ninety people—lawyers, relatives, criminals, friends of criminals, and cops—milled around. The courtroom smelled very much like the lockup, including the smell of tension and anger and dampness. They could even smell vomit.

"There he is," said DeVito. "Hiya, Tommy." Tom Ryerson was Norman Frank's public defender. He and Mario had gone to school together, to St. Patrick's on the old West Side.

"Hiya, Dago," said Ryerson. "Hiya, Jack. I'm all screwed up today."

"Like always," said Mario with a smile. "What's up?"

"They called for my man ten minutes ago in the lockup. And he isn't there."

DeVito grinned. Ryerson glanced down at his manila folder.

"They just sent over to the jail to see if they forgot him."

"Jerks," said Donovan

"I got a theory," said Mario. "When a guy flunks out of mailman school because he can't read zip codes, they make him a jail guard."

Ryerson nodded. "Well, as long as we got a minute, what are you guys gonna do on this one, anyway?"

"Swing for the fences, Tommy. A home-run blast." DeVito was still smiling.

"Don't gimme that shit, Dago."

Donovan glanced at Ryerson. "What deal you wanna make, Tommy?"

"Drop the rape and let him plead to a lesser on the other thing."

"You mean the murder?" asked Donovan. "The other thing is a homicide."

Ryerson turned to his old neighborhood pal. "Come on, Mario. You guys don't have enough for that."

"Shit," said Donovan. "Murder. Downtown. In a public park. And a white woman. No. More than that—a tourist. Are you kidding us?"

"Hey, people get killed all the time," said Ryerson.

Mario said, "But they is mostly our black brethren."

"That's prejudice," said Ryerson.

"That's life," said Donovan.

"What deal you really wanna make, Tommy?" asked Mario.

"Voluntary manslaughter," said the P.D.

"You're dreaming, Tommy," said Mario.

"Hey, come on. He's had a hard time already. Some of our black brethren over in your jail really reamed him."

"Maybe he was flirting," said DeVito. He was not smiling now. His voice was very harsh. Donovan noticed that the instinctive guttural, clipped sounds of the West Side accent had surfaced in the speech of both men.

"You know you just pinned it on him. You ain't got shit."

DeVito said, "Whatever you say, Tommy. Nice talking to you."

"If that's really all you've got."

Donovan broke in. "Hey. We play by the rules. You got what we got. And we got a bloody shirt and a bum in the park and Maj Kirsten's blood type."

Ryerson looked disgusted. "You got diddle. Stop playing this game. I'm trying to do you a favor and my client a favor. Maybe even throw in a little justice just for laughs."

"Whaddaya say, Jack?"

Donovan responded on cue: "We'll drop the rape to assault and we've got to go for murder and he pleads to everything. At least twenty."

Ryerson shrugged. "Everything sounds okay except for the twenty. He won't go for that. How about a recommendation for a minimum." The minimum for murder was fourteen years.

"Hey, this guy is a convicted felon," said Mario.

"Auto theft. Ten years ago. Come on, Dago, you're talking to the Irish Terror." He tried to smile.

Donovan shook his head. "This was a public murder,

Tommy, all over the front page. How the hell are we going to go for a minimum on this? I'd be out selling shoelaces the next day. I'm sticking my neck out now. You know that. We ought to go to bat all the way."

Ryerson shrugged. "I'll talk to my client."

"If you can find him, you Mick bastard," said Mario DeVito with affection. "You couldn't find your ass with a flashlight and a map."

At that moment a deputy sheriff waved to Ryerson and edged over. All around them in the noisy courtroom cases were being called for trial dates, and the hubbub seemed perpetual.

"We can't find him," the deputy said.

"The fuck," said Mario DeVito.

"He's on the list. They said they moved him over this morning before court. We got his name but we ain't got him," said the deputy.

"Check the other lockups?"

"Sure."

"Other courts on this floor?"

"I'm telling you, he ain't around."

"Who was guarding the lockup?"

"New guy named Jackson."

Donovan broke in impatiently and leaned into the deputy's face. "You know who we're talking about, don't you? We're not talking about a disorderly conduct charge."

"Take it easy," said Mario.

"What's this shit, 'He ain't around'? You think I'm asking where the fucking men's room is?" Donovan's face glared red.

"I don't have to take this shit," said the deputy.

"Sure you do," said Jack Donovan. He looked as though he would strike the deputy.

"Who the hell is this guy?" the deputy asked Mario.

"God," said Mario. "You know Norman Frank killed a Swedish woman in Grant Park a month ago."

"Yeah, I know who you mean," said the deputy. "But I still don't have to take this shit."

Ryerson said, "Well, if you boys find him, let me know. I was going to the P.D.'s office anyway. Give me a call."

Ryerson seemed unnaturally cheerful. Mario was as angry as Donovan, but he pulled Jack aside. "Leave Hopalong Cassidy alone. It isn't going to solve anything."

"You know what happened, don't you?" asked Jack Donovan.

Mario nodded. They both understood.

"It gives us a little breathing room, though," Mario said. Norman Frank had made a deal with one of the other prisoners in the lockup, and they had switched calls. "Maybe we can figure out what the hell is going on."

"The bastard is on the streets now, Mario "

"Unless he detoured to the lunchroom and died there of ptomaine poisoning."

Donovan let it go. Without another word he turned and shoved his way out of the courtroom and went down the two long flights of stairs to the state's attorney's office.

When he reached his own office, he closed the door, sat down at the desk, and dialed the sheriff.

"This is Jack Donovan," he said and waited to be put through. Finally he heard Jacobs's deep voice boom on the line.

"Jack, whaddaya say?"

"I say your prisoner Norman Frank is missing."

"Who?"

"Norman Frank who's supposed to go to bat for killing Maj Kirsten."

"Who?"

"The woman in the goddamn park last month."

"Oh. What happened?"

"He was due in court this morning and he's missing."

"Shit." Pause. "He break out?"

"No, it looks like the same old shit. He made a deal with someone and switched calls."

Jacobs was silent and Donovan could not stand it. "Goddamn it. It's happened four times in the past year, but this is the first white guy. You got so many prisoners in the lockup behind the courtrooms that the goddamn bailiff doesn't know who's who."

"I know how it happens," said the sheriff.

"Terrific," said Jack Donovan. "You run a jail like a nympho runs a whorehouse. You don't know who's fucking who and if there's any money in the till."

"That's unkind, Donovan," the sheriff said mildly.

"How come your prosecutor didn't spot him?" asked Jacobs finally.

"He was just getting his date changed. That assistant was juggling thirty cases down there. How the hell is he supposed to know who's who?"

"And the P.D.?"

"They got stand-ins, same as we do. Nobody knows the players except the players."

"Well, it wasn't our fault."

"How do you figure that?"

"Well—"

"Fuck this. Norman Frank is up on murder, rape, armed assault, everything but intent to commit mopery, and he walks out of court today because he's not important enough to your gorillas in the jail to make sure he shows up in court."

Jacobs said, "You aren't going to say that, are you?"

"What do you think I'm going to say?"

"Come on, Jack. We'll hang the guard at the lockup for you, if you want."

"For starters. I'm certainly not letting the office take your beef when the newspapers come around," said Donovan.

"Bud is a friend of mine," said Jacobs.

"Good. If you think Bud Halligan is going to put his balls in the chopper for you, then he must be a pretty good friend."

"Listen, Jack," said Jacobs. The tone had changed. But Donovan felt sick and angry and he couldn't talk to the sheriff anymore. He hung up. He stalked to the window and tried to look up the air shaft at the sky. He hit the window ledge with the side of his hand.

A half hour later Mario DeVito entered the office. Mario threw his thick dark body onto the old leather couch and put up his feet on the chair next to it.

Donovan had finished his schedule, letting the anger and frustration be drained by playing with the problem of numbers on a legal pad. He looked at Mario.

Mario held his nose with his thumb and index finger and began an imitation of a police radio dispatcher. "Be on the lookout for a white, male, Caucasian, nonblack, un-Negro escaped killer named Norman Frank, who walked out of the Criminal Courts today like he owned the joint. That is all."

"Did you get anything?"

"He traded with a fellow shitkicker named Micky Joe Strong. Ole boy Micky Joe was up for grand theft and wanted a bond hearing. Ole boy Micky Joe's lady comes in with the bond and grabs hold of ole Norman and says, 'This here's my beloved Micky Joe.'"

"Norman Frank is certainly a caution," Donovan said.

"He probably went down on Micky Joe twenty times for a favor like that. Ole Micky Joe he say he don't know what happened, didn't hear his name called, says it weren't his fault."

"They were just good friends," said Donovan, who had regained his calm. It was all absurd, he realized. All of it.

"So we got two murders and one fugitive who may or may not be guilty of one of them," said Mario. Jack Donovan realized Mario was getting angry now.

He waited.

"This is really bullshit, you know that, Jack? You ever get the feeling that nothing works?"

"All the time."

They each waited for the other to say something.

"I couldn't remember what Maj Kirsten looked like," Donovan said. "When I was talking to Ryerson. All morning. Even when I was talking to you and Flynn."

Mario reached into the manila case folder and pulled out a small Polaroid picture. It was a photograph of Maj Kirsten, taken at the scene. Her eyes were staring and bulgy and her face was covered with blood.

"Yes," said Jack Donovan. "I forgot."

"It doesn't matter," said Mario.

Donovan got up and went to the couch and sat down next to Mario. He returned the photograph and Mario looked at it. "Sure it does," Donovan said quietly.

Mario stared for a long time at the picture.

Donovan said, "I suppose we ought to talk to Matt at the hospital this afternoon. About this whole thing. After we get a call from Terry Flynn. I suppose we just didn't go at it the right way."

Mario didn't say anything. They sat together on the couch, looking at the photograph for a long time.

6. IT HAD ONLY BEEN THE FLU.

MATTHEW SCHMIDT, HOMICIDE LIEUTENANT IN POLICE AREA One, entered his small office in police headquarters building at 1121 South State Street shortly after eight A.M. Tuesday.

He hung his straw hat on the hook he had driven into the office wall twelve years before when he had first been assigned the office. With satisfaction he looked down at his desk: the top was covered with bulletins, notices, copies of arrest sheets, and messages from other homicide units and shifts, and all the other debris accumulated during his four days in the hospital.

Influenza. They gave him pills for it.

He touched his chest and coughed again experimentally. He wiped his hand across his dry lips and found saliva. He examined it. It was clear.

Gert had wanted him to stay home for a few more days. To rest. She really couldn't understand that after those four days in the hospital and the days of fear that preceded them, going back downtown to work was a kind of miracle, like a child's Christmas morning.

He took off his blue suit coat and arranged it on the back of his chair, then sat down and began to go through nine days worth of accumulated papers. Though he seemed to proceed slowly, in a few minutes his wastebasket was full. He mashed down its contents with his foot and continued to feed it. There were always so many papers to read and fill out, to sort or throw away, to file. He looked down the coroner's list from the past week, and his finger stopped at one line:

"Unknown. WM, approx. 35. Stabbed. Chicago River at Michigan."

He circled the entry and put it on the side of his desk. If it was in the river, it might have been Area One's responsibility.

He had been at home the week before he went into the hospital. It was as though the week was a piece of memory surgically removed from his mind.

He went through the arrest sheets like a priest listening to confessions. All these terrible sins were the same; he had heard them all before.

Gert read Agatha Christie at home as a kind of sleep-inducing drug; he read arrest sheets. But they did not induce sleep, only a sense of life, as though he touched the circle of reality from anarchy to order. This man had killed his wife. He had taken out his butcher knife from the drawer in the kitchen and driven it into her heart and her belly. He had said he was sorry, explained to police that he was drunk at the time.

The absurdity of the tragedies moved Matt Schmidt, as did the stilted police prose: "Perpetrator" and "he proceeded" and "he commenced an assault with a deadly weapon upon." The cops who wrote the reports on battered old typewriters groped with English as though it were a foreign language, but in their inarticulateness, Matt Schmidt found a kind of truth he could not really grasp anywhere else.

Gradually he made order out of the chaotic pile of papers.

He read that morning's daily police bulletin. There was a mug shot of Norman Frank on it, and Matt Schmidt read of his escape slowly, while humming an old dance tune.

It surprised him to think of the sad little man called Norman Frank finding a way out of the machinery of justice he was enmeshed in. After finishing the bulletin, he put it down and turned to the copy of the FBI wire. It had been received on Friday. He wondered if Terry Flynn had read it.

The FBI wire identified the man in the river, and something in the identification nagged at Matt Schmidt.

Finally he picked up a copy of Sid Margolies's report on the body found in Grant Park on Monday, the day before. The newspapers this morning had treated the matter sensationally but had been sketchy about details.

Matt Schmidt was disappointed to find that even Sid Margolies's painstaking report had little more to offer. A dead woman, about twenty, stabbed and raped. Time of death fixed at sometime Sunday morning.

He put the report down just as Margolies himself entered the little office.

Sid Margolies never talked in the morning unless he was forced to. He nodded at Matt, went to the window, and looked out at the bright hot street. Sid took off his felt hat—he wore it summer and winter—and threw it on the desk. He had a little potbelly, and he drank Amaretto as a cocktail. He knew everything about Chinese cooking and was quite expert himself. He had taken the sergeant's exam only once, and never again; he had sad eyes and sallow skin and he always carried his notebook in the pocket of his shirt.

"I want to ask you about the body in the park." Schmidt was as reluctant as Margolies to break in on his morning's silence, but it had to be done.

"You want cream?"

Schmidt nodded and Margolies went down the hall to the communications room where they ran a coffee concession. He brought back two cups and a sweet roll. He tore the sweet roll apart, took half, and began to munch.

Matt Schmidt did not find it unusual that Sid Margolies did not mention his stay in the hospital. Sid did not make small talk before noon and seldom thereafter.

"Is it the same man?" Matt asked quietly.

"Some things are the same," said Sid Margolies. He took out his notebook. "She was stabbed with a big weapon, like a butcher knife or a bayonet. Something very big. She was apparently first stabbed in the right side of the neck, like Maj Kirsten. She was raped and he really tore into her, just like Maj Kirsten. In the park, that's the same. But he took her clothes this time, why's that? And he killed her on a Sunday—why would he figure he'd find a woman in the park on Sunday morning?"

Margolies was finished. He sipped his coffee.

"I didn't see a picture in the morning papers."

"We had to clean her up a little. The morgue released a picture last night, but no one was around to pick it up. It'll probably be in the afternoon papers. We ran her fingerprints but got nothing."

Something nagged at Matt Schmidt's consciousness, but he realized it was not the woman found in the park. He didn't press it; it would come.

"Are they going crazy over at the state's attorney's office?"

Margolies shrugged. That was small talk.

Sergeant Terry Flynn entered the room. He picked up the half of the sweet roll which Matt Schmidt had not touched and started to eat it.

"Hot as vinegar piss," Flynn said.

Margolies walked to his desk and sat down, savoring the bad coffee.

Matt Schmidt stared at the calendar on the wall from the Federation of Police.

"So what'd they say, Matt?" Flynn asked, finishing the roll.

"Flu."

"Flu. Son of a bitch."

"What do you think of our latest park murder?"

"Nothing." Flynn took off his sport coat and threw it on the desk. He had large muscular arms that peeked out of the short-sleeved shirt. His tie was already askew. Though he had brown hair, a fuzz of reddish hair covered his arms. His .357-magnum revolver was on his belt, attached by a small clip on the side of the gun.

"That body in the river ours? I didn't see a report," Schmidt said.

"Oh. Last week? No. Snagged on the other side so Area Six is handling it. Just a wino, I guess. I talked to Haggerty up at

78

Area Six, says the guy had a liver like a dried balloon, lot of booze when he died. Nobody's pressing them."

"And what about our other wino?"

"Who? Norman? He's got the state's attorney's office shitting little green apples."

"What about us? We recommended they prosecute."

Flynn shrugged. "We made a mistake. Maybe. But he killed someone. Even you said that."

"I could be wrong."

Flynn didn't say anything.

Then Matt Schmidt understood. He swung out of his chair and went to the file drawer and opened it. He thumbed back through the reports until he found the one he wanted. He looked at it and then replaced it.

When he sat down again, he was smiling.

Terry Flynn, perched on his desk top, his feet on his chair, watched Schmidt.

"Where'd Norman come from?" Schmidt asked.

Flynn looked across at Margolies, but Margolies was working the *Tribune* crossword puzzle. He wouldn't be any help.

"Is this a Wally Phillips quiz?" He referred to a local radio program.

"Where?" Schmidt repeated.

"Tennessee. Do I win?"

"Not yet."

Schmidt threw across a piece of paper and Terry Flynn read it. "Yeah. I saw this. I told you it was handled by Area Six."

"Nothing connect?" asked Matt.

Terry Flynn hated this. "Fuck this shit," he said. He got up from the desk top and went down the hall. When he returned, he had coffee in his mug. His mug said, "Chief Flynn" on it. It had been a present from his ex-wife when they had first married. He didn't keep it for sentimental reasons; he kept it because it kept the coffee hotter than a paper cup.

"Come on, Flynn."

Flynn thought he had gotten to know Matt Schmidt in the six weeks since they were pulled together on the Maj Kirsten case. Schmidt ran an independent wing within Area One, and Flynn had looked forward to moving into that wing and learning from Matt. But now he was frustrated by Schmidt's tutorial approach.

"This says this guy comes from Red Earth, Alabama," said Flynn harshly. "And Norman Frank came from Tennessee. So what the hell does it mean? Two shitkickers. The city's full of them."

"I'll bet you the guy they found in the river wasn't bigger than five foot five," said Matt Schmidt. "I'll lay money on it."

Flynn gaped at him. Even Margolies put down his pencil and stared. Finally Flynn said, "You saw the report."

"No. Honest," said Matt Schmidt. "Call Area Six and you'll see."

Flynn knew he was being suckered, but he picked up the pax line, the internal police telephone, and called Area Six. "Yeah, this is Flynn down at Area One. Is Haggerty around?"

He waited. "Hiya, Jimbo. I got a question for you. How tall was the stiff you guys got out of the river last week?"

He waited.

"Yeah. I know. But my Supreme Allied Commander says he was under five foot five, and he's going to buy lunch for everyone at Diamond Jim's if he's wrong."

Again Flynn waited.

"Yeah? Yeah? How 'bout that shit, sports fans. Okay, Jimbo. Yeah, I will. Yeah. Yeah."

He hung up the phone. "Five foot two, eyes of blue."

"So now what does that tell you?"

"He was short, Jack."

"Short," said Matt Schmidt. He waited.

Flynn wanted to punch Matt Schmidt in the middle of his gray face.

"Terry, use your head on this. Connect the dots."

Margolies stared at Schmidt. He was thinking about it now, and his eyes were focused on a middle distance which was not in the tiny squad room.

"Norman Frank killed someone," Matt Schmidt said at last. And then both of them understood.

Margolies even spoke: "And where was Norman Frank born?"

"The same town," said Flynn. "He came from Tennessee, but he was born in Alabama. They came from the same town."

"Two good ole boys," said Matt Schmidt, satisfied with the progress of his students. "Two shitkicker winos."

"Shorty," said Terry Flynn "We never found Shorty because he was in the river."

Matt Schmidt nodded. "And Norman Frank had a bloody shirt because he killed someone. His ole buddy who he liked to fight with—in that tavern next to the Red Lion Hotel, and even in the hotel. They'd get drunk together and start telling each other bullshit stories and pretty soon one or the other of them would get mad."

"So Norman was eighty-sixed from Krause's saloon because Shorty was a good customer."

"Just a wino killing after all," said Sid Margolies.

"We got the right guy for the wrong murder," said Terry Flynn.

"We don't have him," said Matt Schmidt. "Not since yesterday morning."

"Matt, now how the hell did you do that?"

Schmidt felt pleased but tried not to show it. "Elementary, Flynn."

"We got to make this positive," said Flynn. "I'll get a photo of our dead man and go back up to the Red Lion and Krause's bar and Top's and show the picture around. If we really got it right, we got Mr. Norman Frank."

"When we find him," said Matt Schmidt.

"So who killed those women?" It was Margolies, and his voice was so unexpected that the other two lapsed into surprised silence.

Margolies got up and went to the window and looked out. "We got two murders now in six weeks in Grant Park and we're on square one."

"You suppose he killed anyone else?" Flynn asked.

"Or tried to?" Schmidt added.

Margolies joined in again. "They were both of a type. Blond and blue eyes. You hear about blonds getting killed. He didn't kill anyone else. But maybe he tried to."

"In the park," said Matt Schmidt.

"I'll go down to First District and look up the assault records." Margolies got up.

"And put out a message to the other districts. In case. And the homicide units."

Margolies nodded.

"He might have struck closer to home. Wherever he lives. Maybe in one of the neighborhoods. Hell. I suppose we'll have to go through the rape reports."

"Except we can leave out the black neighborhoods," said Flynn. "If the guy is black, then we won't be able to figure out the killing from reading reports on black rapes."

"But what about black rape-murders in the past few months? Maybe he was practicing," said Schmidt. "Maybe he wanted to try out his technique."

"This will take a couple of days," said Margolies. He looked forward to the work. It involved patience and an eye for detail, and he was suited for it; also he would not have to talk to anyone in the mornings.

"And I better call Jack Donovan and Leonard Ranallo."

Flynn shrugged. That was Schmidt's job, to run interference, to handle the political parts of the business. The murders in the park were very hot and very public, and Matt Schmidt was paid to take the heat and the glare.

"Let me know something by eleven. I'll call Ranallo and Donovan then," said Schmidt. "If we can throw them something—clear the murder in the river—then we can get a little bit ahead on the park murders. We got to get a little time."

"What about Area Six?" Flynn said. "It's their case."

Schmidt smiled. "But we solved it for them. We'll let them know after we talk to Ranallo. Part of this little game is figuring out who to tell. And when."

Flynn looked at him and nodded. Matt Schmidt was one hell of a detective.

Though detectives on a case despise interference from the brass or the state's attorney's office, Lieutenant Matt Schmidt had guessed correctly that interference was going to come in any case, and he might as well be prepared to meet it. Schmidt talked to Chief of Homicide Leonard Ranallo about the second park murder shortly before ten, and Mario DeVito called Schmidt right after. The meeting was arranged for three. Because he wasn't sure then about the identity of the man found in the river, he did not say anything about their speculations.

At three-ten P.M. the chief of homicide was sitting in Matt Schmidt's chair in the little office. Schmidt was sitting in Terry Flynn's chair. Margolies was not present—he was still in statistics, pouring through arrest sheets.

Flynn sat on the edge of Matt's desk behind Ranallo. And Mario DeVito was left standing at the filing cabinet, leaning on it with one arm.

It had been a bad day for the brass. The newspapers had screamed in the afternoon about police incompetence and about arresting the wrong man for the wrong crime and about terror in Grant Park. The radio stations were full of the same messages, and that night the television stations would join in.

"So. What's new on Norman Frank's whereabouts?" began Mario DeVito. He had eaten spaghetti with clams for lunch at La Fontanella on the West Side. He still savored the meal while he probed his strong flat teeth with a toothpick.

Ranallo lifted his thick brows and looked a question at Schmidt but Schmidt shook his head. He was waiting for them to finish. "Nothing. But he'll turn up."

"That's what they said about Judge Crater," said Mario DeVito, referring to the famous 1930s' disappearance.

"We usually get them back," said Matt Schmidt.

"That's because you have so much practice," said Mario. He was feeling feisty and enjoying himself. He threw the toothpick into the wastebasket. "Two points," he said.

"All right. We're all here to get some answers and to find out what we're going to do on the case," Ranallo said.

"I think we've solved one murder," said Matt Schmidt.

They stared at him. His face was gray and his voice was quiet. "Last week Area Six pulled a body out of the river later identified as Albert C. Rogers. He had been stabbed and dumped in the river. The report says they also recovered a weapon believed used in the murder. We've solved that case."

"I'm sure Area Six will appreciate that," said Leonard Ranallo. "But we're interested right now in the park murders."

"We now believe that Rogers was killed by Norman Frank. Which would explain his bloody shirt and other indications that he had killed someone on the day or night when Maj Kirsten was murdered in Grant Park."

Mario found another toothpick in his shirt pocket and began to chew on it. Terry Flynn took a Lucky Strike out of his coat pocket and lit it. He threw the match on the floor.

"You got a blood type on Rogers?" DeVito said at last.

"Type A. The same as that found on Norman Frank's shirt. And the same as Maj Kirsten's. It's very common."

"How did you clear this, Matt?" asked Ranallo.

"Terry Flynn did most of it," said Schmidt. "At the time we were investigating the Maj Kirsten murder, he got a number of witnesses who said Norman Frank had a buddy he quarreled with frequently. Naturally we tried to find the buddy, but he drifted out of the picture, which was not that unusual. They were both transients. But all of the witnesses identified the buddy as 'Shorty,' and they all told Terry Flynn that Norman Frank and Shorty came from the same town in the south and that they quarreled together frequently when they were drinking."

He paused and did not look at Terry Flynn. "We didn't connect any of this, of course, until the business of Norman Frank's escape and the second murder in the park."

"Shit," said Ranallo. "You mean that Norman Frank is the wrong man."

"No," said Matt Schmidt. "It means he's the right man for the murder of Shorty Rogers."

"We're going to look like fools," said Ranallo.

Schmidt didn't say anything.

"So the cops are saying now that Norman Frank didn't kill Maj Kirsten," DeVito said.

Schmidt waited. He could see that Ranallo and DeVito were tensing, verbally squaring off with each other.

"So it seems," said Ranallo.

"Jesus Christ," said DeVito. "You wanted to prosecute and

now you don't, is that it?"

"Look," said Ranallo. "The police uncovered new evidence linking Norman Frank with another murder. We serve the innocent as well as the guilty." They all stared at him as though he were an idiot. In fact he was trying out the statement he would give to the newspapermen.

"We still have two murders," said Schmidt.

"Important murders," said DeVito. "And we're six weeks behind on them because we fucked up, because we thought it was all solved."

"We didn't all 'fuck up,' DeVito," said Leonard Ranallo. "The police don't prosecute." He felt uncomfortable. He twisted in his chair and pulled at the seam of his trousers so the legs would not wrinkle while he sat. The chief of homicide dressed very well.

"The police don't prosecute and justice is blind and the tooth fairy is real," said DeVito. He didn't like Ranallo; he had once told Jack Donovan that Ranallo dressed like a mob hood from Melrose Park.

DeVito wanted to continue the quarrel. "You guys steered us the wrong way."

"Poor baby," said Ranallo. "Let's stop pissing on each other."

Schmidt broke the tension. "We need surveillance in the park. And I think we should run a decoy operation. In the meantime Investigator Sid Margolies is going through reports to see if there were any assaults or attempts in the past few months that might give a bigger picture of what we're dealing with."

"We're dealing with a guy who goes into the park from time to time and kills women," said Mario DeVito.

They were silent at that.

Ranallo said, "When did this Jane Doe die?"

Schmidt winced. "The victim apparently was killed sometime Sunday morning. The coroner can't be precise yet but it was probably late morning."

"He's an early riser," Ranallo said.

Now they were all offended. Flynn threw his cigarette

85

down on the floor. He had been at both murder scenes. "Both women were killed in the morning. There has to be some reason."

They all looked at him. It seemed very logical. Schmidt was pleased.

"They were both of a type—blond, young, blue eyes," Schmidt said. "We need a decoy. Terry Flynn went down to personnel this afternoon and made a request for some names. Someone from patrol, of the type attacked in the park."

"For how long?" asked Ranallo.

"I don't know," said Schmidt.

"I suppose—"

"The mayor has seemed upset by the park murders."

Ranallo made a gesture. He considered himself a political animal and did not want to be reminded of the obvious. "I understand the situation. But we don't have that many people."

"We have to do it," said Schmidt. "We can't have another murder in the park."

"We're six weeks behind on this. What makes you think you'll get a break now—unless he has the chance to kill someone again?" It was Mario.

Ranallo frowned. He touched the sleeve of his chalk-striped suit coat. A woman manicured his fingernails every two weeks, and his hair was styled. Ranallo thought DeVito looked like a common Dago.

"Why do you think it's the same guy?" Ranallo asked. "This second broad was naked."

The two policemen winced. The word "broad" made the dead woman seem meaningless. Ranallo had spent only a little time in homicide before commanding the division; he did not understand the tenderness with which the detectives addressed the victims of murder. To cheapen the dead cheapened their search for the killers.

"We have to assume for the moment that it's the same man," said Schmidt. "We have to find a pattern to it. And we might catch him before the next time if we have a decoy. We can work the parks with a policewoman and a team behind her. And at the same time if Margolies comes up with any assault victims in the park in the frame of the last few months, we'll pursue it from that end."

"So we should drop the indictment against Norman Frank," DeVito said.

"Quietly," said Schmidt.

"It'll only make a bang big as a headline. Halligan won't be happy," said DeVito. "But he's going to have to bite the bullet. I'm glad I didn't have anything to do with this fuckup."

Terry Flynn laughed.

DeVito smiled. "But if we throw the papers that Norman killed Shorty Rogers, it might keep them off our backs. They can't concentrate on two ideas at the same time."

"Is the killer a colored guy?" asked Ranallo.

Schmidt shrugged. "I don't know. There's nothing to tell us."

Then Flynn saw it. While they were talking, he had chewed on the thought and now he understood. He blurted it out in an unfinished form: "Who'd go to a park near the Loop on Sunday?"

They stared at him.

Flynn reddened. "The park. I mean, Grant Park."

"Everyone goes to the park on Sunday," said Leonard Ranallo, who had never gone to the park on Sunday in his life.

"No, not that kind of park," Flynn said rapidly. He stood up and paced to the door of the little office and turned. "I mean Grant Park in the Loop. On Sunday morning. There's no reason to be in the park. Not for the girl. And not for the killer. No reason at all for either of them to be there. So why the hell were they there? And why Grant Park?"

Schmidt nodded at Flynn and permitted a little congratulatory smile.

Mario nodded as well. "Flynn is right. The Loop's deader than Kelsey's nuts on Sunday except for the flops and the downtown hotels. And the sailors from Great Lakes training center who come downtown in the afternoon."

"And colored guys," said Ranallo.

"There's no black downtown on Sunday in the Loop, not that early," said Mario.

"Not in the park," said Schmidt.

"Not that early. They'd be picked up just for being there."

"So maybe the killer is a lover."

"He takes them down to the park to kill them," said Ranallo.

"But what about our Swede?" asked Mario.

Schmidt said, "We got a statement from a guy she dated the night before she was killed. She had gone to bed with him. Maybe we should talk to him again."

"Maybe the killer lives downtown, in Outer Drive East or something," said Flynn, still in a trance of his own making.

"Or the victim," said Mario. They nodded at that. Suddenly, after a quagmire, they were back on solid ground. There were leads. There were questions to be asked.

"So does that mean you won't need the decoy now?" asked Ranallo, who seemed a little lost.

"Goddamn it, yes we will," said Schmidt, who rarely raised his voice.

Ranallo stared at him coldly. Schmidt had cancer; maybe he was going to die. He was pretty old.

"So the guy works nights," said Flynn in his last revelation of the day. DeVito stared at him in surprise. In the weeks they had prepared the Norman Frank case, DeVito had not been impressed by Flynn; he had seemed just another loud cop who sometimes drank too much.

Schmidt said, "Go ahead, Terry."

"Maj Kirsten was killed on Tuesday morning. The second victim was murdered on Sunday morning. The guy has got to work sometime, it would seem. So he works nights."

"If he's employed," said Ranallo.

"And he works shift work. Odd days off, like cops," said DeVito.

Ranallo glared at him.

"Yes," said Matt Schmidt. "One on a Sunday, the other on a Tuesday."

Schmidt almost felt Flynn's excitement; the room seemed to tingle with it. Schmidt never really believed in the hunt, only in the result, only in the closing of the circle that ran from the anarchy of the act of murder to the solution, the reaffirmation of order. Flynn was a different man; he only believed in the hunt, in the everyday.

7. THEY LEARNED HER NAME EARLY WEDNESDAY. IT CAME FROM AN OLD MAN WHO WOULD NOT STOP CRYING. He walked into the Jefferson Park police station on the Northwest Side shortly after midnight. He went up to the desk sergeant and, without a preliminary remark, began to repeat the name. Large tears fell down the ridges on his brown face; the desk sergeant thought the man was drunk because he couldn't understand him and because his breath stank of beer and cigarettes.

One of the beat men came around the desk and put a hand on the man's elbow. It was not a particularly threatening gesture, but the old man shoved his hand away. Then he said the girl in the park was named Christina Kalinski, and she was his daughter.

Then he said he knew the man who killed her.

At first they didn't know what to do.

The desk sergeant called for the watch commander who came out of his office eating a doughnut. The commander listened to the crying man and to the desk sergeant and then

89

suggested they call Area Five Homicide on the Northwest Side.

The homicide divisions had been asked by Ranallo to call Matt Schmidt on anything involving the Grant Park murders. The homicide sergeant called Schmidt. It was nearly two o'clock in the morning, and Schmidt was asleep. His wife, Gert, would not wake him but gave him the number for Sergeant Terrence Flynn. The Area Five man shrugged and called Flynn.

Which was why, shortly after three A.M., a bleary-eyed and hung over Sergeant Flynn entered the Jefferson Park police station.

The man who said he was Christina Kalinski's father was still sobbing.

He sat in a corner of the station, near the pay telephone. One of the policemen had gotten him a paper cup of coffee, but he had let it grow cold without touching it. The remains of cigarettes littered the floor around his feet. Flynn looked at him a moment while the watch commander said: "His name is Michael Kalinski. He says his daughter is Christina and that she's the one they found in the park Monday. That's all we know now. Some guy named Schultz was supposed to be called in—"

"Schmidt."

"Something. Kraut name. So they sent you, huh? You're Finn?"

"Flynn."

"Helluva thing in the middle of the night. You'd think the guy could have waited until morning."

Flynn blinked.

The watch commander, whose name was Burnett, went on: "We really ain't got nothing out of him. He's just on this crying jag. I think he got stiff someplace before he came here. But he keeps saying he knows who killed the broad in the park."

"Christina Kalinski," corrected Flynn. He really did not want to hear any of this. He went over to the man and put his hand on his shoulder. "Come on," he said. Without a word the crying man got up and followed Flynn into the empty locker room. They sat on a bench. Flynn offered him a Lucky Strike, and the crying man took it in strong, trembling hands. He cupped the light and blew the smoke quickly out of his nose.

"My name is Sergeant Terry Flynn. I'm working on the case in the park. You say it was your daughter?"

"On television. My daughter. Jew bastard kill my daughter."

"What's her name?"

"I tell you name." The accent was thick. The blue eyes of the old man burned.

"Okay. Tell me."

"Jew bastard."

"What was her name?"

"Christina."

"Christina. Christina what?" He wrote down the first name.

"Christina Kalinski."

"How do you spell that name?"

"I kill Mr. Weiss."

"Who?"

"Mr. Fancy Weiss."

"Who's he?"

"He Jew bastard, kike son of a bitch. Kill Christina."

"Slow it down, will ya? Look Mr. Kalinski. Just slow up. Sit there a second and have a smoke."

The man looked up as though coming out of a trance. "Who you?"

"Sergeant Terry Flynn. From homicide."

The words seemed to start the tears again. Flynn was embarrassed. He reached for his handkerchief and realized he didn't have one. The tears rolled down the old man's face.

Finally there were only sobs.

Terry Flynn said, "Tell me about Mr. Weiss."

"I kill him."

Flynn said, "Look, Mr. Kalinski. Someone raped your daughter and stabbed her to death. We'll get him."

Raped and stabbed. The words cut through the sobs. For the first time the old man was silent. He had gray hair which grew in spiky clumps on his head, and thick gray eyebrows.

"Tell me, now."

So the old man began: "My daughter is Christina. Good girl. Momma die ten years ago, my daughter then is good girl. Go to mass, go to communion, always. Everything. She is only twenty-two years old." He seemed on the verge of tears again.

"How do you spell that last name?"

The old man pulled out his worn wallet and passed it over. Flynn opened to the driver's license. He wrote the name down on his pad and then flipped the pages of the wallet. There was a picture of a little girl about ten years old. He really couldn't see the resemblance between the picture and the body in the morgue.

"Your daughter lived with you?"

"No. Mr. Weiss. She live with that kike. She whore now. She sleep with him."

"Who is Mr. Weiss?"

"Mr. Weiss. You cops know place. Cops all know. I tell them, they do nothing."

"What place?"

"Place Susy."

"Susy?"

"Yah. Susy, Susy, Susy. I tell cops. You know."

"Where is it?"

"Downtown. Bad place."

"Susy?" Flynn thought a moment. His mind scoured the streets of downtown in his memory. And then he thought of Rush Street, the heart of the sleazy, faded nightclub district. Susy-Q Lounge.

"Susy-Q."

"Ya. Susy."

"On Rush Street?"

"Ya, ya. Dhat place."

It was a strip joint.

"She work in Susy-Q?"

"Yah. I tell you cops this before, you do nothing. You no get my daughter. My Christina." His eyes filled again. "Now he kill her. I kill him."

"Take it easy, Mr. Kalinski. She a stripper?"

92

"No clothes."

Flynn didn't understand.

"No clothes," the old man repeated. He was not talking to Flynn.

"What's no clothes?"

"On television," he said.

"What about television?"

"Christina on television. Her face. My daughter. Man say, she got no clothes. No clothes. My daughter. She whore." He started to cry.

"On the news last night."

"Shame to me. They say she have no clothes."

"Yeah," said Flynn. He was bone tired. His head threatened to drop onto his chest. He wanted to sleep or he wanted a drink, but he didn't want to talk to this old man in his inarticulate grief.

"You cops do nothing."

Flynn waited.

"Cops. Pigs."

Flynn thought, fuck this. "Someone raped and stabbed your daughter. And her body is down at the morgue right now and you're going to have to go down and see it. So don't tell me about your daughter being a whore. What's the matter with you, man? She's dead. Dead. Now tell me who the hell Weiss is."

The old man was stunned. It was as though someone had struck him in the face with a shovel. The tears stopped. "Mr. Weiss. Four months ago she meet Mr. Weiss. I don't know other name. She run away from home."

"A runaway?" At twenty-two?

"She go away, no tell me. I tell cops. They no look for her. One day, then, she come home. She strange. She come home, no talk. She take clothes. I hit her then. She cry. I go away, work, I come home, she gone. Christina."

"Was she on drugs?"

The old man shook his head. "I don't know."

"You met this guy, Weiss."

"One time only. He came with her when she take clothes,

put in car. But he wait outside. I not know. I go outside, go to work. I see him. Cadillac. Jew bastard. I tell my friend then, he have daughter too, she run away. We find car is Mr. Weiss."

"How'd you do that?"

"I not tell you."

"You traced the license."

"Why you ask then?"

"How'd you do that?"

"Friend."

"Policeman?"

"Bah. No police friend. Cops. Pigs. Fuck cops."

"Fuck you too."

"We go down to see Mr. Weiss."

"How'd you find him, I asked."

"Collection man."

"Friend of yours in a collection agency?"

"We find him."

"Where'd you find him? Home?"

"No. We go to Susy place. The place you said."

"So you followed him."

It was obvious the car was registered to this Weiss man, with the address listed at the Susy-Q Lounge.

"Bastard cops," Michael Kalinski said. "We go, me, my friend. And she is there."

"Why not call the cops?"

"I do call." The old man stood up. "Cops say she is twenty-two, can do nothing. What rule is this? She is my daughter. She call me name in this place. Place of devil. She not my daughter, she is whore. Man throw us out."

He paused and then: "Big nigger man at door. Mr. Weiss send him."

"The bouncer?"

"Ivan take me home."

"Ivan who?"

"My friend."

"Yeah. Ivan who?"

"I not tell you."

Flynn got up. He thought he couldn't take any more of it. He let his cigarette drop to the floor, and he crushed it with his shoe. He left Kalinski standing by the lockers and went into the front room of the station. Commander Burnett was eating another doughnut.

"I need someone to take him down to the morgue for an identification."

"So that was her?"

"Looks like it."

"Why can't you take him down?" asked Burnett.

"I got to see a man. I'd appreciate it," said Flynn.

"Who you gotta see?" asked Burnett out of curiosity. Nights were slow and long in Jefferson Park district.

"A guy named Weiss who was shacking up with his daughter. Who is ninety percent sure to be the corpse we found in the park Monday."

"You solved it?"

"Who knows?"

"I'll get Gloves to take him down. Gloves?" He called into his office. A man wearing white gloves came out.

"You gotta take Mr. Kalinski down to the morgue to eyeball his daughter, the broad they found in Grant Park on Monday."

"Shit," said Gloves.

"Why are you wearing those gloves?" said Flynn.

"Eczema." The man had a sour look on his face.

"Oh." Flynn lit another cigarette.

"All right. Who's who and what's what?"

Flynn gestured toward the locker room. "Guy named Michael Kalinski in there says that was his daughter we found in Grant Park on Monday. So I need a positive ID before I talk to this other guy. What time is it? I left my watch."

"I dunno," said Gloves. "Big clock on the wall there says the time is three thirty."

"Shit. I'm not going to make it."

"Okay. Say, what do we do when he eyeballs the stiff?"

"Call me. No, I'll call you at the morgue. And then take him home."

"Shit," said Gloves.

Flynn flushed. "Look, you're not doing me a favor, you know."

"Sure he is, Flynn," said the commander mildly. He had finished the doughnut.

"Look. This is a very hot case, as you know, Commander. I got to have that ID one way or the other by four A.M. I'm going over to the guy's club and betting it has a four o'clock license. It's a joint on Rush Street. I gotta have a positive ID before I talk to him."

The commander shrugged. This guy Flynn was a pain in the ass, but Burnett didn't know how much clout he carried downtown and he didn't want to get into any trouble. Not for Gloves's sake. "Take him down, Gloves," he said.

Flynn called the morgue from a pay phone outside the Susy-Q Lounge at four-ten A.M. and neither Kalinski nor Gloves had arrived. Flynn cursed Gloves roundly to the startled morgue attendant on the other end of the line and then hung up.

Rush Street was fading fast. It would be dawn in an hour.

The hookers were booked or going home; the drunks were weaving down the streets, making final pickups. The cabbies prowled for conventioneers who wanted an after-hours drink joint or a black whore in a blond wig who'd be willing to go down on them in the back seat for twenty-five dollars. The hustlers and pimps and strong-arm boys lounged in the shadows of the garishly lit buildings, waiting to pick off the drunks or fools or both. The "he-shes," black gays dressed in women's clothing, pranced their final tired poses beneath the glittering marquees.

Flynn realized he might get into trouble moving in on the club without a search warrant and without even a positive identification from Michael Kalinski that the girl in the park was his daughter and that she was "Weiss's" mistress or employee.

But there was no question that he was going in.

He banged on the front door for several minutes, but there was no answer. He went around the gangway to the alley in back and knocked on the rear door. No answer. He knocked again.

"Get the fuck out of here," came a voice.

"Police," said Flynn. "You better open that door, you son of a bitch."

Silence.

"Police. I want to talk to Weiss."

"He ain't here."

"Open that fucking door."

"Who says you're the cops?"

"I say."

"Go way."

"Listen, you son of a bitch, if you don't open that motherfuckin' door right now, no one's going to open any doors tomorrow. I'll get your fuckin' license pulled so fast you won't be able to fart in there in the morning. You understand what I'm saying?"

"Go 'way."

"I'm from homicide," Flynn tried. The door was steel.

"What say?"

"Murder. Open the goddamn door."

He heard the bolt at last and then the deadlock. He thought he heard voices. For the first time in months he felt for the .357-magnum pistol tucked into his belt near the base of his spine.

The door opened on a thick chain. He saw a face in the dim light of the alley.

"What you want?"

He flashed his star. "Open up. I want to talk to Weiss."

"What do you want? We take care of them over at the district. We're okay with vice. So what do you want?"

"Son of a bitch," said Flynn.

"Hey, man, that's no way to talk. You talk to Lieutenant O'Connor on vice, that's my man."

"But I ain't your man. My name is Flynn and I'm in homicide and if I don't talk to Weiss in about ninety seconds, you're going to the fucking shithouse for obstruction of a murder investigation. Can you dig it, shithead?"

It appeared the black man at the door was a little drunk. He wore a shiny black velvet suit. "You shaking me down, man, or what? Whaddaya want? Ya want some whiskey, my man? You want some Johnny Walker Red Label or what?"

Flynn shoved his wing-tipped black oxford into the crack of the door opening. He said it again: "I want to see Weiss."

"Sure, baby."

The face disappeared into the blackness beyond the door. Flynn felt angry and foolish standing in the alley with his foot wedged in the entrance.

Then headlights flooded the alley, and for a moment Flynn froze. He couldn't see. His instinct was to duck into the service basement steps to his right and pull his pistol. He waited. And then the car door opened.

"Stand right there. Police."

It was absurd.

Flynn stood still. He was aware of a figure beyond the blinding headlights.

"Put your hands away from your body," the voice said.

A second voice said, "Turn and face the wall. Slow. And assume the position."

It was even embarrassing. Flynn pulled his foot from the door and turned to the brick wall and threw out his arms and spread his feet.

"Wider," came the voice.

They patted him down.

"Shit, he's got a gun, Joe," one of the voices suddenly cried. "Watch him, watch him."

They freed his pistol. Then one of them hooked one wrist with a handcuff and the other tripped his ankle. Flynn went sprawling on the floor of the alley and skinned his cheek. They dragged his left arm back behind him and snapped the other wrist into the cuffs. Then they roughly pulled him to his feet.

"You tore my coat, you stupid bastards," Flynn said quietly.

"Shuddup," said the first uniform. He took a step toward Flynn and cuffed him on the face. At that moment the back door of Susy-Q was thrown open.

"Whaddaya doin' here?" said the second uniform.

"I'm a police officer," said Flynn.

The two hesitated. The first one said, "Where's your star?"

"I wish it was sticking up your ass right now," said Flynn. "Left-hand inside pocket."

The beefy one—the first uniform—stepped forward and reached inside Flynn's coat and gingerly removed the black wallet. He flipped it open and saw the five-pointed shield which Chicago police call a "star."

"Let him go, Stan," said the beefy one. "Why the hell didn't you tell us?"

"Why didn't I pull my pistol and blow your fuckin' stupid heads off?" said Flynn. "Nobody'd notice it was missing for days, least of all you guys."

The drunk in the door of the Susy-Q was watching all this and now he said, "Turns out he was a cop, huh?"

"Goddamn it, Luther, you asshole," said the beefy cop.

"It wasn't my fault."

Stan was having trouble removing the cuffs.

"Get these cuffs, you moron."

Stan finally clicked them open, and Flynn grabbed his wrists and massaged them.

"What's your fucking name?" he asked the beefy cop.

"Tom Turner." Then he thought to add: "Sergeant Flynn."

"You're wrong. Your fucking name is Shit. Mr. I. M. Shit."

"We didn't know who you were," said Turner.

Flynn snatched away his pistol and replaced it on his belt. "You get your fucking kicks shoving around citizens, do you, you stupid jagoff? You're going to eat turd pie until your eyes are brown, Turner. What's Micky the Mope's name here? And how come you guys aren't wearing your nameplates?"

"Stan Barza," said the other cop.

"Which one of you guys tripped me?"

They didn't speak.

"Assholes," dismissed Flynn.

"Say, officer, no need to be angry," said the man in the doorway. "Shit. Just a mistake. How about a bottle of very fine whiskey? How about a little something for your trouble?"

"How come you know this guy?" Flynn said.

The two cops looked at each other. "We get around the district."

"How could he call you? He's got to go through the dispatcher downtown. He can't ask for the cop he likes. Can he?" asked Flynn.

"Oh, shit," said Luther. "I seen these fellas eating cross the street. I always know they's there right now, having their lunch. So I just called across to them."

"Is that right?" said Flynn. "You boys are in a jam."

The two men looked at Flynn with white faces.

Flynn turned to the door. "I still want to talk to Mr. Weiss."

"You can't come in here without no search warrant—" the black man began.

"Is that right?" grinned Flynn. "Turner—Mr. Shit—did Luther here call you?"

"Yes," said Turner.

"What'd he say?"

"Said someone was breaking in," Turner mumbled.

"Investigate then," said Flynn. "Go ahead."

"Shit, man," said Luther. "You can't—"

Flynn leaped at the bouncer and pushed him back inside and slammed him against the wall. The bouncer instinctively brought his hands up, and Flynn chopped him hard on the shoulder. He heard a crack.

"Listen, motherfucker," said Flynn. "I want Weiss in five seconds. Four." He pulled his pistol. "Three. Two."

"He's home. He went home. He had the flu."

"Where's home, asshole? Four. Three. Two. One."

"Man, don't do that stuff. Outer Drive East. The cat lives in Outer Drive East. You killin' me—"

Flynn let go. "Bingo," he said. Downtown. In Grant Park. Not three hundred feet from the body of Christina Kalinski.

The two policemen stood in the doorway, the light from the alley silhouetting them. At that moment Flynn heard a noise from the darkness inside the club.

He pushed Luther aside and cocked his pistol.

"Lights," he hissed.

"No one there, man," said Luther.

Flynn turned suddenly and Luther flinched. "Lights."

The man fumbled for the switches in the darkness. Two large ugly spotlights glowed on. There were brilliant shadows in the tawdry half darkness of the lounge. The stage was bare.

"Who's there?" said Flynn.

He was sure he heard the noise again.

Cautiously Flynn moved into the lounge. The two uniformed men hung back by the door. Both had drawn their pistols.

Flynn saw the door on the far wall and moved toward it. He felt along the wall for a light switch. He suddenly shoved the door open but held back, pressed against the wall. The room beyond was dark, but someone was there. The presence of another human was palpable.

He tried to find the light switch.

He realized he was silhouetted in the dim light. His hands were wet. He moved suddenly into the darkness of the inner room and dropped to one knee, holding the pistol out in front of him with both hands.

"Police," he bellowed. "Who's there?"

"Don't shoot, for God's sake," a voice screamed.

"Turn on the fuckin' lights now," Flynn cried.

"Don't shoot," the voice said.

"Turn on the fuckin' lights," Flynn repeated. He was very frightened.

He thought he heard another sound, like weeping. "Don't shoot!"

"I ain't gonna shoot if you turn on the lights," he said. He was aware that someone in the inky room was moving.

And suddenly the lights flashed on and Flynn blinked. His eyes and his pistol scanned the room. Then he stood up, feeling sick. His hand went limp and the pistol barrel pointed at the floor.

Standing on the other side of the room, near a light switch, was a middle-aged white man with a sagging belly and breasts. He was dressed only in undershorts. His gray hair was matted with sweat. Flynn thought he would vomit just looking at him.

The girl was on the bed, naked.

She had long black hair. Her genitals were small and very nearly bare of hair. Her arms had been stretched above her, tied to the rail at the head of the filthy cot. She had a leather gag in her mouth, and her legs were spread wide.

There was blood on the dirty sheet and a plastic object protruded from her anus. Her buttocks rested on a pillow to lift them, and her ankles, tied to the rail at the foot of the couch, were raw where the leather straps bit into them.

She appeared to be crying—that was the sound he had heard—but he could only see the convulsive rising and falling of her ribs.

She had small breasts, hardly larger than those of the man who stood behind her.

Flynn stepped toward the man and slapped the barrel of the .357-magnum on the side of his cheek. The man fell back, spitting blood. The two uniformed men crowded the doorway with their pistols drawn.

The girl on the bed appeared to be about fourteen years old. She looked at Flynn, and Flynn could not look back at her. He looked at the tear on the sleeve of his sport coat. No one moved. The man in shorts began to sob.

Flynn looked back at the door, at the two uniformed men. "Get out of here," he said. They backed away.

He went to the bed, untied the girl, and took the leather gag from her mouth. As he covered her with a blanket, he felt her thin body shake.

And then they all heard her begin to cry.

8. THE TELEPHONE BEGAN TO RING, AND JACK DONOVAN EMERGED FROM A DEEP, RESTLESS SLEEP LIKE A DRUGGED MAN. HE rolled over in the bed and dragged the covers with him, but the phone wouldn't stop. He opened his eyes and saw morning light streaming through the blinds in the bare little bedroom. Finally the phone stopped ringing.

He was awake and his mouth was thick. An empty glass sat on the nightstand beside the bed; Donovan looked at the glass and tried to remember the night before. He closed his eyes. The telephone started ringing again.

This time he pushed himself up, dragged the covers around him, and stumbled to the kitchen. In the living room the television set was on, but only a white static sound came from it; there were no images.

He pulled down the receiver on the fifth ring. Beneath the covers, drawn around him like the robes of a king, he was naked.

He did not speak.

"You told me to call you." Goldberg. What had happened

now? He looked at the kitchen clock. It was nearly six A.M.

"This is about the Kalinski murder. Sergeant Flynn just arrested a guy and he says he thinks the guy killed her."

"What the hell are you talking about?"

Goldberg sounded excited, which was not unusual. Donovan leaned his forehead against the cool kitchen wall.

"I'm sorry, I forgot. It's all happened overnight and I forgot.... You didn't know her name. We got an identification a couple of hours ago on the girl in the park. The second body. Her name is Christina Kalinski, age twenty-two. Her father made the identification. She was apparently a B-girl down on Rush Street and was shacking up with some guy named Seymour Weiss. So Flynn went down to Weiss's joint—"

"Slow down, Goldberg."

Goldberg seemed annoyed. "Sergeant Flynn," he began slowly, as though talking to an idiot. "He went down to the place where Christina worked, which is a club on Rush Street owned by this Weiss character."

Donovan nodded to himself. His forehead was still pressed against the cool kitchen wall and his eyes were closed.

"So when he got down there, you know what?"

Donovan waited.

"He rousted Weiss and found a fourteen-year-old girl there, a runaway, all tied up. You know, in an S and M scene. And she was strung out on some kind of drugs. They got her at Henrotin Hospital now. And we got Seymour Weiss down here. They haven't talked to him yet about the Kalinski woman."

"I'm coming down." Donovan kept his eyes closed. "Did Flynn give him his rights and everything?"

"Sure. Everything was careful. They're going to charge him with deviate sexual assault, rape, contributing to the delinquency of a minor, imprisonment . . . shit, we can hold this bastard until doomsday."

"Just take it easy on the park murders. Tell Flynn I'm coming down."

"Sure," said Goldberg. "He even got to call his lawyer. Guy named Larry Hopewell. You know him?"

"Yeah," said Jack Donovan. "An outfit lawyer." He referred to the crime syndicate.

"Oh. This guy Weiss in the outfit then?"

"It wouldn't surprise me," said Donovan. "Did Weiss say anything after he got his rights?"

"He said he didn't know the girl was underage. Oh, yeah. Flynn rapped him, I think. They had to take a stitch at Henrotin."

"Shit," said Donovan. "What's wrong with these guys? They got shit for brains?"

Donovan hung up and went into the bathroom. While he shaved, he wondered if Flynn had really broken it open.

In the kitchen he found a half carton of milk. He opened it and sniffed at it. It did not smell bad so he drank all of it and threw the carton in the garbage can.

He turned off the television set in the living room and left the apartment.

"You look like hell, Flynn," Donovan said as he walked into the squad room next to the interview room.

"I feel like hell," said Flynn. "I called Matt twice, but I can't get through Brunhilda to talk to him. He's sleeping and she won't wake him up. She pulled the gizmo out of the receiver so now I can't get through at all." He handed the arrest sheet to Donovan.

"How good does it look?" asked Donovan.

"Very good. The bum lives in Outer Drive East. The Kalinski girl is found one hundred feet from the building, practically. Bingo. And this little creep was shacking up with her. Bingo again. And the guy is into beating up girls. He gets his kicks from whips and stuff. You oughtta seen that poor kid he had tied up in his club. So bingo number three, and we get a free game on the pinball machine. I think he is candidate number one for the park murders."

"Just like Norman Frank," said Donovan.

Flynn frowned.

"He's been processed and we've got him stewing next door in the interview room."

"You slugged him?"

"I had to." Flynn looked back steadily at Donovan. Now they were policeman and lawyer. "He resisted arrest. I had two other coppers with me at the scene, and they'll back me up. Both of them already made statements."

"Well, that's a relief."

Flynn smiled. They were on the same side again. "See, the little creep tore my coat." He indicated the tear in his jacket.

"Anything else? Where's his attorney?"

"He had to leave a message. The attorney has got an answering service. I asked him if he wanted to call anyone else, but he ain't talking. See, everything is neat. He got his call, got his rights, got everything."

"Okay."

"One more thing. We also got a colored guy named Luther Jones. He's a bouncer at the Susy-Q Lounge for Weiss, and he's the guy that let us into the club to talk to Weiss. We think he was also into helping Weiss tie up little girls. We got him locked up."

Donovan frowned. "So you didn't have a search warrant for the club. Says here you effected the arrest after hours. What was the pretext for entering the property after hours?" Donovan was testing the strength of the legal web surrounding the arrest.

Flynn still smiled. "Luther Jones called police to investigate a reported break-in at the club."

"Really?" Donovan was surprised. "Who broke in?"

"No one. False report. It was me at the back door. The guy was a little drunk and decided to fuck me around by calling the cops when I banged on the door." Terry Flynn grinned and lit a Lucky Strike. "We got a lot of shit on Luther Jones too. He's gone down twice for very heavy stuff. Armed robbery fifteen years ago and attempted murder and aggravated assault five years ago. Luther's on parole."

"So Luther Jones is our wedge with Weiss and our cover in case we made any mistakes."

"More than that," said Terry Flynn. "This Susy-Q has got to be an outfit joint, especially with Weiss calling this Shyster,

Hopewell. Luther Jones just might like to talk 'bout all kinds of things."

"You're dreaming," said Donovan. "Luther would rather go to the joint again than end up on a meat hook on the West Side."

Flynn shrugged.

"Well, let's talk to him before Hopewell gets around to coming down," said Donovan. Flynn led him into the interview room.

Weiss looked up from the table where he sat. The room contained only the table, four folding chairs, and a chain attached to one wall. The chain had cuffs at one end and was used when questioning violent prisoners.

Flynn thought Seymour Weiss had diminished in size since his arrest. He appeared now to be a little man. He looked at Flynn as the two men entered. One eye was swollen and had turned blue, and there was a bandage on his cheek.

"What now? You gonna beat me up some more?" The sniveling man found in the room with a naked girl on his bed had also changed; he was a mean-voiced man now with flat, crafty eyes.

"Shut up, asshole," Flynn said amicably. "You want another cup of coffee?"

"I don't want shit. I want my lawyer."

"Did we let you call him?"

"I ain't saying nothing."

"Did we let you call him?" Flynn repeated and this time Weiss felt he should answer. He nodded.

Donovan said, "We're going to ask you some questions."

"I ain't talking. I told this one here I ain't talking, so you can ask questions and you won't hear nothing but echoes."

"Very hard case," said Flynn in the same amused tone. "You want a cigarette?" He offered the pack and this time Weiss took it. "You ain't got filters?" he asked.

Flynn chuckled and held out a light. His mood was maddening to Weiss.

"We want to know about Christina Kalinski," said Donovan quietly.

Weiss seemed to freeze in the act of puffing the cigarette to life.

Flynn and Donovan both knew in that moment that Weiss was afraid.

"Who?"

"Christina Kalinski."

They fell silent and Weiss drew hard on the cigarette and lost himself in blue smoke.

"What about her? She used to work for me but I ain't seen her," Weiss said at last. His voice had lost something in the past few seconds.

"Since when?"

"All week," said Weiss. He suddenly tried out a smile on Flynn. "Hey. Come on. Look, I know you gotta do what you gotta do. Look, you know Lieutenant O'Connor with vice? That's my man. Really, long as I been on Rush Street, O'Connor and I know each other. We go back, you know? I really run a clean joint, you know? Man? You figure I could talk to O'Connor, maybe we could straighten all this out? Look, I know you got your job to do and I got mine and sometimes we get a little misunderstanding, you know—"

"O'Connor's my brother-in-law," said Jack Donovan. Even Flynn looked surprised.

"No shit?" said Weiss, the smile widening.

Donovan beckoned Weiss into the squad room. He picked up a phone and dialed. He waited for a long time and then spoke. "Hello? This is Jack. I got a friend of yours I'm talking to. Tell him who I am."

He handed the phone to Weiss. Donovan said, "We want to make sure you get all your phone calls."

Weiss took the receiver as though it were a hand grenade with the pin pulled.

"Hello? This is Weiss. Morey Weiss. Who's this?"

"What the hell is going on, Seymour?" asked the sleepy voice at the other end. "What the hell did you get me into?"

"O'Connor? Is that you? They got me down here, this guy says he's your brother-in-law. I got troubles, big—"

"Lemme talk to Jack."

Weiss handed the telephone receiver back to the thin,

red-haired man sitting across the table from him. Donovan put the receiver to his ear and watched Weiss's face.

"Jack?"

"Yeah?"

"What's the beef with Weiss? He's a good guy."

"How much does he drop to you?"

"I don't know nothing about what you're talking about. You talk like a goddamn fed, for Christ's sake. You keep your nose outta my business, Donovan."

Silence.

"Jack? Are you there? What's the beef with Weiss?"

At the wedding O'Connor in a jovial, free-handed way had lent them his car for the honeymoon and then he had drawn Jack aside in the pantry of her mother's house and given Jack a hundred-dollar bill. Sixteen years ago. He and Rita had driven away as though they would never come back. They spent the first night in a Holiday Inn just over the state line in Indiana. They didn't even know where they were going and it didn't matter. They couldn't wait to touch each other, to release all the energy pent up during all the years they had known each other. O'Connor. He smoked cigars and drank whiskey and talked loud and he always bought at the bar. He had a red face and four kids and his children loved him. He played Santa Claus at Christmas when they were young.

"Jack?"

Donovan spoke quietly. "Weiss is going away for a little while."

Weiss said, "Christ." He shrank back into the doorway to the interview room.

"What's going on, Jack? You down at the state's attorney's office or what?"

"Weiss diddles little girls, Tom. Did you know that? He ties them up and he sticks things up their ass and he fucks them until they bleed, did you know that? And he strings them out on dope. Runaways, Tom, that nobody really gives a fuck about in the first place. Your buddy, Weiss."

"I didn't know nothing about that."

"I believe that." He was talking to O'Connor, but it was for Weiss's benefit. "But your man Weiss is in serious trouble and he wants to be a tough guy. He wants to be very standup, he won't even say his name. We want to ask your buddy just a couple of questions about a girlfriend of his named Christina Kalinski, and he doesn't want to talk to us. So he started throwing your name around."

"Hey, wait a minute," said Weiss.

"Wait a minute," said Tom O'Connor.

"You wanna come down and do a character witness for your buddy, Tom?"

"Hey, come on, Jack. I don't mess with guys like that. You know that. Hang the little sheenie bastard."

O'Connor sounded afraid and upset and that pleased Jack Donovan. And then he remembered something else: when Rita went crazy, finally, O'Connor and his wife took in Jack Donovan's two little children while he tried to put things together. The kids always told him they had had ice cream almost every night.

Donovan cupped the receiver and stared at Weiss. "He says to hang you, Morey."

"Fuck this shit, fuck this shit," Morey Weiss said, repeating the words like a charm. "What the hell?"

"You made him unhappy, Tom," said Jack Donovan. And he replaced the receiver on the cradle.

Flynn, who had been standing behind Donovan, said to Weiss, "You wanna answer a few questions about Christina Kalinski?"

Weiss shrugged and entered the interview room and sat down at a table.

"I didn't kill her."

They waited, afraid to speak.

Morey Weiss broke the silence. "I saw her picture in the paper yesterday afternoon. I knew it was her. She was missing since Sunday. I didn't know what to do. Maybe she went home to her old Polack father. I didn't know."

"You wanna wait around for your lawyer?" Flynn asked quietly. "We just wanna ask you a few questions of your own free will now."

"Sure," said Weiss. He slumped in his chair, looking like a dead man.

110

The interview room door was open, and Jack Donovan stood framed in the entrance. Flynn sat down at the table across from Weiss.

"What happened about Christina Kalinski?"

"You gonna hang this on me too?"

"No," said Jack Donovan. "We need some information about her."

"Hey, Morey," said Flynn "When you get up to Stateville, you're going to like it. Really. They got guys up there who like to put their pricks up your ass, you know what I mean? And you'll love it too, you know that? You like to tie up little girls? Shit, they won't tie you up. They'll make you love it, they'll stand in line for you. You'll get calloues on your knees, you'll give so many blow jobs. You'll get so you'll go down on them for breakfast, lunch, and dinner, you're gonna love it so much. And you won't never think about girls again unless you want to be one."

Donovan waited. He thought Flynn was wrong. It was the wrong approach. Weiss was shrinking into himself, slouching more, turning a deathly white.

"I didn't kill no one," he said at last.

"We know that," said Jack Donovan.

"I didn't, I swear—"

"Hey, take it easy," said Donovan. "You want to talk to us? Is that right?"

"Sure, sure. Just—"

"Just what?"

"Can I have a cigarette?"

"Fuck him," said Flynn.

"Give him a cigarette."

Flynn pulled out his pack and threw it on the table. Weiss took a cigarette and lit it nerviosly and threw the match on the floor. His hands shook.

Flynn watched him.

"You don't have to talk to us," said Jack Donovan quietly.

"No. I know that. I know that."

"You want to talk to us?"

"Sure. Sure I do. Listen, I didn't have nothing to do with that thing in the park."

"What thing?"

"Christina. Getting killed."

"I can't really talk to you about that, Mr. Weiss." Donovan turned as though to go. He looked back. "Unless you're willing for us to talk to you about Christina without your lawyer being here."

"Maybe I should wait."

"Fine," said Jack Donovan. "Take him into the lockup. We won't talk to him until he's appeared before the judge this morning. You know we aren't going to recommend any bail."

Weiss looked up. "I didn't kill anyone."

"We don't need to talk to you," said Jack Donovan. "Why not send him to the lockup."

Flynn smiled. "Sure. He can get practice up there sucking off cocks. It'll be just mild stuff compared to Stateville but you gotta start small."

Weiss cried, "Man, don't send me to jail."

"Listen," said Donovan. "First you want to wait for your lawyer, then you don't want to wait for your lawyer. I don't really give a shit. I'm trying to be a nice guy in this, and you aren't letting me."

The tension was unmerciful. Morey Weiss squirmed as though the chair was red hot.

"I wanna stay here. I wanna talk to you. I gotta talk to you. You gotta understand me."

"Fine," said Donovan.

Flynn got up and went into the next room. He returned with a Sony tape recorder. He pushed it on.

"My name is Jack Donovan and I'm an assistant state's attorney assigned to the criminal division of the Cook County state's attorney's office. This conversation is being recorded with the permission of Mr. Seymour Weiss of Four Hundred East Randolph Street in Chicago. Police Sergeant Terrence Flynn, assigned to Area One Homicide, is a witness to this conversation. Mr. Weiss has freely granted permission for us to interview him and waived his right to have a lawyer present. Is that right, Mr. Weiss? Don't nod."

"Yes."

"You know you can consult with an attorney and that you can have an attorney present during questioning?"

"Yeah. It's all right."

"Do you want to delay this conversation until we can reach your attorney?"

"No, I can't reach him myself."

"You have been charged today, July 27, with crimes not relating to this conversation. You are now in an interview room in police headquarters at 1121 South State Street. You have not been coerced into permitting this conversation, have you? Don't nod."

"Yes. I mean no. I wasn't coerced. I want to talk to you."

"Did you know Christina Kalinski?"

"Yes."

"How did you meet her?"

"I met her in a bar. On Rush Street. It was the Follies."

"When did you meet her?"

"About six months ago."

"What happened after your first meeting, if anything?"

"I offered her a job."

"Doing what?"

"Doing some waitress work in my place."

"What place is that?"

"Susy-Q Lounge. On Rush Street."

"What were her duties?"

"Wait on tables for the drinks. Give the customers a good time."

"Was she hired to perform acts of prostitution?"

"Fuck no. Not that."

"Did you become her lover?"

"That. Yeah."

"When?"

"I don't remember."

"Was it part of her condition of employment?"

"What the hell are you talking about?"

"Did she have to go to bed with you to keep her job?"

"No. I wouldn't say that. She wanted to get away from her old man."

"She found you attractive."

"I got a certain style."

"Where do you live?"

"You got it on the sheet. Outer Drive East apartments."

"Around ten A.M., on Sunday morning last, Christina Kalinski was murdered near Monroe Street Harbor, within a quarter mile of Outer Drive East."

"I didn't kill her."

"No one said you did."

"Were you a gentle lover?"

"What's that mean?"

"Did you and Christina play games?"

"Sure. Gin rummy."

Even Flynn laughed.

"Did you ever whip her? Or tie her up?"

"Sure. Sometimes. She liked it that way. You find most broads are like that, underneath. You know, a little kinky. Puts some spice into it. Me, I can take it or leave it. But you know, you throw a fuck into a broad and that's it. It gets boring after awhile."

"Did you beat her?"

"Not beat. I slapped her around once or twice but so what? You never slap a broad around? They need it once in awhile, you know? They expect it. You treat a broad like she's the Queen of Sheba, they get to be a pain in the ass."

"Did she live with you?"

"After her old man threw her out. A crazy man, an old-country Polack. You know what I mean? He come down to my joint one time with this other guy and they wanted to cause trouble, you know? They called the cops on me, checking everyone's ID, everything. But my joint is clean, and my broads weren't doing nothing illegal. The Supreme Court says you gotta let them show you their cunts if they want to.

"But these two old Polacks come down and they accuse me practically of kidnapping Chris. I told her right there she could go home with the old man any time she wanted to. She says she wants to stay with me. Look, I was nice to her. She's free, white, and twenty-one—so what the fuck? Listen, I took care of her. She wanted a dress, I give her a dress. I gave her a coat. I didn't have to do that. Besides, she's a nice piece of ass. I mean you guys are older. It's nice to have a little young quail once in a while, right?"

"I was over at Outer Drive East and talked to the doorman.

He said Christina left the building last Sunday a little after nine A.M. and that you followed her about a half hour later."

"I was wonderin' when you were coming to this part. This is a lot of shit. This is where you try to pin this thing on me. Well, you can shut off the machine because I ain't saying no more. You wanna talk to me, talk to my lawyer."

"Sure. Fine. I think we got enough."

"Now what's that mean?"

"That's fine. Shut off the machine, Terry."

Flynn obliged.

"Hey, you guys," said Weiss. "She was goin' to church. Went to church every Sunday. Don't ask me. Long as I know her, she goes to church over to St. Peter's on Madison Street."

Flynn didn't speak.

"Hey, honest," said Weiss.

"And you went to church too," said Flynn.

"Not me. I'm Jewish."

Donovan said, "Just went out for a walk."

"Sure," said Weiss. "I'm an early riser. I like to walk. Besides, I usually go up on Rush Street, get some eggs, read the paper, you know. Sunday morning."

"Who was Maj Kirsten to you?"

It was Flynn. Weiss looked startled.

"Who?"

"Maj Kirsten."

"Never heard of her."

"She was murdered last month in Grant Park."

"Hey, you guys trying to clear the whole roster with me? What the fuck, do I look like a shine?"

"Christina's father says you killed her."

"Why would I want to do that?"

"Why do you want to tie up little girls?"

"I ain't going to talk to you about that."

Donovan said, "We don't need to talk to you, you little scumbag. What do you think we're playing? I don't want to talk to you anymore, you smug little shit. You think you got outfit clout and you think that's going to save your miserable ass. Well, I got news. You think the outfit is going to bat for a queer son of a bitch like you? You think they're gonna defend you against molesting little girls? The worst thing that could happen to you, you son of a bitch, is to get out. Go ahead, walk out on bail, and you'll be in a trunk in three days or hanging on a meat hook somewhere. You think the outfit guys don't have little girls at home? You give them a bad name. You're between a rock and a hard place, and no matter what you call it, you're dead, Morey. Real dead. So you go on back to your cell and wait for your lawyer and you talk to him and then go to court. And you think, Morey, you think about how you're going to get out of this one. You want to be a standup guy? Good. You be that because you're going to have to take all the shit that goes with it."

"I didn't kill no one."

"I don't want to talk to you anymore," said Donovan.

"Listen to me—"

"You spend a little time and think about if you want to get on our good side. Think about what kind of plea you want to cop to get easy time. Because right now you're booked on the next train to Joliet, and when you get to Stateville, they're going to have a welcoming committee for you. And you never knew time was going to be so hard."

"Listen. Can we work something? Can we hang it on the nigger, on Luther?"

But Flynn led him out of the room without another word.

9. THOMAS P. HALLIGAN AND LELAND HOROWITZ ARRIVED AT THE CRIMINAL COURTS BUILDING ON THE WEST SIDE SHORTLY AFTER eleven A.M. This in itself was unusual. Though Bud Halligan had been the state's attorney for nearly seven years, no one in the Criminal Courts building, where much of his office was located, could recall his ever visiting the place.

Halligan preferred to govern his sprawling little empire from a more comfortable office downtown in the Civic Center. There was located the polite and comprehensible civil division of the office, and Halligan liked the men who worked in the civil division. They had pocket calculators and gray suits and wore shirts that always looked clean. When they returned from lunch, their breath did not reek of garlic and cheap Italian wine like those on the West Side who liked to eat in the old Italian section around Twenty-fourth and Oakley streets. Halligan also preferred the downtown office because it was physically closer to the source of political power in the city—just across the street from City Hall.

Frankly Halligan did not like the atmosphere on the West

Side. And he did not like or comprehend the strange, snarling men and women who worked as prosecutors in that sprawling criminal division. They did not have pocket calculators, only brown case envelopes. They did not speak, they shouted and laughed—too loudly. And the corridors of their domain seemed perpetually crowded with evil-smelling people. It was chaos.

Shortly before Halligan took office there had been a judge in the old court building who sentenced a young black criminal to ten years in prison for armed robbery and rape; the young man became so upset by the verdict that he suddenly pulled a pistol from his suit and blew the top of the judge's head away. Before they shot him to death in the court, he also managed to wound the court clerk, a young assistant state's attorney, and his own lawyer. Halligan thought at the time that the incident symbolized the madness of the place. Who would willingly work in such conditions?

Besides, Horowitz pointed out to Halligan from time to time, the mayor of the city (who was also head of the vast political machine to which Halligan owed allegiance) liked to see Halligan's face occasionally when he dined in the Bismarck Hotel downtown. That alone was justification for his preference for the downtown office. In fact, Halligan was so seldom a visitor to the West Side building that the guard in the lobby ordered him to open his briefcase and patted him down. The weapons search was routine, instituted years before after a berserk gunman had entered the lobby one afternoon and gunned down two witnesses on their way to a courtroom where they were to testify against the gunman's brother in a murder trial.

Halligan and Horowitz took the elevator to the state's attorney's office which occupied a large section in the eastern part of the second floor.

Horowitz led the way. He was a dapper man with impeccable taste in clothes who had first been a young lawyer in the same building forty years before. He thought the offices were immutable. Horowitz liked the old building and, as a native of the tough West Side of the city, he liked the atmosphere. But Horowitz had always played a power game,

118

and now at the age of sixty-eight, he stayed downtown where the power was.

Mrs. Farrell was startled to see the two men appear in Jack Donovan's outer office and she gaped openmouthed for a moment while Halligan smilingly extended his hand. "Hello, Mrs. Farrell," he said. He never forgot a name but in Mrs. Farrell's case, it was easy to remember. She had been secretary to the past twelve chiefs of the criminal division.

"Mr. Halligan," she said. "I'll buzz—"

"That's all right," said Lee Horowitz. He again led the way into Jack Donovan's office.

Donovan looked up from his desk. He didn't appear surprised.

"Hello, Jack," said Bud Halligan, like a man looking for votes.

"Hello, Bud."

Horowitz stood by the door and closed it. Halligan went to a chair next to Donovan's desk. Donovan got up and walked to the window and looked out at the air shaft. Then he turned and sat on the ledge.

"What brings you out here, Bud?"

It was Horowitz who answered: "We wanna know what the fuck you're gonna do with this Weiss character?"

"He appeared this morning. We decided to tack kidnapping on him instead of imprisonment. That'll put us in a better bargaining position later. It's pretty solid all around and we can go to the grand jury in the next couple of days."

"I'm not talking about that stuff," said Horowitz.

"What are you talking about, Lee?" Donovan glanced at Halligan. "And who am I talking to?"

"You're talking to both of us," Halligan rumbled. "When are you going for charges on those park murders? That's why we came down here."

Donovan shrugged. "There's no need to right now. We don't have anything, but Weiss isn't going anywhere. His bond is three-hundred-thousand dollars. That's because we leaked it to the *Tribune* when he was going up, and they sat in the courtroom the whole time." Donovan smiled.

Lee Horowitz nodded. "Good trick for an amateur."

"But we've got to wait on the park murders. The cops talked to him a little bit but, we really don't have anything."

"Nothing?" Horowitz spat. "You got nothing? You had nothing on that guy Norman What's-his-name, but you sent him up to bat before he walked out of this fuckin' building. You got us holding a sack of shit downtown and smiling about it."

"Are you with the sheriff's office now, Lee? I thought the sheriff took the rap on the escaped prisoner."

"Yeah, but we got to say it's the wrong guy and then it's the right guy for the wrong murder. Shit. What a mess you got us into," said Lee.

Halligan held up his hand. "All right, you guys. Take it easy. I don't wanna see a fight." That was true, in fact.

Horowitz said, "We want an indictment. Right away."

"There isn't anything there to indict."

"So?"

"We can't indict."

"Who says?"

"Come off it, Lee. Look at it. I talked to Weiss this morning." He knew this surprised Lee. "We got him as solid as shit in winter on that little girl. We go to the grand jury, we've got it. And he knows it too. And we've got another guy we arrested with him, a black guy named Luther Jones, and we're going to work on him because he's gone down two times already. What I'm saying is, we don't have to move on Morey Weiss on that Grant Park stuff yet. Until we get more. Until we're sure."

"Sure?" Horowitz looked disgusted. "We get an indictment now. If it doesn't hold up in three months, who's going to remember? They remember now. They pick up the paper and they read about the politicians fuckin' up the country and they read about the state's attorney can't even solve a fuckin' murder when the cops hand him the killer on a silver platter. You wanna know about the public? They remember the girl in the park, two days ago, she was dead and Norman Who-Ha walks out of the Criminal Courts building and they say, 'Same old shit. These guys are fucking up, cutting deals.'"

Donovan waited.

"So where does all that leave Bud? Bud is all alone downtown. The mayor called him up this morning. And it wasn't to talk about next year's Saint Patrick's Day parade either."

Donovan said, "You don't want this, Bud. We don't have anything on the park murders, nothing to tie it to Weiss. You announce an indictment now, and even the public is going to see holes in the thing. You don't want that kind of publicity." He looked at Lee. "I take the responsibility for the Norman Frank mess. I moved on it when I shouldn't have. But this is different—"

Horowitz started screaming. "Bullshit! What do the papers know about anything? That's the public, you know. Who gives a fuck about the public? You bring an indictment, you got the guy, he's guilty. You don't have to apologize later. Even if he walks in three months, you won. No apologies. Three months from now, who gives a fuck? He's guilty anyway. And we clear the murders."

"What if he didn't do it?"

"Cut the crapola, Donovan. You're not the fuckin' jury, you know. You're the prosecutor."

"That's right, Lee. I'm the goddamn prosecutor." The mild response, delivered in Donovan's usual flat tone, seemed to infuriate Horowitz. The little man looked as though he would strike Donovan.

"Lee's right, Jack," Halligan said unhappily. He hated the wrangling. "We really need an indictment on this. The mayor's man called me before the mayor called. They're taking heat at City Hall."

"That's right," said Lee.

"I'm going to give you a little scenario," said Donovan mildly. He got up and went over to the couch and squatted on his heels beside it so that his face was on a level with Halligan's. He tried to talk directly to the state's attorney, shutting out Horowitz. The old man was forced to come around the couch to listen.

"We indict Weiss. This guy killed Christina Kalinski. At least. Maybe we can even tag him with Maj Kirsten. Good enough for a grand jury anyway. We don't have a weapon, a definite motive, but we indict. But everyone is happy. The papers praise thy name. The TV guys hang him on the air. Everyone is happy, from the cops, who think he did it, to the mayor, who now can get the Streets and Sanitation Department to stop chopping down all the foliage in Grant Park."

Halligan's eyes were soft. He was seeing it, just as Donovan laid it out.

"And suddenly, about three weeks from now or maybe four weeks from now or five, some blond, blue-eyed woman of twenty-four is strolling in the park one day and a man grabs her and rapes her and stabs her to death."

He got up. His knees cracked. He went back to the window while they waited in silence. He turned: "Suddenly, everyone says, 'Hey, I thought Bud Halligan said he caught the killer of those women.' Now it turns out we got a phony indictment and Weiss and his lawyer use it to mitigate the little girl case which we've got solid. He'll say there was no little girl, that we set him up just like we set him up on the other thing." Donovan stared at Halligan. "You want that kind of trouble, Bud? Or do you want to ride out the trouble you got now?"

"You really think he didn't do it?" said Halligan at last.

Donovan shook his head. "I don't know."

"That's all bullshit," said Lee.

Halligan shrugged. "What if it isn't, Lee? What are we gonna do then?"

Horowitz was still worked up "Crapola. I think this cocksucker has gone soft since he fucked up on the Norman Ho-Ho thing. Fuck this shit. We wanna indict. I talked to Leonard Ranallo this morning and he wants to indict. The cops want to clean this one up. This ain't Saint Joan of Arc you got. You got a miserable little prick in there. You got a soft spot for him?"

Donovan flushed. "Who are you gonna indict with? You gonna walk in there with a prick in your hand and say 'Boo' to the grand jury?"

"You can say black is shit to the fucking grand jury and get an indictment," Lee Horowitz screamed. "You are the fucking prosecutor. That's your jury. I can indict Snow White on charges of blowing the Seven Dwarfs. So what the fuck is this?"

"He didn't do it."

Halligan said quietly, "What do you mean, Jack?"

"I talked to him. He didn't do it." He was sorry he had blurted it out, but now it was there on the table for them all to pick over.

"Did he tell you he didn't do it?" Lee mocked.

"All right. I feel about this one the way I felt about Norman Frank and I didn't even see Norman Frank. I made a mistake. I let the pressure carry me along. I won't do it again. You can't indict and there's no percentage in it for you anyway, Bud. But while we take the heat off, the guy who is killing those women is going to set up his next murder."

"Ranallo says he thinks it's Weiss," said Horowitz.

"Ranallo doesn't know his ass from third base," said Donovan. "He's beginning to believe what he reads in the papers. He hasn't seen either victim and I doubt he's seen Weiss."

Halligan said stubbornly, softly, "The mayor really wants this cleared up."

"And where's the mayor gonna be tomorrow when you're standing up there with an indictment that looks like Swiss cheese and another park murder?"

He looked at Halligan and Halligan winced. Donovan suddenly knew he had won. He was aware, for the first time, that his shirt was soaked with sweat.

Horowitz understood too. The tension seemed to drain out of the room like a storm disappearing to the east.

"Okay," said Halligan finally. "If that's the way you see it right now, Jack, I'll back you up."

Donovan nodded. Halligan's words were worthless.

"Yeah," hissed Horowitz. "But I'm against it, remember. If it turns out okay, Donovan, you know I'll be the first to say it. You know that."

Donovan stared at him.

"But if you're wrong, if we don't get this guy, then I can't stand by you."

"That's nice to know, Lee," Donovan said. "I appreciate

the support. Nice to have you drop by and talk about it."

"All right there, Jack," said Halligan. He was on his feet. He sensed the smell of the old building closing in on him. He wanted to get away, escape downtown. Have a gin and tonic at lunch. Maybe with Charlie O'Neill from the civil division. He looked at Donovan. Maybe, he thought again, he really wasn't the man for the job.

"See you, Jack," he said vaguely. "We got to have lunch sometime soon."

"Anytime you say, Bud," said Jack Donovan.

"Soon," repeated Bud Halligan. "I'll check my calendar when I get back and call you. Come on, Lee, we got to leave the man alone. We've got things to do. You know what it's like, I don't have to tell you, Jack."

Donovan shook his head.

Bud Halligan didn't have to tell him.

10. HER NAME WAS KAREN KOVAC.

MATT SCHMIDT LOOKED UP AT HER STANDING IN THE DOOR-way of the special squad room, smiled, and waved her to a chair. She sat down. Schmidt glanced at the papers in front of him on the desk for a moment, then swiveled his chair and looked at her. She rested her hands on her lap and looked steadily at him.

"Do you know about this?"

"A little," she said. "They said it was a decoy operation. I put in my name. They said you wanted me."

Schmidt smiled. The squad room was empty.

"How do you like patrol work?" he asked.

"It's fine," she said. Her voice was flat and husky as though she had grown tired of talking but that was the way she always spoke. She had blue eyes. Her hair was blond. That had been the description on the personnel form they had first consulted, and it turned out to be true.

"You're married," he said.

"Divorced."

"Children?"

"I have a son." She wasn't going to say any more than she had to. She had learned that. She was not nervous and her hands did not fidget on the lap of her standard blue wool skirt. The sleeve of her blue uniform shirt said she worked in the Nineteenth District on the mid-North Side.

"I'm asking because there is an element of risk in this operation," he said. He tried out a smile.

"There's risk in patrol," she said.

"You know this is about the murders in Grant Park."

"Oh," she said. "No. I didn't know." She looked at the piece of paper on his desk.

"We're working a special investigation with the state's attorney's office. You probably read about Seymour Weiss."

"Yes. You picked him up yesterday."

"Yes. At first, we wanted to talk to him about the murdered woman. About Christina Kalinski, found Monday in the park. But then the other thing came up." He meant the tortured girl found in the club Susy-Q.

"Did he kill her?"

"Who? Oh. Christina Kalinski? We don't know. Some think he didn't kill her."

"So you want to go ahead with the decoy operation. As long as you can." This time she smiled.

"Right," he said. "There were two women murdered. Maybe Weiss killed Christina and maybe he killed them both. But that seems unlikely."

"Okay." She nodded to him.

"We want to work the decoy in the mornings. Both women were killed in the morning, within an hour of each other. One on Sunday, one on a Tuesday. But I'm afraid because of that, we'll go at it seven days a week. For as long as we can."

"Until they don't let you," she said.

Yes, he thought. He liked her. "That's it."

"A woman comes in and watches my child."

"And there's an element of risk," he repeated.

She shrugged. Her shoulders were thin, and Matt Schmidt thought her breasts were probably small. But Schmidt mostly looked at her eyes. They were set wide in her head and her face had a certain strength and sharpness of feature that is uniquely Polish. She did not blink while he examined her, and he was sorry he was so obvious about it. She did not move her hands from her lap.

"We talked to three woman, including a young student at the Art Institute, who have been attacked—or reported they had been attacked—in Grant Park in the past few months. When we found Maj Kirsten—we never told this to the press—she had marked down next to the entry on her guide that said, 'Art Institute' she had marked, 'Must see.' We don't know if she was going to the Art Institute the morning she was murdered. We've been talking to a few people at the Institute since her murder." He did not want to say since Norman Frank was ruled out as the killer, only a few days before.

She nodded.

"If you want to sign on, we'll talk with the state's attorney's office this afternoon to coordinate, and then we can start in the morning."

"How long will it be?"

"I don't know. The superintendent isn't that crazy about the idea. And Ranallo thinks it's a waste of time. He thinks we've got the killer."

"Do you?"

"Think we've got the killer or that it's a waste of time? No to both."

"Why do we have to talk to the state's attorney's office?"

He smiled again and this time he didn't have to try it on. "Some of them were on it from the start, and they've been okay with us. Besides, this whole thing has gotten so political that it spreads the heat around. And Jack Donovan asked in. He's the chief of the criminal division. Apparently he stuck his neck out yesterday when the brass wanted to indict Weiss. If that had happened, we would have lost the chance of running this operation at all."

"Fine," she said. "I only wanted to ask." She did not sound delighted. "What will I do?"

"I don't know. I suppose walk in the park."

"Is that all?"

"That's all we know to do. They were both killed in the

park and in the morning, and we don't know anything else. We know less than we knew when the first woman was murdered because we don't understand the killer—if it was the same man. There's a psychologist from the University of Chicago who's supposed to be putting together a profile of the killer. I don't think he'll have anything because he's working with the same things we have. Nothing."

"Why do you think he killed them?"

Schmidt shrugged. "He wanted to. He hated them. Why do people kill people like that? It's become a strange world. Men hate women and women hate men for it. I don't know." He paused. Why was he talking so frankly to her? "He must have hated them. He raped them and he was very cruel. And he stabbed them. Viciously. As though he were angry."

"It must be more than that," said Karen Kovac.

"Why?" asked Matt Schmidt. And then he said, "You're probably right. Fortunately or unfortunately, we don't have to be the psychologists of the world in this thing. There is chaos, and all we have to do is make order again. We don't have to solve the sexual problems of the society. Just murders."

"Why did you pick me?" she asked.

"We didn't have many choices. You seemed the type. They were both blonds, they both had blue eyes, were young."

"I'm thirty-three."

"But you look younger. Also, your watch commander said you were very quick, very smart."

She nodded. She didn't blush.

"It probably won't matter in the long run. We'll wait for weeks, or for as long as we're allowed to do this, and he won't strike again or it'll turn out we're wrong and Weiss will confess. Or maybe he'll kill someone else, but not in the park. It's the only thing we can do, though."

"Is there anything else I should know?"

"No. There was no apparent connection between Maj Kirsten and Christina Kalinski. We thought both might have been taken to the park by a mutual boyfriend, but now that we know Christina lived with Weiss, that appears unlikely. Not impossible but unlikely. Christina came from the

Northwest Side and Maj came from Sweden. One was stabbed to death and raped and the other was stabbed, stripped, and raped. Why did the killer take her clothes?"

"It was Sunday, wasn't it?" asked Karen Kovac.

"Yes," said Schmidt.

"Perhaps he had the opportunity."

Schmidt stared at her.

"I mean," she continued. "Perhaps because there was no one around, he could take her clothes. And couldn't before."

"Of course," said Matt Schmidt. "That would be logical."

Karen Kovac waited.

"That's very good," Matt said at last.

She appreciated it but did not smile. "It's not like 'Kojak,'" she said. "It's mostly just detail and boredom."

Matt Schmidt smiled.

By the time the six of them could arrange to meet, it was after three P.M. and the throbbing morning life of the Criminal Courts had eased into the daily afternoon coma.

Mrs. Farrell asked them if they wanted coffee. She was almost human, Jack Donovan thought, and then decided it was because of the presence of the policewoman. Except that she couldn't know Karen Kovac was a policewoman since Karen had changed back into civilian clothes.

But no one wanted coffee. It was too late in the day for that.

Karen Kovac sat on the old leather couch next to Matt Schmidt, who had wanted the meeting.

Terry Flynn sat on the chair next to Donovan's desk. Donovan had taken his usual position sitting on the sill of the grimy window that faced the air shaft. When it became apparent there was no other place to sit, Sid Margolies had finally decided to take Donovan's desk chair. He looked uncomfortable behind the large desk.

Mario DeVito, standing next to the filing cabinet, was staring at Karen Kovac's legs. He decided they were too thick.

Strictly speaking, there was no reason for the conference at all. And Mario DeVito had better things to do, as he had told Jack Donovan. And yet the meeting was inevitable. For one

129

thing, a new member had joined the group. For another, they were all feeling the official heat generated by the two public murders in Grant Park. The three regular Criminal Courts reporters—from *City News*, the *Tribune*, and the *Daily News*—had pestered Mario and Jack all day about Seymour Weiss and when he would be charged in connection with the park murders.

And there had been two telephone calls from Lee Horowitz essentially asking the same thing.

Leonard Ranallo had told someone that Matt Schmidt ought to be retired. He was too old and there was the problem with his cancer. The word had gotten back to Matt and he resented it.

Even Terry Flynn had been ragged at by his old boss at Area One. He had said nothing because the last time he had told a lieutenant to go fuck himself, he had very nearly been suspended for two days. But he had carried the resentment all day.

So now there were six of them, including the woman.

Flynn started: "I got the profile from the guy at the University of Chicago just before we came over. The guy says the killer is a black who is taking out his hatred of the white world on blond women. He says that's why he rapes them; not because he really wants to screw them, but because it's a symbol of renewal in his own mind of his black manhood and a way of asserting black claims on white America."

"What a lot of crap," said Mario DeVito. He flicked his toothpick into the wastebasket. "Two points," he added.

"There's more," said Flynn. "He says the killer is of above-average intelligence."

"How can he tell that?" Donovan asked from the windowsill.

"We haven't caught him," said Flynn. They all smiled.

"Miss Kovac," Jack Donovan said.

"Yes."

"Did Matt tell you about all this? That it might not work at all?"

"Yes."

"And that if it works, you will be in great risk of your life, however briefly?" Donovan did not like the sound of his own voice; it was too pompous. Even supercilious.

"I'm going to carry a pistol."

"Not your service revolver?"

"No," she said. "Something smaller."

"Something you can put in your purse," said Matt Schmidt.

"It's a twenty-five caliber automatic." She took it out of her purse. The automatic was small and the barrel gleamed dully in the dim office light.

They all seemed relieved to see the pistol. She returned it to her purse.

"Maybe you won't be able to use a pistol," said Margolies. They looked at him.

"I learned hand-to-hand combat at the academy. And I took a course in martial arts at the YMCA before I even joined the department," she said. "I get practice." They gaped at her. "Riding the El to work," she said.

Flynn laughed out loud.

Schmidt said, "Terry Flynn and Sid Margolies are going to alternate your surveillance on this operation."

Flynn said, "I'll be in the car. We'll set up a regular route, from where Maj Kirsten was found over to Monroe Street Harbor and then back. Obviously I won't have you in sight at all times. But we ought to be able to arrange for a portable radio for you."

"I don't know," said Margolies. "I already asked around and everyone is either using theirs or they're in the shop."

"What crap," said Flynn.

"It'll be all right," Karen Kovac said. She found the discussion embarrassing. She did not want this.

"You have a boy at home," said Mario DeVito. "Do you want to think about this?"

"What do you mean?"

Jack Donovan said, "Go home and think about this."

"Why?" she asked.

Matt Schmidt looked at Donovan. Donovan felt foolish but tried to console himself that he was only being chivalrous. That he was only thinking about the child. It wasn't true, of course.

"Look," she said in that flat, husky voice. "I'm a sworn officer and I know I don't have to do this. But I want to do it. I want to get into homicide."

"What?" It was Matt Schmidt.

"I don't want to be on patrol all my life," she said.

"I can see that," said Schmidt but it was plain he could not. She laughed then. It was the first time she had laughed that day. They were all so foolish.

Flynn grinned. "Sure, Matt. Why not? Give a little class to the operation. Besides, there's no heavy lifting."

She smiled at him.

"Well," said Schmidt in a lieutenant's voice. "That's later. We intend to start tomorrow morning at eight A.M. We'll work the park until noon."

"Tomorrow," said Margolies. "Day off for me."

"Then I'll take it," said Flynn. "I'm working through the weekend."

"Tomorrow's Friday," said Mario DeVito.

"So what?" said Flynn.

"Nothing. I just didn't think this week was going to end." They all understood that.

11. LILY PROVIDED A COMFORTABLE ARRANGEMENT FOR JACK DONOVAN AND IT SOMETIMES OCCURRED TO HIM THAT HE was just as comfortable for her. She did not want to get married again, that was clear. She had been married three times in her thirty-nine years, and each marriage had turned out worse than the last. Lily had an ability to select the wrong man at the wrong time. When Jack Donovan told her this once, when both of them were very drunk in O'Rourke's Pub on a Friday night, she said that must include him as well and she wouldn't go home with him.

Now Lily reached again for him across the unmade bed. He felt her hand reach for his penis and slowly awaken it.

Comfortable for both of them. She had her place and he had his. She had two cats and he had none. She owned her own small travel agency which catered to independent women like herself who, nonetheless, were reluctant to travel alone. And he—what did he have exactly?

"Jack, I want you," she said.

Lily could be disconcertingly direct. He met her a year

before at a political fund-raising dinner in a downtown hotel. She was sipping a Manhattan at the cocktail hour, and he was not drinking, merely standing near the bar and watching the scene. She asked him where his campaign button was, and he said he did not have one and did not want one. Why attend the dinner? she asked. He had had to purchase a one hundred-dollar ticket from the party and so he wanted to see what one hundred-dollars worth of food looked like.

Don't bother, Lily had responded. Was he a politician?

No, just a lawyer, he had explained. She seemed interested and he had warmed up enough to have a drink with her, and then two, and when the announcement came that they were all to shuffle into the grand ballroom, she suggested they skip dinner and go to another place. It turned out to be her own, a townhouse on Grant Place on the North Side. They ate bread and cheese and apples there and drank wine. And they made love. After it was all over, Jack Donovan thought it might have been a dream.

But he met her again, a few weeks later, at Sterch's Tavern, and this time they talked to each other like old friends who had missed each other's company.

You're really a fucked-up guy, she had said that time. Later. After love again. He agreed and said she seemed to screw up her own life just as well. Yes, Lily had replied. That made it easier on both of them. No one could ever get hurt, she said, because it was too much of a comedy.

Now he slipped into her, feeling again the pleasant wetness of her; she kissed him on the neck and her thighs squeezed his narrow buttocks. She grabbed his behind. "I love your ass," she said. "You've got an ass that a broad would be proud of."

"Stop it," he said and kissed her. "You're making me feel inferior. You've got a very nice ass too."

"Too," she said. "You bastard."

He wanted to laugh, and yet he wanted to make love to her more. He raised his chest a little and she gasped then. "Yes," she said.

Afterward, he rolled over to her side and she held him.

"Jack, that was nice," Lily said.

"Yes." He felt very tired. The bare bedroom—it was his

bedroom this time—was dark but there was a light in the hall that slanted through the open door and made them barely visible to each other on the bed. He thought her black eyes glowed in the darkness like those of the cats she kept at home.

It really had not been a satisfactory evening, though it had ended in bed. He was late for dinner and she had not been very interested in his explanation. The state's attorney's office bored her.

"Where are you?" she said now.

"Here. In me own bed with me own woman beside me."

"Celtic humor. Very funny. You're still worried about that case."

"Yes. I was wondering if you'd need any help in the travel agency. I could lead tours of single women."

"To where? Monasteries in Ireland? You'd be hopeless on a tour. Are you going to lose your job?"

"It's possible."

"Does that bother you?"

"Yes. And that's what bothers me. I really didn't want it in the first place. And now I can lose it and I don't want to lose it. They always get you, don't they?"

"That's why I work for myself. Why don't you get out and put up your roof or whatever it is that lawyers do."

"Put out a shingle," he said. He smiled and kissed her.

"Well, why not?" She got up from the bed and found her dress and shrugged it on.

"You're going?"

"If I was going, I'd put on my bra, dummy. It's cold in this place. I never understand people who have the air-conditioner on full blast. Turn it down."

"You're cold-blooded."

"I'm going to get a drink."

"Get me one."

She brought two glasses back and sat down on the bed cross-legged. He had propped his head on the pillow. He felt pleasantly dissipated. He took the drink.

"Why not?"

"What?"

"Open your own place."

"I don't know."

"I do."

"What?"

"You're afraid you won't make it."

"No. It's not that. I'll make it. I've got too many years in the office not to make it. Too many connections."

"Then do it."

"I don't want to."

"Why not?"

"I don't know. I'm thirty-eight years old and I'm not even sure I want to be an attorney."

"Well," she said. "What do you want to be when you grow up?"

He smiled. "A cop. I want to catch the bad guys."

"You've done that. You were a cop."

"Yes."

"You want to be a cop?" she repeated. "What the hell's the matter with you?"

"Oh," he said. "I don't want the bullshit that goes with it. I couldn't go back in the department. Even if I did want to go back, I don't think it would be very easy. And then what would I do? Back on patrol? Or at tactical? Writing parking tickets? Doing Friday night shootouts with the West Side cowboys? No. But being a cop—I mean, Lily, I liked being a cop without liking most of it."

"You're just another pig. You like to push people around."

"But that was it," he said softly. "That was the part that made it mean something. I was a good cop. I didn't take. I played it on the square. I didn't push John Q. around, even if he was black. Shit, Lil, you should have known me. I was a good cop."

"I couldn't have stood you. You were a little Catholic boy from the South Side playing cops and robbers, going home every night to your little Roman Catholic wife and the little family shrine she had set up there..."

He didn't answer. She was sorry about that but sometimes he seemed to drive her to it. She wondered if that were true. Lily touched him on the chest. "Jack," she said. "You make yourself lost, you know."

He nodded.

"No, you don't know but I do. I like you, Jack, I really do but thousands wouldn't. You're morose and you really are a drunk, you know. Really. And you're going bald."

"I am not going bald," he said.

"And you think you drove your wife crazy a long time ago and while you take the guilt, you won't take the responsibility."

"That's just crap, Lily," he said.

"Okay. Maybe it is. I've been drinking too much tonight, being with you."

"Thanks."

They sipped their drinks silently for a long while.

"What are you really thinking about?" she said.

"About him."

"Oh," she said. She waited. She didn't like to hear this.

"Is it one guy? Or was it Seymour Weiss and someone else? Or won't it happen again?"

"Jack, that just depresses me."

"We got a woman. From patrol division. Her name is Karen Kovac, she's divorced, got a kid, I think you'd like her."

"I don't like kids and women with kids."

"She's very...something. Very sure of herself. Or she seems to be sure of herself."

"Polish?"

"Kovac isn't Polish but that was probably her husband's name. Yes. I'd think so."

"And I don't like Polacks either."

"You're the most prejudiced bitch I know."

"I am. I don't like niggers either or fags. In fact, I hardly like anyone but red-headed Irishmen. And the odd Dago."

"How many odd Dagos have you had?"

Again they were silent.

"Why would I like her?"

"I just think you would. She's going on a decoy operation tomorrow. In Grant Park."

"Is she crazy?"

"No. I think she wants to move up."

"An ambitious bitch. That's why you think I'd like her.

You're wrong. There's only room for one ambitious woman in my life and that's me. I like them dumb and passive. It makes me stand out more."

"You'd stand out anyway. Especially with those tits."

"Do you want to screw again?"

"You're insatiable. I'm afraid men don't have the staying power women have."

"Yes. That's too bad." She added, "Do you think this creep, this guy is going to go for her?"

"We hope so."

"Oh."

"You see how it is?"

"Yes. That's why I don't like to talk about what you do. It really is all like that, isn't it? Nothing clear, nothing clean, just this kind of temporizing, patching up your plans day by day. I really don't like to think that's the way it is. I like to think it's a lot clearer."

"Yes." He got up and pulled on a robe. "I like to hope it would be all a lot more clear. That's what's wrong. That's why I really don't like it either."

"Jack, you are home," she laughed.

"I know. I'm going to the bathroom."

"I'm tired," she said.

"Will you stay tonight?" he asked.

She said she would.

The telephone began ringing at midnight, but he did not hear it until Lily poked him in the ribs. He grunted and awoke. He pulled the alarm clock near his face and looked at the time and then got up. The telephone kept ringing and it sounded shockingly loud in the silence of the flat.

Lily was right. It was too cold. He stood naked at the telephone and picked it up.

"Dad?"

The voice was small, afraid, almost a whisper.

He could not speak at first.

"What?"

"Dad? It's me, Kathleen."

"Kathleen. What's wrong, baby?"

"Mom," she said. She sounded so afraid. His hands were shaking.

"What's wrong," he repeated.

"She's gone again."

He steadied one hand on the sink and looked at the half-empty bottle of Scotch whiskey standing nearby.

"Grandpa's gone to look for her."

He glanced at the kitchen clock.

"When did she leave?" he said at last.

"Maybe this morning. I was in summer school and Brian was out early because he was working at the drugstore."

"Where was Grandpa?"

"He went out early like he does. Down to the tavern. He says she was home."

Arthur O'Connor had his shot in the morning before anything else. And rarely drank the rest of the day.

"He doesn't know where she went," Kathleen said.

"Don't cry, baby."

"Now they both went out. They didn't want to call you. But I'm here alone, Dad," she said. "I'm not a baby." She knew she didn't have to add that, he thought, but she did. Did he treat her like a baby? Of course.

"Did anyone call the cops?" he asked.

"No. I don't know. They treated me like a baby. They said I should stay here, that everything would be all right, that they would be back soon. But she's gone, Dad. I know she went away again."

"Don't cry, Kathleen," he said.

"I'm not."

"There's nothing to be afraid of."

She waited. He could hear her not crying.

"Maybe she's down at the tavern."

"No," she said. "They never saw her. She's left like she did before. Dad, I'm afraid."

He didn't know what to say. Rather, he knew what he should say. He waited.

"Daddy," she said. She broke his heart.

Lily was in the hallway now, watching him. He cupped the receiver. "Rita."

"Her? At this hour?"

"No. It's Kathleen. Rita ran away again."

She saw how white his face was.

"What are you going to do?" she said.

"Hello? Dad?"

He put the receiver to his ear. "I'm here. I'm coming down, Kathleen. I'll get you."

"Will you?" she asked.

"I'll be there right away. I want you to do something."

"What?"

"Until I get there. I want you to turn on all the lights. And wait for me. And turn on the TV. I'll hold on while you do it." He knew Arthur O'Connor's house; he knew it was dark because the old man preached economy in all things. And he could see Kathleen, being very grown-up and thirteen, sitting in the half darkness, talking to him on the telephone.

"Okay," she said and put down the phone.

While he waited, he thought: yes. He'd get her and Brian. That was what he had to do. All the rest was just bullshit, all the self-pity. This was his daughter. Kathleen.

"I turned all the lights on," she said.

"Wait for me, baby," he said.

"You don't have a car."

"Wait for me." He looked at Lily again, standing naked in the hall, watching him. "You're coming home with me. For now. Pack some things, we're going to wait until your Mom comes back. Okay?"

"Am I?" she asked. She sounded much better, he thought.

"Yes."

"I'll be ready, Dad," she said. "What if Grandpa comes home?"

"You tell him what I said. But don't fight with him. Just tell him what I said."

"Yes," she answered. And he broke the connection.

Lily was watching him.

"Rita's gone and Kathleen's been left home alone while that old fool went out looking for her. He didn't call the cops, and he wouldn't call me. So Kathleen called me now. This is bullshit." He went back into the bedroom.

140

"You're going to bring your kid back here?" Lily asked.

"Yes," he said. He pulled on his shorts and went to the closet and found a pair of pants.

"Where's your boy now?"

"Brian's out with the old man. I don't know where they're looking for Rita. I can't imagine."

"Poor kid," she said.

"Who? Kathleen? Or Rita?"

"Or Jack," she said.

"I want to borrow your car. I'll bring it back tonight."

"Do you want some coffee? To sober up?" she asked.

"God, no." He found a shirt and pulled it on.

The streets were brilliantly orange under the lamps. One environmental group had said they killed the trees by fooling them into thinking it was perpetual daylight; trees needed to rest. When he had heard about that, Jack Donovan thought: only people don't need to rest.

He found the car at the end of the block, opened it, and got in. It smelled of Lily or Lily's perfume.

Within five minutes he was on the Kennedy Expressway heading for the South Side. There was still much traffic. As he sped south, the skyline of the Loop loomed up in the darkness and then fell away as he cut into the South Side. He was on the wide Dan Ryan Expressway and the other cars were behaving erratically; some straddled lanes or burst ahead inexplicably. He supposed at that hour most of the drivers were drunk.

Forty minutes later he turned off the Ninety-fifth Street ramp and headed west to Oak Lawn, the suburb where Arthur O'Connor lived. Where Rita lived. He looked at the darkened houses along the way. Where are you, Rita? Are you cold? Or happy? Or have you forgotten us for the night?

The first time Rita ran away, she was gone more than a year and they thought she was dead.

No crisis had precipitated her disappearance. One day she had merely gone. He had been working the night shift at South Chicago district tactical and the desk sergeant had received a call from a neighbor. When he called the neighbor back, she told him that Rita had left the kids with her for an hour to go shopping and that had been at four o'clock and the kids were crying and Rita hadn't returned and there must have been an accident and—

She came back fourteen months later and said she didn't know where she had been or what she had done. She agreed to go into the hospital. It was very hard for her, and it was hard for him and the kids.

She suffered. Sometimes, the doctors told him, she woke up screaming and when they asked her what she had dreamed, she saw her children dead. Not only Brian and Kathleen but the others. She had names for the fetuses she could not carry to term. The first was Michael and the second was Ann and the third was Sean. Sean, she would tell them, called her. Over and over, in her sleep.

He turned down the block where the O'Connor home sat.

There was no car in the driveway. He turned the engine off and went to the door and rang the bell. Kathleen opened the door and her face seemed pale.

"How are you, baby?"

"Dad." She let him in. "I made coffee for you."

"All right." He let her lead him to the kitchen. He sat down while she poured him a cup of coffee. It didn't taste very good.

"They didn't come back yet."

Jack Donovan nodded.

"I'm ready to go with you. But what about Brian?"

"It'll be all right. I'll leave a note if they aren't back yet."

"But what about summer school?"

"It's all right. We can call them up."

"Okay."

"I'm calling the cops first," he said.

She nodded. "Do you think this is like last time?" she said. "Or is Mom in trouble, in an accident?"

"I don't know."

Ten minutes later the two policemen entered the home and sat down on the plastic-covered couch. In that precise house, they seemed large and heavy and threatening in their uniforms, full of pistols, bullets, mace cans, and truncheons and handcuffs.

He told them everything, all the facts. He left out the anguish. They understood the anguish was there, but they didn't need to hear about it. He gave them a picture of Rita. "When she came out of the hospital, she seemed all right for a while and then she ran away again, this time for only a week. They found her in Evanston, working as a waitress. I don't know if she'd do that again."

"Is she under treatment now?"

"Medication. Maybe she stopped it."

"She's not dangerous?"

"Only to herself." What a mess life turns out to be, he thought. Little Rita O'Connor in the first grade, standing in the playground in her snowsuit, her breath smelling of milk. "I'm gonna have babies," she told him then. She didn't even know where they came from.

"So what about you, Mr. Donovan?" One of the officers looked up from his note pad.

"I'm taking Kathleen home with me tonight. I'm leaving Arthur O'Connor a note. And my boy. I don't want Kathleen left here alone."

They looked at each other. It was family business and the two policemen didn't want a part in it. They got up and one of them shrugged. "Sure," he said. "That's okay with us."

Kathleen fell asleep on the way back to the North Side, but she awoke when he turned off the expressway and went down the bumpy side streets back to his apartment. He wondered if Lily would be there. He didn't think so and she had not said.

"Hi," said Kathleen. She snuggled next to him.

"Hi," he said. It was nearly three A.M.

They were silent for a little while. Then she said, "When do you think Mommy will come home this time?"

"I don't know."

"Why does she do it?"

He couldn't think of an answer. "Sometimes, I think, she gets unhappy. Inside. And she has to go away until she can work it out for herself."

"She's crazy, isn't she?"

"Sometimes," he said. "Sometimes she is." They had stopped at Halsted Street and Fullerton Avenue and Donovan glanced at the bright exterior of the Seminary Restaurant and Lounge. They waited for the light to change.

"Am I going to be crazy?" she asked.

"No."

What a pitiful answer, he thought. The car was pleasantly cool and the city was silent outside the windows, as though it were a film without sound.

"I worry about it," she said. She touched his arm.

"Don't worry, baby," he said. He always said that and it didn't mean anything.

"Okay."

"It'll work out." Everything he said sounded hollow and unconvincing to him. Did it to her as well? Why did he say these things? Why was he so worried? Was it for Kathleen? Or Rita?

"She'll be all right," Kathleen said. She was soothing him and he realized how frightened she was.

"Yes. She's a tough Irishwoman, Kate. She'll survive."

He realized he felt sorry for himself. He extinguished the feeling the way he might clear his throat. Gone.

"Why did she run away the first time?" Kathleen asked.

Because of the dead children.

"Dad?"

He waited.

"Is that when you're crazy? When you have to run away?"

But he didn't answer.

12. THEY HAD STARTED THE DECOY OPERATION AS PLANNED. KAREN KOVAC AND TERRENCE FLYNN MET AS THEY HAD arranged Friday at seven A.M. on the corner of Jackson and Michigan, across the street from the Art Institute. It was at the edge of the park and within a mile of the places where Maj Kirsten and Christina Kalinski had been murdered.

Terry Flynn had borrowed a portable radio transmitter from Area One Burglary, and they tested it for a moment before Karen Kovac put it in her purse. The radio, which emited a constant stream of official chatter, was too noisy to leave on. It would be worthless at the moment of attack, but it might be useful at other times. They were both vague on what the other times might be.

Karen Kovac was to begin her stroll from the Art Institute, across the railroad bridge, to the comfort station where Maj Kirsten had been killed seven weeks before. From there she was to cross the Outer Drive at the Monroe Street traffic lights and continue down the sidewalk to the harbor.

All this time Sergeant Flynn would be in the unmarked

police car, trying to follow her visually or at least according to the planned schedule. Once she had walked to the end of the Monroe Street Harbor, she would turn and repeat the route.

They would rendezvous again at the Art Institute once an hour. They agreed they had thought of everything.

If there was an element of risk—as Donovan and Schmidt harped—then it was probably a small one, and Karen Kovac was determined to ignore it.

At seven forty-five A.M. she marched off briskly from the Institute building, went across the railroad bridge and into the park. As she went deeper into the park, she could hear the thunder of rush-hour traffic from Michigan Avenue merging with the sound of traffic on the Outer Drive.

Unfortunately, in planning the decoy operation, everyone had forgotten about the rush-hour traffic.

Within five minutes Terry Flynn's car was hopelessly entangled in a traffic jam caused by the collision of a CTA bus and a private car which had attempted to turn into the same lane at the same time. Within a few minutes hundreds and then thousands of autos miles from the scene of the slight accident on Lake Shore Drive were mysteriously halted by the jam, like disturbed waters rippling away from the epicenter. Flynn's car was trapped in a curb lane.

He could not see Karen Kovac. And because her radio was not on, he could not call her.

Lieutenant Schmidt, while valuing Terrence Flynn's insights and occasional acts of courage, still was under the impression that his subordinate often had mental lapses in which he acted instinctively, without regard for the consequences of his actions. In this Schmidt was correct; even Flynn would agree. But Flynn never saw this part of his character as a defect. He trusted his instincts. Given a choice between what he felt and what he thought, he would choose his feelings. And those instincts rarely failed him.

Flynn gunned the accelerator on his car and swung the front wheels sharply onto the curbing and into the grassy park. The big Dodge lumbered across the grass and crashed finally into a row of bushes. Flynn considered himself parked and jumped from the front seat. He began running across the grass to the comfort station where Maj Kirsten had been murdered.

Karen was not there.

The ground was dusty around the comfort station, and the air was heavy and sweet smelling. Flynn was sweating already. He stood in his shirt sleeves and rumpled tie and looked down at the ground where he had first seen the body of Maj Kirsten. He wiped his head with a handkerchief, then stuffed it back into the pocket of his trousers. His lungs ached from his sprint across the park. He lit a cigarette and then threw it down on the ground and began again to sprint along the grass path he had taken from Lake Shore Drive. Cars were stalled in a miles-long jam on the drive, and he did not have to wait for the lights but ducked across the middle lanes. What a mess, he thought.

He smelled the lake.

Flynn found the sidewalk leading down alongside Monroe Street Harbor. Hundreds of little pleasure boats bobbed on the water as far as the concrete breakwater.

He ran past the bushes where they had found the body of Christina Kalinski and then he stopped. It was all right.

He saw her.

She was standing at the far end of the sidewalk, talking to a uniformed policeman. A three-wheeler sat nearby, its police radio squawking out morning commands.

He walked up to them and he was not puffing as badly when he arrived. Karen Kovac began to speak, but he waved her words away and looked at the policeman.

"What the hell is going on?"

"Who the hell are you?" asked the cop.

"Who does it look like I am?"

Recognition came to Officer Clarence Delancey's face. "Oh. Sarge. You. I didn't recognize you because your face was all red like that."

Karen Kovac said, "He was going to arrest me."

"What?"

"This is no place for a woman at this time of day, I was telling her," Delancey said. He seemed quite firm about it, as though the obvious had escaped both of them. "There were women killed here, don't you know that?" He was addressing Karen. "I told her she had to go on back, or I'd have to run her in. But I wasn't really going to arrest her."

"You goddamn idiot," said Flynn.

"I'm a police officer," said Karen Kovac. "I didn't get a chance to tell him. He came out of the bushes and told me to halt and then he started talking."

"Idiot," was all that Flynn could think of to say in front of the woman.

"I didn't know she was an officer," said Delancey. He sensed for the first time that something might be wrong.

"Even if she wasn't, what the hell right do you have to go around telling people they can't walk in the park?" asked Flynn finally.

"Orders," said Delancey.

"What?"

"Well, the watch commander said I should try to discourage people from being out in the park until they catch this guy that's killing the women. I just followed orders is all."

"That's terrific," said Flynn. "A guy kills someone in the park, so what do we do? We keep everyone out of the park instead of catching the guy. Brilliant police thinking."

"Well," said Delancey. But Flynn had grabbed Karen Kovac by the arm and was starting away up the sidewalk. Delancey shrugged and got back on his motorcycle and slowly putt-putted up to Lake Shore Drive.

"He's an idiot," said Flynn. "I wish to Christ they'd transfer him down to the South Side and get him out of my way. He's the one who found Christina Kalinski. And he found Norman Frank, the cause of all our troubles."

She smiled. She liked Flynn. "A regular sleuth."

"An idiot, you mean," he repeated.

"What happened to you?" she asked.

"More brilliant police thinking. We forgot about the rush hour, it just happens every morning. I got caught in a traffic jam on the Outer Drive and lost you and I got a little panicked. So I pulled up on the curb and came after you. This won't work the way it is. We're going to have to have a different operation. I hate to say it, but I think I'm going to have to walk.

Maybe I can disguise myself as one of those goddamn joggers."

She smiled. He was big and beefy and his face was red. She thought he was rather sweet. "I don't think anyone would be fooled."

"Especially when I light up a Lucky," he said. Which he did at that moment while they waited for the lights to change at Monroe Street. Traffic was moving again.

"Do you know they originally built this as a pleasant little motoring drive through the park?" she said.

"They must've been perverts," said Flynn.

The lights changed and they walked across the broad expressway to the park. When they reached the unmarked car on the grass, it was just after nine o'clock. In ninety minutes the third murder would be committed.

Tiny Preston was very tired and that made him very hungry. He wondered if it were too early for a cheeseburger; not that it would be unseemly in his eyes to eat a cheeseburger at nine A.M., but he wasn't sure he could find a place nearby that served them this early. He had arrived at the theater shortly before seven o'clock which meant he had arisen a little after five A.M. and that was too early for anyone.

He stood at the back of the ticket booth where Gloria Miska now sat. Usually Gloria didn't come in until the afternoon, but this was a very different day and, in the spirit of the occasion, Gloria had worn a new dress and new dark nylons. Earrings, too.

Tiny Preston glanced again around the lobby to see if everything was set. Again his eyes rested on the large poster-picture of Bonni Brighton in the center of the dismal little foyer.

The picture revealed a blond with bright, even teeth and a long, sensual tongue which, at the moment the picture was made, was blatantly extended from her mouth. The picture showed a woman with large eyes, and the expression on her face was undoubtedly meant to be sexually appealing. Because the photo was taken with black and white film, Tiny Preston could not determine the color of Bonni Brighton's eyes, but he guessed they were blue.

He had erected the poster the day before when the picture made its unofficial Midwest premiere. *Bonni's Brass Bed* had been preceded by waves of favorable publicity.

A prominent cinema critic for a New York newspaper had first pronounced the film an appealing, serious work of art, despite the fact that it was essentially a pornographic picture. The same critic had stated that Bonni Brighton played her role as the lesbian prostitute with humor and élan. He also stated that the picture was not pornographic in the usual sense but rather an excellent parody of the pornographic genre and that one scene involving two men and three women engaged in various group sexual activities was particularly devastating in its artistic and social comment.

Other film critics either agreed or disagreed with the original commentary on the movie but, in all, they unconsciously conspired to make *Bonni's Brass Bed* a cause célèbre.

The film was banned in Milwaukee, and a prominent prosecutor in southern Ohio reportedly was determined to get a grand jury indictment for conspiracy against the makers of the movie. Everyone connected with the movie was properly outraged and delighted with its success. Bonnie Brighton had been asked to pose naked for two men's magazines and a third combined the pictorial offer with a promise to interview her in the same issue on the role of nudity in art.

Most delighted of all was Bonni Brighton, now on a nationwide publicity tour on behalf of the movie. She had already appeared on the cover of one newsweekly, and a prominent paperback publisher was committed to bringing out her autobiography. She was twenty three years old, and at noon she was due to make her Chicago appearance in the theater managed by Tiny Preston.

Her agent, Maxwell Hampstead of New York, had arranged all the details of the appearance in Chicago, down to the velvet rope line on the sidewalk where it was expected the noon throngs would be contained during Bonni Brighton's appearance.

Tiny Preston took his dark darting eyes from the poster

and looked at the popcorn stand. Maybe he could have some popcorn to tide him over.

"Everything looks okay, I guess," he said.

Gloria Miska shrugged.

"She's gonna show up around ten thirty because she's got this interview set up with some newspaper creep who's gonna write a column about her. I don't like all this publicity for the house, I tell ya."

"It was okay by Mr. Rocca," Gloria Miska reminded him.

"Yeah. So it's his house, so he can do what he wants. But I don't like it. The creeps don't like it. Hey, any creeps in there now?" He thumbed toward the door of the theater, which had opened at eight A.M.

"Some. The usual bunch. I sold fifteen tickets this morning."

"I better check 'em out."

"Whatever," said Gloria Miska.

Tiny entered the theater and stood in the back, beneath the buzzing exit sign, letting his eyes grow accustomed to the darkness. The usual creeps. Old men and men in raincoats and lonely night workers slumped in their seats, killing time until they had to go home to sleep. The usual morning bunch, in fact. He thought he had seen some of them before.

He went back into the lobby.

"I hope there ain't no trouble."

"How's trouble?" asked Gloria Miska.

"Ah, you know. Crowds and stuff. I don't wanna have to have no cops here. No heat."

Gloria Miska shrugged.

Jack Donovan awoke his daughter gently at ten thirty in the morning.

She sat in bed and looked at him. He had slept on the couch. Lily had gone home but not before making the bed and putting away the liquor bottles.

"I have to go to work for a little while," he said.

She opened her eyes and looked around at his room. She had not been able to go to sleep at first. The bedroom was strange and so bare. But it was his bedroom. And it was cool.

She felt comfortable and tired under the covers. She wanted to go back to sleep.

"What about Mom?"

"I talked to the police this morning. Brian and Grandpa are home now. They didn't find her."

"Poor Mom," she said.

"Brian wants to stay down with Grandpa for now, but it's okay for you to stay with me awhile. If you want. I have to go downtown now for a little while. We're working on some special business. But I'll be home early and if you want to get up later, there's eggs in the icebox and some tea. I don't think I have any milk."

"That's okay," said Kathleen. "I don't drink milk anymore."

He smiled at that.

"If you go out, there's a key on the dresser. There's three locks. Downstairs door and two locks on this door. It's a pretty safe area, I guess. I see kids on the street. But don't go too far, will you? There's a grocery up the street if you need anything. There's some money." He put a twenty on the dresser. "You'll be okay."

She reached from under the covers and touched his freckled hand. Poor Dad, she thought. "Are Brian and I going to live with you now?"

"I don't know," he said, standing up. He didn't want to talk to her about it.

He left her and she went back to sleep.

They arrived at the theater shortly before ten-thirty A.M.

Bonni Brighton was, on closer examination, a rather ordinary-looking woman blessed with even white teeth, a firm chin, and wide eyes. She seemed tired this morning and was chewing gum. Robert Fredericks, a prominent cinema critic with a Chicago paper, was with her. Tiny Preston thought that Bonni Brighton looked pretty flat in the ass department. She wore a blue jersey dress and no underwear.

The film crew from a local television station arrived just behind them while the star and her entourage stood in the cramped lobby. Two men, without a word, began setting up the camera and sound box. Another man with shiny hair stepped forward and grasped Bonni's arm.

"I'm Tom Bruce with Eyewitness News," he began. "We'd like a few minutes for the early news."

"Sure," Bonni Brighton said laconically, snapping her gum.

"Maybe we can finish our interview," said Robert Fredericks to the television reporter. "I've got a first-edition deadline."

"You can use the office there," said Tiny Preston, who, despite his reluctance, was now caught up in the mood of excitement.

"No," said Robert Fredericks. He was known as a reporter and critic who liked to create mood in his stories as well as mere fact. "I think it'd be great if we'd finish in the theater, watching Bonni's picture together. Waddaya say, Bonni?"

"I don't care," she said as though she meant it.

"Why not let me get my film first?" said Tom Bruce. "We've got a murder on the South Side right after this."

"I got a deadline," argued Robert Fredericks, and he grabbed Bonni by her arm and led her toward the door to the theater. Tom Bruce relinquished his grip.

"How long?" asked Tom Bruce.

"Gimme ten minutes more," said Robert Fredericks, who intended to take as much time as he wanted.

They closed the lobby door, and Bonni Brighton and Robert Fredericks were in the darkness of the theater. On the screen a woman was on her back with her legs spread; she was naked. The set was apparently a sort of bedroom. Between the woman's legs could barely be seen the face of another woman who was performing a sexual act with her tongue. It was Bonni Brighton.

"That's Sandy," said Bonni Brighton. "She's okay."

They went halfway down the darkened aisle and stumbled into two seats. Bonni took the aisle seat.

Fredericks flicked on his tape recorder.

On the screen a man entered the room. He was naked and he said something to one of the women on the bed. She opened her mouth.

Bonni Brighton leaned back in the theater seat because she was tired. They had gone to Arnie's Café the night before for a party. She had thought Robert Fredericks was a twerp at the party and in bed but she supposed he was important.

Tomorrow she would be in Minneapolis. The chief of police there had threatened to close the theater down, and Bonni had been instructed by Maxwell to try to get arrested.

Maxwell said her book might sell half a million copies.

Fredericks touched her leg and began his question: "Do you think that art in film is—"

The tape recorder clattered to the floor when Bonni Brighton's right hand suddenly lashed out and struck the machine.

It was an instinctive gesture, caused by the knife tearing down into the back of her neck, so deep that it severed the main arteries and ripped her vocal cords in one sweeping arc. The knife plunged again into the muscles of her upper back and tore down until it was snagged by a rib. As she arched back into the seat and slowly sank down, blood began to form on her lips. Her mouth was open wide as though she were silently screaming.

Blood spilled down the front of her jersey dress.

Her eyes were wide open, and blood streamed from her nose. She did not die for nearly forty seconds as the blood welled into her throat and lungs and drowned her.

The two knife blows had taken less than a second. It was ten thirty-two A.M.

Robert Fredericks screamed in that second and heard the noise of the blow and felt the presence in the aisle behind them. Seeking safety, he tumbled onto the floor beneath the theater seat and kept screaming.

Bonni Brighton was dead. Her body sprawled back in the seat, her knees pressed against the seat in front of her. Her body was prevented from sliding down to the floor on top of Robert Fredericks by the handle of the butcher knife which had wedged itself on the top of the theater seat while the knife blade was snagged between two bones of the upper rib cage.

There were other panicked screams.

Door were flung open and the sparse audience began to run toward the two exit doors. At the same time people from the lobby rushed into the theater. Someone flung open the fire exit door and stumbled into the alley, and others wasted no time following.

13. DESPITE HIS PROMISE TO KATHLEEN, JACK DONOVAN DID NOT GET HOME EARLY.

He had intended to go to the state's attorney's office downtown in the big steel Civic Center and arrange to take a few days leave to straighten out his family affairs.

But first Lee Horowitz corralled him as he walked into the main office on the fifth floor. Then he was rushed into a special conference room where state's attorney Bud Halligan, the police superintendent, and chief of homicide Leonard Ranallo sat waiting. Donovan did not recognize a fourth man, who sat in the corner. The man did not bother to introduce himself, but Jack Donovan discovered he was from the mayor's office.

"Jack, we're going to take you off administrative duties for the next couple of weeks and set up a special state's attorney's task force to try to get to the bottom of these park murders," Halligan began pompously.

It was shortly after eleven A.M., and no one in the room was aware that Bonni Brighton, a porno movie starlet, had just been killed less than three blocks away.

155

"I came downtown this morning to get some time off. For personal matters," Jack Donovan said.

"What about?" asked Lee Horowitz.

"It's personal and urgent. I'll tell you later," said Donovan.

Leonard Ranallo spoke now. He looked unhappy. "The mayor feels we haven't gone after this business the right way. He thinks there's too many cooks in the pie."

Donovan smiled. The man from the mayor's office lit a cigarette and said nothing.

"He wants a special force to deal with this, so he can announce it. We got word this morning—well, the mayor got word, that the upholsterers' convention has decided to cancel its meeting here next spring. The mayor says the city is getting a bad reputation with these unsolved murders."

"That's hard to believe," said Donovan. "Is he talking about Al Capone's day?"

"Cut the crap," said Lee Horowitz. Again Halligan looked uncomfortable.

The police superintendent spoke for the first time. "Politically these are very uncomfortable crimes for all of us. You know that and we all know it. Actually the police have a very good record in clearing murders but it's the spectacular crime, the random crime like this, that is so difficult. And gets the public's attention."

Donovan decided the superintendent was talking to him. It was hard to be sure. He stared at a pad of paper on the table and never glanced up. The superintendent's eyes were swimming behind thick glasses.

The superintendent cleared his throat. "This doesn't reflect well on any of us. The police department has even been under fire in this matter. Compounding the crimes themselves is the unfortunate . . . er . . . disappearance of Mr. Norman Frank from the Criminal Courts building. Well, none of these murders would mean that much in another context. But those women were murdered, as we know, in Grant Park. Right downtown. We had one suspect and he escaped, and now we have another, a strong suspect, this person, this man . . ."

The police superintendent finished speaking and gestured ineffectively with his left hand. The gesture was meant to convey the whole crime surrounding the imprisonment of the young girl in the Susy-Q Lounge.

"There really is nothing more to be done," Jack Donovan said quietly. "The police, as you know, began a decoy patrol this morning in Grant Park involving two homicide detectives. And our office is still working on aspects of the Seymour Weiss case as well as the case of Luther Jones. I really can't see what else can be done—"

"Godamnit, Donovan," cried Horowitz. He pounded the table, and this startled even the phlegmatic police superintendent. "We want results. The mayor expects results. You stonewalled us on Weiss and you told us he didn't do it. Okay. You get who did it."

"For Christ's sake, Lee," said Jack Donovan. "We had to bend Ranallo's arm even to get a decoy set up."

"That's not true, Jack," said Ranallo. His face was flushed. Both the superintendent and Halligan looked away.

"All that's changed now," said the mayor's man. It was the first time he had spoken. They all looked at him. His voice had the trace of an Irish brogue.

"You got priority, Donovan," the man continued. "The mayor said for you to run the operation."

Donovan flushed and Halligan stared at him.

"He doesn't even know me—"

"He reads the papers. He read about you. He checked around." The mayor's man chuckled. "You come from the right side of town." Meaning the Irish South Side where the mayor had his roots and where the power elite of the city mostly came from.

There was a knock at the conference room door.

"Excuse me," said the secretary who opened it. "There's an urgent call for you, Commander." She nodded to Ranallo. The homicide chief got up gratefully and went to the other room. While he was gone, there was silence. No one knew what to say.

Halligan kept staring at Donovan. The mayor knew him. Maybe Donovan was a better man than Lee Horowitz made him out to be. He'd have to talk with Lee about Jack.

When Ranallo returned, his face was white.

"A movie star just got murdered in a porn theater. In the Loop. About three blocks from here, on Washington."

"For Christ's sake," said the superintendent. He was obviously disgusted. He tore off the pad of paper and threw it in the wastebasket at his feet. "For Christ's sake."

14. BY ELEVEN THIRTY A.M. THERE WERE TOO MANY POLICE-MEN IN THE THEATER. THEY BUMPED INTO EACH OTHER passing in and out of the seating area; they clogged the tiny lobby and some of them had even managed to squeeze into the one-desk office of the theater manager where they used the single phone constantly.

Tiny Preston, who stood behind the popcorn machine, looked miserable. He stood and stuffed popcorn into his mouth and watched the policemen trudge back and forth. It was all worse than he had imagined trouble could be. In front of the theater a police squadrol waited at the curb. And blue-and-white squad cars blocked traffic on Washington Street, with their blue Mars light rotating.

At the same time four unmarked police cars were parked at crazy angles in front of and on the side of the theater, blocking three lanes of Washington Street and the service alley. Special barricades marked "Police Line—Do Not Cross" had been erected on the sidewalk alongside the velvet rope line. The barriers forced pedestrians to cross the street to the opposite walk to pass the theater.

It was spectacular and all largely unnecessary.

And it annoyed Traffic Policeman James McGarrity whose beat included the street in front of the theater. The situation was ruining business at the parking garage up the street. Still, he supposed, it couldn't be helped. Like any interested spectator, he stood in the street and watched the comings and goings of the medical examiners and homicide investigators.

Matthew Schmidt and Terrence Flynn had arrived at the theater at eleven thirty-five, along with Karen Kovac who had been in their office when the call came in from the beat man sent to the theater. The police had received their first call—placed, as it turned out, by Gloria Miska from her booth—at ten fifty-one A.M. The squad from First District station had arrived three minutes later. After a preliminary investigation they had notified Area One Homicide.

Schmidt thought to call Sid Margolies at home. Sid had the day off but went back on duty without reluctance. His wife was in Buffalo, New York, visiting relatives, and Sid Margolies did not like to sit at home alone.

Now Margolies stood in a corner of the lobby, talking to Maxwell Hampstead, Bonni Brighton's personal agent, who had arrived from New York that morning and gone straight to the theater.

Karen Kovac had been asked to talk to Gloria Miska. She was delighted with the assignment—her first—but she did not show it.

Three other homicide investigators from Area One were stalking the small shops along the street to see if anyone had spotted those who fled by the alley fire-exit door when the murder occurred.

Flynn sat on a corner of the desk in the office and tried to question Robert Fredericks. The diminutive movie critic was still shivering as he spoke.

It appeared Matt Schmidt had nothing to do.

He stood by the ticket booth and surveyed the confusion. He felt in his shirt pocket for a toothpick, found it, and began to elaborately pick his yellowed teeth. He wondered what he was not doing which should be done. He was sixty-one minutes behind the killer.

A moment before, he had ordered two burly uniformed men from First District to seize the film can from the television camera crew. It had attracted his interest after one of the cameramen told a detective he had instinctively turned on the film when the theater doors were flung open by the panicked audience. Tom Bruce protested the seizure, and Schmidt ignored him. He told the patrolmen to take the film to the lab and get it developed.

Perhaps they had a picture of the killer.

"Look, Lieutenant," said Tom Bruce. "I can't go back to the station and tell them you took my film."

"Sure you can," said Schmidt. "You're aiding the police in an investigation. Eyewitness News is to be congratulated."

Bruce brightened. "Will you say that?"

"I just said it," said Matt Schmidt. He threw the toothpick into the can of sand.

"No, I mean on camera."

Schmidt considered it. If he didn't, there might be a real howl from the station. You could never trust the media in a thing like this, seizing notes and film and such. On the other hand, Tom Bruce appeared to be a moron, and if Matt Schmidt congratulated Eyewitness News for aiding a police investigation by turning over important film, it would square any potential beef.

"Sure," he said. And Tom Bruce rushed away to set up the camera crew.

At that moment Jack Donovan and Leonard Ranallo strolled into the lobby.

Schmidt nodded to Ranallo. "Why are you here, Jack? Want your old job back in the department?"

"It's about the park murders," Jack Donovan said. He looked glum.

"As you can see, we're into movie murders now."

"Yes. They want to set up a special task force combining you guys and the state's attorney's office. To deal with the park murders. Mario DeVito is running the criminal division for now. I'm detached."

"Christ," said Schmidt. It wasn't that he didn't like Donovan. He glanced at Ranallo who looked equally glum.

"I know," said Ranallo. "I don't like it either. But we got pressure from City Hall."

"I see," said Schmidt.

"What do you have here?"

"Bizarre," said Schmidt. He mentally recalled the awkwardly sprawled body of Bonni Brighton. "A movie actress. Or a whore who plays in movies. Strictly porn. She was in the film they're showing here." He made a face. "Making a personal appearance. God." He glanced at the office. "Anyway, about ten thirty this morning she arrived at the theater and went into the theater with blubber-boy over there, the one talking to Flynn. He's with one of the papers. He says he was doing a story on her, on the 'art of the porn film.' These people can be real assholes, you know."

Ranallo nodded.

"So someone came up behind them and damn near cut her head off and left the knife sticking in her. No one saw him, of course."

"Did the reporter do it?"

"No. Unfortunately. He doesn't appear to be strong enough to stab anything tougher than a rare steak. Whoever did it must be an iron man."

"The park murders," Donovan said. "Can we talk about it tomorrow?"

"Sure. If we don't get this guy in the next four hours, we'll have all the time in the world. We'll be able to put this down with the park killings. All open cases, forever. I even called up Sid Margolies at home because I thought—well, when I heard the call, I was confused, I suppose. I thought it was another park murder."

"But in a theater."

"I was confused," said Schmidt. "I've had those murders on my mind all week."

"You sound down," said Jack Donovan.

"Yeah," said Schmidt. He stared at Karen Kovac who was still interviewing Gloria Miska. "The decoy didn't work worth a damn this morning. She and Flynn got separated, and she almost got arrested."

But Jack Donovan did not hear. He was staring at the large black-and-white poster in the lobby.

"Is that her?"

"Who?"

"Bonni Brighton."

"Yes. Except she doesn't look like that any more."

"Blond?"

"Yeah."

"And blue eyes?"

"Yeah."

"Killed with a knife."

"Yeah."

"Where did the killer get her?"

"In the neck," said Matt Schmidt.

"The same as the others."

Schmidt looked at Donovan. He shook his head. "I told you I was confused."

"Maybe I'm confused now too."

"We can't tie together every unsolved murder of a blond woman."

"Sure. Just a random killing, a murder without motive."

Schmidt bit his lip. "There's nothing to tie them together."

"You did it unconsciously, Matt. That's why you called Margolies at home."

Schmidt thought for a moment.

Donovan said, "We tied together the two women in the park because they were both in the park. But there's more to tie this murder with the other two. The same type of victim. The same method of murder. And in the morning. Friday morning. Around the same time the others were killed."

"I don't know," said Matt Schmidt. "Let's go into the theater and you take a look at her before they carry her out."

Two spotlights had been set up in the semidarkness of the theater. Though all the interior lights had been turned on, it was not bright enough for the evidence technicians and the police department photographer.

The spotlights flooded the body of Bonni Brighton with light. They had not moved her yet. She was still sprawled, the knife hooked on the seat back. Her mouth and eyes were open, and her dress and face and the seats around her were splattered with her blood.

"Damn it," said Jack Donovan. He would not be sick, but he would not forget the sight either.

"It looks like a butcher knife, doesn't it?" said Ranallo.

Schmidt nodded.

"Hey, Loo?" said one of the uniformed men. "Loo" was common departmental slang for "lieutenant."

"Look it. There's a tape recorder. It was on and the battery ran down."

"Where was it?"

"Under her chair. There was some blood on it. One of the guys just found it."

"Watch it for prints but I'll bet it belongs to the reporter in there talking to Sergeant Flynn. Go see. And see if someone can find a battery, go see if there was anything on it."

"Well," said Jack Donovan. "What are we going to do, Matt?"

"Whatever you say," said Schmidt. He looked sour.

"It's not my fault," said Jack Donovan. "I didn't want to interfere."

"The brass is turning all this into a circus. It isn't going to catch a murderer."

"I know," said Jack Donovan.

Schmidt nodded. "Like you said, it isn't your fault. You've been square with me since this thing started."

"There's heat on the park case now," said Ranallo. They stood near the body. He looked at it again. "This isn't part of the park case. We don't need more heat by tying it in. Let's just get someone like Flynn or one of the other investigators to handle this, and you guys get on the park murders."

Schmidt didn't say anything. Jack Donovan looked at him and tried to figure out what Schmidt wanted him to say.

"Look, Chief," said Donovan at last. "I think there may be a connection and they put me in charge of the investigation, so I think we should investigate. Let Matt go after this one and if there's no connection, we'll drop it and go to the park case. But if there is a connection, maybe we'll be more lucky this time."

Ranallo said, "Okay. It's your neck."

"I know," said Donovan. "Everyone keeps reminding me."

"I'm going to leave you both then."

Schmidt turned to Ranallo. "Chief, there's a TV crew out there. They made a film by accident when the doors of the theater were flung open right after the murder. It's a million to one, but maybe we have the killer on the film."

Ranallo gaped at him. "You want me to ask the TV crew to turn over the film?"

"Not exactly. I took it already."

"Jesus Jumping Christ, Schmidt, are you crazy?" Ranallo said.

"Just a minute," said Matt Schmidt. "It's all right."

"It's not all right," said Ranallo, who was very sensitive to the rights and privileges claimed by the press.

Schmidt explained that Tom Bruce could be easily mollified and Ranallo, once convinced that the seizure of film had been patched over, readily agreed to be interviewed for the camera. He left Donovan and Schmidt in the theater and walked out.

"How will you recognize the killer if he's on film?" asked Donovan.

"He'll look guilty."

Donovan waited.

"I'm sorry. It's not your fault, I guess. But I hate this goddamn interference all the time. First it's Ranallo, then the state's attorney's office. It isn't your fault, I know, but you're part of the problem."

Still Donovan waited.

"When Maj Kirsten was murdered," he said at last, "I had this little black kid. He's listed in the report. He discovered the body."

"His name was Washington," said Donovan.

"Yes," said Schmidt. "You remember the name. I wanted to know why he decided to pee in the bushes more than a quarter mile from where he was playing ball. That's how he discovered her body, you see."

Donovan nodded.

"He said he didn't see anything. I talked to him a long time afterward. And Sid Margolies talked to him. Sid is very patient with kids. He can talk them out of their circles—you know how kids always talk in circles? Margolies can think like that. But that kid wouldn't say shit. Which I think means he saw something. Or someone."

"So you think he'll identify the killer?"

"No. We couldn't hope for that. All I want is for the killer to be on that film. And for Washington to see it and maybe, just for a moment, flinch. Or give some indication he has tripped his memory back to that day in the park. The same with the others, the girls who have been assaulted in the park—Angela Falicci was a student at the Art Institute. It happened right after the Kirsten murder. I don't know if any of this will work, but it's a helluva lot more solid than anything we've had before."

"And if he ran out the alley entrance?" said Donovan, indicating the open exit door.

"Then maybe there's something else. Maybe the knife can be traced. Maybe that pile of rotting flesh in there—that theater manager—can remember something. Jack, I feel it. I really feel it."

"Yes," said Donovan. He was elated. "So do I. I think you're closer than you've been. Than we've been."

"All right," said Matt Schmidt with a smile. He considered shaking Donovan's hand but rejected the thought. "We've been."

"When can we arrange our movie?"

"You want to do it on the West Side?" He meant the Criminal Courts building.

"Fuck no. Let's do it downtown. Halligan has a big conference room and a projector. We can run it there. Can you get the film developed by tonight?"

"Sure."

"Seven o'clock then?"

"Sure," said Schmidt. "Now you can do me a favor, if you want."

Donovan nodded.

"I want to bring Karen Kovac in on this. All the way. Attach her to the special investigation or whatever the hell they're calling it."

"Why?"

Schmidt shrugged. If he said he liked her, Donovan would get the wrong impression. "She could use a break."

Donovan nodded. "Done," he said.

"You're not too bad for a lawyer," said Schmidt.

"Speaking of that, Mario told me late yesterday that Seymour Weiss is getting a trial date tomorrow and his lawyer wants to plead down. You can tell Flynn that."

"What are you going to do?"

"He knows he's got to do some time. I think we can make it easy on him. Three years minimum."

Schmidt nodded. It was the way things worked. If the state's attorney's office and the defense did not agree on a plea before trial, there would be a long, expensive trial after many continuances and, if there was a conviction, there would be an equally long appeal of that conviction. But in this case, Flynn—a policeman—and two other cops were the key prosecution witnesses, and because Flynn would not go away or be frightened away, the defense wanted to plead guilty to reduced charges. And the state would make the deal to clear the case from the books. It was a form of plea bargaining and, in an imperfect way, it made the criminal justice system function.

"Three years," said Matt Schmidt. "I better wait to tell Flynn. He won't like it, and he was almost human today."

Donovan nodded.

"The girl?"

"Turned out she was a runaway like we thought. From Rochester, New York. Thirteen years old."

Kathleen's age, Donovan thought.

Schmidt said, "They brought her down gently at Henrotin. She was on drugs pretty bad. They think she might be a little mental; they're going to give her tests."

"I'm surprised Terry didn't just shoot him," said Jack Donovan.

Schmidt shrugged.

15. SID MARGOLIES FOUND THE LIGHT SWITCH IN THE WHITE-WALLED ROOM AND TURNED THE LIGHTS OFF. AT THE same time the projector flickered on, and the sixteen-millimeter film began to unwind slowly through the machine.

The first scene was of women on a beach. It appeared to be the Oak Street Beach and they could see the tall buildings of Michigan Avenue in the background. One woman in a bathing suit posed for the camera and smiled. Though there were men on the beach, the pictures were mostly of women.

Then they saw Tom Bruce with a microphone in his hand. He was obviously speaking, but there was no sound.

"We didn't bother about sound," said Terry Flynn. "It's funnier this way."

Karen Kovac smiled.

In the next sequence of the unedited film the camera focused on a poster in the lobby of the movie theater, the black-and-white photograph of Bonni Brighton.

"They must've shot that when they came in," said Margolies. He stood along the side wall; the others were seated.

They saw the door of the theater suddenly flung open.

"Stop," said Matthew Schmidt.

The film stopped. The first face, grainy and blurred, seemed to belong to a dark man. He had black hair, cut close to the scalp; his eyes were wide and frightened.

"Looks like a black," said Sid Margolies. Margolies lit a cigarette, and the plume of blue smoke filtered across the intense light of the projector.

"I don't think so," said Terry Flynn. They all stared at the freeze frame. "More like a Dago. He was the first one out of the joint."

"You know what this reminds me of," said Karen Kovac. They waited.

Her voice was clear and low. "When they showed the movie about Kennedy. From Dallas. When he was killed."

They didn't say anything.

"Is this the door on the aisle where the murder happened?" asked Jack Donovan.

"Yeah," said Matt Schmidt. "That's a break. It would seem most likely the killer would run out of the theater by the most direct route—up the aisle where the murder happened."

The film advanced. The door in the theater seemed to swing nearly shut and then was flung open again.

"Stop," said Schmidt to the deputy sheriff operating the film.

The next man was tall with broad shoulders and he wore a light zippered jacket, gray in color, and a gray work shirt. The focus seemed better than on the first subject. The eyes of the second man were wide too and very blue.

"Can we have this one frame at a time?" asked Donovan.

"This thing will do magic," said the deputy. Click. Click. Click.

"Hold it there," said Schmidt.

The second man had turned toward the camera and appeared startled by it. He had gray hair, cut in a shaggy crew cut; his eyebrows were thick and gray. His lips appeared to be pulled back over his even white teeth in a surprised snarl. He appeared to have a long symmetrical nose.

"Wonderful," said Terry Flynn. "He looks like the hood

ornament on an old Pontiac I owned. Look at that schnozz."

"Listen to the film critic," said Sid Margolies. "Talking to Robert Fredericks an hour and he's ready for Cannes."

"What?"

"Cannes."

"What the hell is that?"

"The second man out," said Schmidt, noting it and breaking up the conversation.

The film rolled forward. The third man was short, and because the camera was fixed and unattended, it missed his face.

The fourth man was black. He had large shoulders which could not be contained in the short focus of the camera. His eyes looked left and right, and then he blundered past the camera's range.

"Stop," said Schmidt.

"Big son of a bitch," said Terry Flynn. "Do you think he hates the white race and takes out his revenge on poor li'l white women?" He was parodying the report of the University of Chicago psychologist.

The fifth man had a beard and when he saw the camera, he grimaced.

The sixth man was very pale and his eyes were watery and looked tired. He was wearing a suit and carrying a briefcase.

"He looks like the police superintendent," said Jack Donovan.

"Maybe it is."

"No, I had a conference with him when the movie was shot."

The film ended. For a moment they sat in the darkness of the room.

"You want me to run it through again?" asked the deputy.

"Yes," said Matt Schmidt.

Karen Kovac was staring intently at the screen. She was afraid to speak, but something had nagged her, something about one of the men. She watched the film a second time, and she could not get it clear in her head.

"Any ideas?" asked Matt Schmidt.

No one spoke.

"Okay." He turned to Margolies. "Catch the lights, Sid." The room was bathed in thin white light.

Schmidt got up. "We got the tape recorder too. This is a sound and light show."

He picked up the Sony. "This belongs to Robert Fredericks, but it's in custody now, evidence. He had it turned on when Bonni Brighton was killed, and it picks up a lot of sounds. We're taking it over to a private lab tomorrow to try and get some of the sounds separated, see if there's anything there."

He turned it on.

The first fifteen minutes consisted of an interview with Bonni Brighton held, apparently, in a restaurant. They could hear the sounds of dishes in the background, and at one point a male voice with a French accent said, "And dessert, sir?"

"Now, this is the part."

There was a brief blank spot on the tape, and then it resumed: "Do you think that art in film is—"

What followed seemed indistinguishable noise—from a hissing sound, a thump, and then a clatter—presumably as the tape recorder fell. After that came the sound of screams. Robert Fredericks'.

"He screams like a girl," said Flynn. "God, you spend an hour with him, you think you're interviewing a fruitcake."

"But he went to bed with Bonni Brighton the night before," said Karen Kovac.

They all seemed a little shocked at her remark, and they were silent.

"Well," said Matt Schmidt. "You can see. It doesn't sound like anything."

"What was that hissing noise?" said Donovan.

Schmidt played the tape again. Again they heard the ridiculous question begun and then the hiss and thump and the clatter.

"That noise. Like a thump. That must have been the knife."

It was Karen Kovac again. They looked at her. "And the hissing noise. What would that be? It sounded like a voice."

They listened again. It might be a voice.

"Maybe it's from the movie sound track."

"No," she said. "It's too close. Too real, too much resonance. If you make a tape of what is essentially a recorded voice, then it loses resonance."

"It might be someone speaking," said Flynn.

"But what is he saying?"

They listened to the hissing sound again. And a fourth time. And a fifth.

"Sshhhh. Verrrrrr." That was Flynn's imitation.

"Like that," she agreed.

"If we can get it to a private sound lab, we'll be able to clean up the background noise a little and maybe we can get a better idea of what it is," said Schmidt.

They were silent again.

"What about the black kid?" Donovan asked.

"He ain't around," said Flynn. "We went out to his house on the South Side. He was staying with his aunt. But after the murder of Maj Kirsten they sent him down South again. To Mississippi. They said they didn't want him raised in an environment like this."

"They were right," Schmidt said. "Damnit. I really thought the kid could do some identification."

"Why don't we get stills made from the film," said Sid Margolies, "and send them down to the cops in Mississippi wherever the kid is?"

"Sure," said Schmidt. "Sid, you take charge of that, okay?"

Sid wrote it down in his notebook.

"Well, I guess that's it." Schmidt stood up and stretched. "We got Angela Falicci coming down in the morning to look at the film. She was attacked in the park right after Maj Kirsten was murdered. I can't figure out what else we can do. I'm disappointed in the film. I thought there would be more there."

"Maybe it is there," said Karen Kovac.

Schmidt glanced at her.

"I mean—" she said. "I don't know. I really think there must be something there. And on the tape."

Flynn said, "Let's roll it again."

The deputy reversed the film to the beginning of the sequence.

"I'm going home, Terry," said Schmidt.

"And me," said Jack Donovan. "Only eight hours late."

Sid Margolies opened the door of the conference room. He turned back, "Then Terry will have the film."

"Yeah," said Schmidt. "Bring it back to the area, and we'll find a screening room tomorrow for Angela Falicci."

"All right," said Terry. He realized he didn't mind waiting for Karen Kovac to see the film again.

They all left the room except for the deputy, Flynn, and Karen Kovac. The room seemed colder; as in most modern high-rises, the air-conditioners took a long time to adjust at the end of the day to the presence of fewer people in the building giving off heat.

The film began again with the ludicrous photograph of Bonni Brighton in the lobby of the theater.

The film rolled slowly through the sequence of people fleeing the theater. Flynn glanced at Karen Kovac and saw she was biting her lower lip. Her teeth were very white and even and small: she had thin lips and angular features that were pleasantly combined.

Terry Flynn lit a cigarette.

"You want me to run it through again?"

"Yes, please," she said. The deputy complied.

The film rolled backward. The sixth man suddenly appeared, walked backward comically, and the door slammed on him. The fifth man backed into camera range and disappeared into the theater. And so on to the beginning of the sequence.

Again there was the photograph of Bonni Brighton in the lobby.

"Stop," she said.

The frame was frozen. She examined the photograph from close to the wall it was projected on. Her shadow blotted out part of the frame. She stared into the image of Bonni Brighton's eyes.

"What is it?" said Terry Flynn.

"I don't know."

She sat down again, and the deputy rolled the film forward. The first man came out of the theater. He had dark close-cropped hair. The second man appeared with his gray shaggy crew cut and dull gray Windbreaker and his teeth bared to the camera.

Terry watched Karen Kovac chew at her lips.

He waited until the end of the theater sequence.

"You want me to run it through again?" asked the deputy. He seemed to be willing to stay all night and run the projector.

"No," she said. She sounded a little tired. "I'm sure there's something there, in the film, and it won't come loose."

"All right, Karen," said Terry Flynn. "We got a day tomorrow. Only this time I've decided to disguise myself as a tourist when I trail you in the park."

"What will you look like?" she asked.

"I'll end up looking like a cop disguised as a tourist," he said.

She gave him a rare smile.

"Come on, kiddo," he said. "Let's have a drink."

"I don't think I can. There's a woman watching my boy."

"Pay her overtime," said Terry. "Come on. We'll go over to Mayor's Row across the street."

They found seats at the end of the bar.

She ordered a Scotch and soda, and Terry Flynn ordered a beer. His latest diet was in shambles and he was in no mood to put it together again. He drank the beer like a man who really liked beer.

She sipped her Scotch. He lit a cigarette and offered her one which she declined.

"I quit when I joined the department," she said. "For training."

"I started when I joined," said Terry Flynn. "It made me look older."

"Where do you live, Terry?" she asked.

"South Side," he said. "Around Ninety-fifth and Lonwood Drive. In Beverly. You know Beverly?"

"No. I mean, I know where it is, but I don't know it."

"Yeah. You talk like someone from the North Side."

"Northwest," she said. "Six Corners."

"Yeah." Terry Flynn didn't need an explanation. He knew

every street in the city and every neighborhood by name; he knew all the parishes on the South Side, for most South Siders identified themselves as belonging to a parish, "Visitation" parish or "John of God" parish. He knew the districts of the West Side as well, and he was an encyclopedia of racial and ethnic change in the city. He knew when St. Ambrose had "gone black" and when the Jews fled the West Side and when the hillbillies started moving in on Wilson Avenue in Uptown. He didn't take pride in his knowledge; it was just part of his education.

"You're married then?"

"No," he said. "I was married and then I wasn't. My ex-wife didn't like cops, it turned out."

"Why not?"

He shrugged. "I don't know. How can anybody not like cops?"

She took another sip of her drink and smiled again.

"Why'd you go on the department?" He was asking her.

"It was a job. And it paid good money. And I had a kid to raise."

"What'd your old man do?"

"He's in advertising. An account executive."

"Yeah?"

She didn't say anything. She was surprised she had said as much as she had. She felt she must like Terry Flynn. She put down her drink.

He watched her, but she made no move to leave.

"I'm seeing them now," she said.

"Who?"

"In the film. It's almost there, I can almost touch it."

He nodded.

"But what is it?"

"It'll come," he said gently. "You see, it almost came that time. You weren't thinking about it and it almost came. I get it that way sometimes. I realize the answer before I know that anyone asked the question."

"That's a clever way of saying it," she said. "Why did you go on the department?"

"What is this? More women's lib?" he asked. "Men aren't

supposed to have reasons. We just do things."

"Okay."

"No, I want to tell you," he said. "I think it's really important. Shows what a clear thinker I was when I was a kid. My father was a cop and my uncle was a cop and my grandfather was a cop. So I wanted to be a fireman."

"Why didn't you?"

"Heights," he said. "So the world lost a great fireman and gained a great dick."

"Heights?"

"I got in training academy and the first time I climbed the hook-and-ladder—that's what we had then—I almost passed out. As it was, I puked on the instructor who was down below. So I washed out."

"So you went on the cops."

"It wasn't that easy. But my old man still had his clout and so I got on. I was on the South Side for the first eight years. Christ. Nothing but war. That was when the black gangs were really being cute. And we had shit. Well, I don't want to bore you."

"Did you ever kill anyone?"

"Not in this country. I killed some people in Nam for a while, but I haven't killed anyone here but a few German Shepherds."

"Kill dogs?" She leaned forward in her chair and he leaned back in his. He was smiling.

"Sure. The brothers keep Shepherds in their flats. All the time. So you go up someplace and you say, 'Is Willie there?' and the next thing you know some goddamn dumb dog is jumping out at you. I ain't gonna be bit by no dog."

"So you kill them?"

"Sure," he said.

She nodded then, silently, as if in a sort of private revery. He waited. Her eyes were staring at some place other than the room.

"Her teeth. They were remarkable," she said. "And her face. So symmetrical."

"Yes," he said. He wasn't sure what she was driving at, but he was sure she was talking about Bonni Brighton.

"One of the men," she said. "Oh, I wish we could see the film."

"You've got it now," he said gently.

"Yes."

"Come on. We'll go back."

"You don't have to. It's late. Maybe I'm wrong."

"Hell, Karen. This is homicide. There's no late in it. We just do it as long as we can."

"Esprit de corps," she said.

"No. Cop macho."

The deputy was gone and Flynn threaded the projector himself. He explained he had seen it done once and that he was very mechanically minded.

Surprisingly the film was affixed properly. He turned on the projector lights and the film began.

Again the bathing beauties on Oak Street Beach.

And then the lobby. And the photograph.

The first man came out of the door.

The second man.

"Stop," she said.

But he fumbled with the switch and the film proceeded to the third man. He stopped the film and the picture froze. Slowly he reversed it and then stopped.

On the wall was projected the image of the gray-haired man in the crew cut.

"Yes," she said softly. "I knew it."

"What."

"Do you see?"

"No."

He stared at the gray man who seemed to snarl at the camera.

"Look at this," she said. She went to the wall and pointed. She appeared to be pointing to his mouth.

"What?"

"The teeth. They are the same as Bonni Brighton's teeth."

He was disappointed. Maybe she was a dud after all.

"You don't see, Terry," she said. She sounded excited.

178

"Look at the eyes. Look at the mouth. Look at the long nose, look how symmetrical it is. Do you have a picture of Bonni Brighton from the morgue?"

No, he did not.

She went to the door and opened it and went out. She returned in five minutes.

"I went down to the newsstand by the bus station," she said. "Here's the *Daily News*."

It was the final edition. On the front page was the banner story of the murder of the porn star. Below was another Watergate headline. And just above the fold was a large picture of Bonni Brighton which resembled the poster in the lobby of the theater.

Flynn stared at it.

She took the newspaper to the wall and held it up next to the freeze frame of the second man.

Then he saw it. "Mother of Christ," he said. "That's really—that's—"

She looked back at him and didn't speak.

"Karen" he said. "I think you've got him."

The two of them stared for a moment in the darkness at the face of the gray-haired man with piercing eyes and a snarl on his lips.

It was so simple.

"He looks like her," she said. But it wasn't necessary to speak.

"He killed her," said Flynn. "Whoever he is, he looks like her and he killed her."

"Look at the shoulders," she said.

"Strong man," said Terry Flynn softly. "When Maj Kirsten was killed, the knife came down from the heart across her body. Three ribs were broken. He cut her like a piece of meat."

"Look at the shirt," she said.

Yes, he understood everything. "A factory worker. He looks like a factory worker."

She let the newspaper fall onto a table and stood back from the wall, still gazing at the freeze-frame image.

"Which is why he killed in the mornings," she said. "Because he worked at night. Somewhere downtown. He killed them after work."

"Her brother or uncle or father or something. The dead women all looked like her. She was the last killing."

"For now," said Karen Kovac. "Until next time."

"Look at him," said Terry Flynn. "He looks like every bohunk factory worker in the city. He's gotta live in the city. Put out his face in the papers and we'll have him in twenty-four hours."

"It isn't real, is it?" she said. She hugged her arms around herself both because the building was very cold now and because she felt the excitement rising within her.

"Sure it is," said Terry Flynn. "It happens just like this. You're chasing a shadow and then there he is. Real as hell, just standing there, waiting for you."

She couldn't say another word. She stood for a few minutes more, staring at the freeze frame. She could hear the buzzing of the projector, and she could hear Terry Flynn calling someone. But they were not real sounds.

She stared at the eyes of the killer.

16. BECAUSE IT WAS FRIDAY NIGHT TERRY FLYNN AND KAREN KOVAC HAD A DIFFICULT TIME IN PROCEEDING TO THE NEXT step of their investigation.

When they called Matt Schmidt at home, there was no answer and they did not reach him until nearly midnight. By that time, of course, his wife answered the telephone and told them not to bother Matt that night because he was tired and was sleeping; she removed the plug on the telephone. This time, though, Flynn sent a squad car to the South Side to get Matt Schmidt at home and bring him down to Area One Homicide. The case was too important for sleep now.

They also had a difficult time tracking down Sid Margolies who had gone alone to a new Chinese restaurant on Clark Street. When they reached Margolies in his house in Rogers Park on the far North Side, he said the Peking duck had not been up to his expectations or to the rave reviews he had read in *Chicago Magazine*.

They had finally managed to assemble the team by one A.M. Of course, they had been busy with other business as well.

Karen Kovac had called on Maxwell Hampstead, Bonni Brighton's agent, at the Continental Plaza Hotel where he was spending the night before returning to New York.

He was not in his room but at the bar off the lobby, and he was very drunk when she found him. She agreed to sit with him for one drink while she asked him questions about Bonni Brighton's family.

"She was born in Cleveland, you know," said the agent. "Poor kid. What a way to end up. Did you see her in the theater? Dead?"

"Yes," said Karen Kovac. She was drinking a glass of white wine. It was clear from the bar bill in front of Maxwell Hampstead's glass that he had consumed at least ten martinis.

"You know, with the buildup she was getting, she would have been a big star. You know? A big star."

Karen nodded. "Do you know anything about her father? Or brother? Did she have any brothers?"

"Yeah. There was one. A guy named Bruno or something. Some name like that. A real family of Krauts." He took a large gulp of his drink. "You'd never know it, but even Bonni has a little accent. I think she spoke German at home until she went to school."

"She was born in Germany?"

"No, she was born here. But you know what some of these immigrant families are like."

Karen Kovac nodded. She knew.

"It was all going to be in the autobiography."

"She was writing a book?"

"Who? Bonni? Are you kidding? She was a sweet kid but writer she wasn't. A good actress but not a writer." He circled his finger at the bartender who brought him another martini. "Silver bullet time," he said and sipped the drink.

"Do you have the book?" asked Karen.

"No. N'York."

"In New York?"

"Yes."

"Does her family live in Cleveland?"

"I don't know. I don't know where they live."

"What was her real name? Was it Brighton?"

"Hell, no. You ever meet anyone named Brighton?"

Karen Kovac waited. Maxwell turned in his chair and looked at her. "You're a good-looking girl, you know that?"

She stared at him.

"Well, you are. Even if you're a cop. Why would you want to be a cop anyway? Lady cops should have muscles and tattoos."

"What was her real name?"

"Who?"

"Bonni Brighton."

"Look. Bonni Brighton is a thing of the past. I hate to say it because I liked her but she is. A thing of the past. Listen, would you like some dinner?"

"No," said Karen Kovac. "I'm here strictly for a murder investigation."

"Okay, okay. You're pulling the Joe Friday stuff, right? Listen, it's okay. God, you've got nice legs."

In fact, Karen Kovac did not care for the shape of her legs. She thought they were too thick. She didn't know what to say now. This was the sort of thing that made her work difficult.

"What was Bonni Brighton's name?"

"If I tell you, will you have a little dinner with me?"

"No, Mr. Hampstead." She stood up. "Do you want to be interviewed here, now, or do you want to come with me to Area One Homicide and be interviewed?"

"What? Are you arresting me?" He started to laugh.

"It's up to you."

"What? Are you going to put me in handcuffs?" It was too funny.

Karen Kovac realized she was very angry. She said, "No. I'm going to call for assistance. And two uniformed men will be here in three minutes. They'll put you in handcuffs and throw you into the back of the squad car and they'll take you downtown. Since you are obviously very drunk, we shall have to wait until the morning to question you. There will be a small charge. Disorderly conduct, I think. And in the morning when you are sober, you will go before the judge and he will fine you twenty-five dollars and sentence you to time served in jail. All because you will not tell me Bonni Brighton's name."

Maxwell Hampstead said, "Sit down. Her name was Mathilde."

She took out a pen and began to write the name down in a little notebook.

"Mathilde Bremenhoffer." He spelled it slowly.

"Is her mother or father alive?"

"I don't know. It's in the book."

"Haven't you seen the book?"

"Look, I'm an agent. I don't have to read what I peddle."

"What is her father's name?"

"I don't know."

"Do you know what he does for a living?"

"No. Wait. Yes. He was a printer. That's what Bonni told me. When we were talking about the book. She said her father might have to print the book and wouldn't that be funny. You're a very tough broad, you know that?"

She ignored him. "And what was her mother's name?"

"I don't remember. They were just names. I never met them. She called Bruno once or twice, I remember. Maybe he lives in L.A. Yeah. It seems that she called area two-one-three, that's L.A. He must live out there."

"How can we see the book? To get the names you can't remember?"

"You have to get hold of Bonni's editor."

"But didn't you have a copy of the manuscript?"

"Not really."

"Who was the ghost writer?"

"Dolores Riddell."

She wrote down the name as he spelled it. "Where does she live?"

"Where else?"

"In New York."

"Of course."

"Do you represent her, as well?"

"No," said Maxwell Hampstead.

"How can we obtain the manuscript?"

"Well, maybe you can't," said Maxwell Hampstead. "What do I get out of it?"

She merely stared at him without expression. Her face was very pale and her eyes seemed a glowing sort of blue. He didn't realize she was furious.

"Come on," said Maxwell.

"Mr. Hampstead, this is a murder investigation. You have important information to contribute to the solution of the crime. If you withhold that information, you are obstructing the investigation of a crime. You are guilty, then, of a crime yourself. You're under arrest."

"Don't come on tough with me, honey—"

She turned and left the book-lined bar. He watched her leave, waited, shrugged, and sat down again.

She telephoned Terry Flynn at Area One and told him what had happened.

"Pinch him," said Terry Flynn. "I'll call East Chicago and get a couple of nonmorons over there. Just wait for them."

"I should handle it myself," she said.

"Fuck no," said Terry Flynn. "We just want to shake him up anyway. We'll give him a ride in the nice blue-and-white car with the sirens and all and when he gets down to the area, he'll be shitting in his pants."

She smiled. "You put it so well."

"I've got an ear for dialogue," he said. "That's literary talk."

Four minutes later two beefy uniformed men from the East Chicago Avenue district station walked into the lobby of the Continental Plaza Hotel. Karen Kovac pointed out Maxwell Hampstead in the bar. They walked inside, and one man stood on each side of the barstool. The bartenders looked up and so did the customers. The place became very silent, as though the presence of the uniformed men were a rude intrusion on a polite world of alcohol and leather chairs and books along the walls. Which was the case.

"Hi," said Maxwell Hampstead.

The first bartender came up. "Is there any trouble?"

"Not yet," said one of the uniforms. "Mr. Hampstead? You want to come with us?"

"He's a guest of the hotel," said the bartender.

"And now he's going to be a guest of the city," said the

uniform. He thought this was very funny.

"What do you men think you're doing?" asked Maxwell Hampstead.

"Mr. Hampstead, you don't want any trouble in here, do you? You want to come with us out in the lobby and maybe we can straighten this out?"

"Of course," said Hampstead. "I'm from New York, you know."

"We didn't know," said one of the uniforms.

They waited while he got up unsteadily and they let him lead them into the lobby. He turned in the lobby and saw Karen Kovac. "So that's it, huh? That little cunt thinks she's going to fuck me around? Is that it? You fucking little slut."

"Oh, shit," said one of the uniformed men. In a moment he grabbed Maxwell's arm and snapped one cuff on it and then twisted the arm behind his back, forcing Maxwell to bend over. The agent made a spasmodic move of protest in that moment, but he was handcuffed in a second. Then one of the uniformed men shoved him against the lobby wall and leaned very close to his face. "You really don't want to do that, do you, Maxwell?"

"You—"

"No, don't speak. Not yet. Really. Believe me. Don't say anything, all right?"

Maxwell felt the pressure of the policeman's large hand on his chest. To those passing by, it appeared as if the policeman were merely restraining a drunk with a gentle hand; but Maxwell knew that the policeman was making it very painful for him to breath.

Karen Kovac came up to him and said quietly. "We really don't want to arrest you. Just call Dolores Riddel in New York, now, and tell her to give us the names of Bonni Brighton's family."

"This pig is hurting my chest," he gasped.

"Yes," she said. "I know."

"You people are really fascist goons; ever since—"

"No," whispered the uniformed man. "We really aren't. And you don't want to talk now."

"I'll tell you. But when I get out of here, out of this fascist town, I'm going—"

"Do you want to call from your room?"

"No, I don't. You'll probably use rubber hoses on me up there."

Karen nodded to the uniformed man and they led Maxwell to the telephone alcove off the lobby. A small crowd had gathered around the policemen. They watched Maxwell being led off.

"Nothing," said Karen Kovac. "Just a drunk." They nodded and some of them gaped at her. She went and joined Maxwell and the policemen at the telephone.

Dolores Riddell was asleep when Maxwell Hampstead finally got through to her, but she was not uncooperative when the agent handed the telephone to Karen Kovac.

"The name of the family is Bremenhoffer," she said.

Karen said, "What about the mother and father? And brother?"

There was a pause for several minutes as Dolores Riddell found the appropriate place in the manuscript. "The name of the father is Frank. Frank Bremenhoffer. He was a refugee from Germany at the beginning of World War II. He had a brother who stayed in Germany and was in the underground but was caught. The brother was shot to death in 1943."

"And Frank Bremenhoffer?"

"He worked for the Allies in England during the war. After the war he returned to his native town, Zehdenick, that's in East Germany, just north of Berlin. He stayed there two years and then, in 1948, he left East Germany and emigrated to the United States. He arrived in Cleveland in 1949. That's where Bonni was born."

"And the mother's name?"

"Ulla."

"Brothers and sisters?"

"We didn't put it in the book but there's a brother, Bruno, who lives in Van Nuys in California. I think he's a production engineer or something for a plastics firm. Very dull. She called him often. She liked him. It's a shame. Just a shame. She was a porn actress and all and there wasn't much she hadn't done but she was okay. Really a sweet kid."

"And what about lovers? Any lovers?"

Dolores Riddell laughed at the other end of the line. "Sure. Plenty. She was a good-looking girl and she really had an appetite. You understand?"

"Yes," said Karen Kovac. "Was there someone now?"

"I don't know. She didn't seem to have steadies or whatever they call them now. God, that ages me."

"Do you know where the family lives?"

"Her parents? I suppose they live in Cleveland. I don't know, Bonni didn't really say. She was reluctant to say anything about the family."

"Her father was a printer?"

"Yes. She did say that."

"Well," said Karen Kovac. "Thank you, Miss Riddell. I appreciate your trouble, waking you up and all. I appreciate Maxwell calling you."

"Any time, Mrs. Kovac. Any time. I want you to find out who did that to Bonni. What a sweet kid, it just kills me to think about it."

"And now there won't be a book," said Karen Kovac.

"Oh? I don't care. But I doubt if my publisher will let a little thing like a murder stand in the way."

They broke the connection.

Karen Kovac looked at Maxwell. She was calm again. "Thank you, Mr. Hampstead."

The two uniformed men understood and they suddenly let him go. Maxwell almost fell and then caught himself. He mumbled something, but they could not understand it.

"Thank you," Karen said to the two uniformed men.

"Sure," they said. "You working homicide?" one asked her. "I didn't know they had any women in homicide."

"Just on this case," she said. "I came in as a decoy. On the park murders."

"Oh. Then this is part of it?"

"Yes," she said. "We think so."

"Sarge says Terry Flynn called and asked us to help. We know Terry. How is that Irish bastard?"

"Fine," she said.

"Terry and I were on the South Side together. And Johnny here went to school with him."

The one named Johnny smiled.

Karen said, "What was he like then?"

"Just as crazy but not as fat," said Johnny. "Sort of a little kid's idea of Robin Hood."

The other man chuckled. "Now he's a fat man's idea of Robin Hood."

She smiled and left them.

It was nearly one A.M. when they all assembled again at Area One Homicide.

Matt Schmidt sat back in his chair. He looked tired, and his face was the color of ashes. He coughed twice, experimentally, into his handkerchief and examined the sputum.

Terry Flynn did not look tired and neither did Karen Kovac. Their faces seemed flushed with excitement.

Sid Margolies stood by the filing cabinet in the back of the room and rested his arm on it.

"Well, what do we have now?"

"We got a face that looks like Bonni Brighton." It was Flynn. "Thanks to Karen. I wouldn't have seen it in a million years. We've got a name. A guy lives in Cleveland. I called Cleveland P.D. three hours ago and they're looking into it. There were two Bremenhoffers in the Cleveland directory, neither of them Frank."

"I don't understand about Cleveland," said Sid Margolies.

"That's where she came from," said Flynn.

"Yeah, but what about here?"

"What do you mean?"

"People move," said Sid Margolies. "She was killed here."

Flynn shrugged. "I checked out the name in the telephone book."

"Telephone books aren't any good," said Margolies. "Call information."

Flynn picked up the telephone and called. He asked for the name. He waited. "Thank you." He replaced the receiver.

Margolies looked at him.

"No such name."

Margolies shrugged. "Maybe he doesn't have a phone," he said at last.

"Everyone has a phone," said Terry Flynn. "Besides, if he doesn't have a phone, how can we find where he lives?"

"If he's a printer, maybe he's a member of the printer's union. Here or in Cleveland," said Matt Schmidt.

"We could call her brother," said Karen Kovac.

"Sure," said Flynn. "I'll do it."

"What are we going to tell her brother?" asked Sid.

"That she's dead," said Karen. "And we want to notify the rest of the family. And need their address."

But though they found Bruno Bremenhoffer's name in the Van Nuys area, there was no answer at his telephone.

"What time is it in California?" asked Flynn.

"A little after eleven," said Sid Margolies. "That's early. People in California never go to bed."

"I was in bed," said Matt Schmidt. "And then all of a sudden there's two gorillas from tactical at my door, pounding away at it and my wife was yelling—"

"I wanted to get your attention," said Flynn. He felt very good, better than he had in a long time. He wondered if his good feeling was all related to the developments on the case.

"You got it then," said Matt Schmidt. "Can we get coffee?"

"I'll pop," said Terry Flynn. "What have we got? Cream, cream, black, black?"

"Make mine black too. They're using that nondairy crap now. I'm allergic to it."

"You're a hypochondriac, Sid."

"So what? One of these days I'm going to be right."

The call from Cleveland police came at two A.M. Neither of the Bremenhoffers appeared related to Bonni Brighton or knew a Frank Bremenhoffer or had anyone in the printing trades.

At two thirty-four A.M. they got an answer at the residence of Bruno Bremenhoffer in California.

Terry Flynn told him what happened to his sister, and there was a long silence.

He then asked him the whereabouts of the rest of the family.

Another silence. "Who killed her?" he asked.

"We don't know."

"You think it was someone in my family?"

"No. We want to notify your parents."

"I see." Another pause. "I suppose." Another pause followed that.

"Hello, Mr. Bremenhoffer?"

"Yes, I'm here. We don't have trouble with the cops, you know."

"Yes," said Flynn.

"My father is afraid of the police, you know. He doesn't like police. It's because of what happened in Germany. Before the war and after, when he had to live in East Germany. I want you to understand that."

"Yes, I understand," said Terry Flynn.

"Actually, it isn't my father. It's my mother I'm worried about."

"I understand."

Another pause. It was maddening. Flynn could hear the line crackle over the two-thousand-mile distance. When Bremenhoffer spoke, it sounded like there was an echo.

"They live in Chicago," he said at last.

Terry made a thumbs-up sign to the rest of them.

"Yes?" he said. He tried to sound calm.

"Here's the address: 4597 North Kedvale Avenue."

"Yes." Flynn repeated it. "Your father doesn't have a phone?"

"No."

"What does he do?"

"What has that got to do with it?"

"He's a printer?"

"Yes."

"Do you know where?"

"What if I do? Why do you have to know that? You want to cause him trouble?" The voice seemed agitated. Flynn said, "Take it easy, Bruno. I just asked. It's all right."

"What are you going to do with Mathilde's . . . body?"

"She's at the morgue now. We'll release her body. After tests."

"Yes. I see." The voice sounded very weary. "Well, you must let me know. What Father decides to do."

"We will. Do you have any other relatives?"

"What? What kind of a question is that?"

"Just a question. Does Bonni . . . did Mathilde have an uncle here?"

"No. There's no one else. Don't call her that name to my father."

"Bonni?"

"Yes. He hated that. More even than what she . . . did."

"He didn't approve?"

"No. Would you? If your daughter decided to run away and become a whore, would you approve? Don't be stupid."

Flynn flushed and seemed about to make an angry retort. Matt Schmidt, who was listening in at an extension, shook his head vigorously at Flynn who saw the movement in time. He took a deep swallow and tried out his calm voice again: "Of course. Did Bonni run away from home?"

"Her name is Mathilde. Was Mathilde. Yes. She went to Haight-Asbury when she was sixteen. We found out later. To become a hippie."

"Did she see your father?"

"Why don't you ask my father?"

"All right. It's just that we didn't wish to disturb him with these questions, we thought—"

"How considerate," said Bruno Bremenhoffer. "I didn't know the police were so considerate."

Matt Schmidt glared at Flynn who was flushing dangerously red again. Flynn said nothing.

"All right," said Bruno. "I apologize. I'm upset as well. I liked Mathilde very much. No, she didn't see my father. He was very unforgiving and she did not bother to see him anymore."

"Or her mother?"

"No. My mother is very much of the old country. My father rules her, if you understand."

Flynn waited.

"I'm sorry to be rude. I am not usually rude. This is upsetting to me. Have I answered all your questions? Can I go now?"

"Yes," said Terry Flynn quietly. They broke the connection.

Flynn turned to Matt Schmidt and the others.

"He sounds screwy," said Flynn.

"Just natural belligerence," answered Matt Schmidt. "You bring out the best in people."

"That isn't fair," said Flynn. "Anyway, we got a name and an address now and I'll bet you a dime to doughnuts that the guy we saw coming out of the theater was Frank Bremenhoffer."

They all stared at him when he said this.

"It stands to reason," he said. "The old man killed her."

No one spoke.

Sid Margolies finally said, "I'm glad you weren't on the Kennedy assassination committee investigation. You'd hang first and ask questions later."

"Sure," said Flynn cheerfully. "I'm not an intellectual like you, Sid. I'm just a simpleton from the South Side who likes to bash in heads first and then find out if they have anything in them."

Karen Kovac was amazed at the mildness in Terry Flynn's voice. He sounded happy.

"What do you think, Matt?" asked Sid Margolies, ignoring Flynn.

"We are basing all this on hunches," said Schmidt. He coughed again into his handkerchief. "Karen has given us a reasonable base of speculation. She noted that one of the men running out of the theater appeared to resemble Bonni Brighton. From this, we proceeded to question her agent who told us what he knew about her family."

"Not really," said Flynn. "But let it go."

Schmidt frowned at him. "From this we learn that her mother and father happen to live on the Northwest Side. The question is: What do we do at this moment?"

It was nearly three-thirty A.M.

"Roust him up," said Flynn. "Talk to the guy."

The others waited.

"I think we ought to call Jack Donovan," said Matt Schmidt.

"Look," said Flynn. "Jack is a good guy and all and you've explained about the problem of this special task force he's suppose to have set up. But for now we've got no reason to wake him up. Let's go get Frank Bremenhoffer and see what he looks like and then we can call Jack Donovan."

"We've got less to go on now than we had with Norman Frank," said Schmidt.

"Yeah," said Terry Flynn. "It's a shame that murder ain't neat."

Schmidt glanced at him but decided not to take offense. It was too late in the night or too early in the morning for anger and short tempers.

They waited until dawn. Schmidt telephoned Gert and told her he would not be home.

"I'm all right," he said.

"It's supposed to rain today," she replied. "You have to take care of yourself."

"I feel all right," he said. They had been married for twenty-nine years, and they did not have a lot to say.

"You don't sound good. Don't catch cold if it rains. You've got the umbrella downtown." He had a downtown umbrella and a home umbrella.

"It'll be good if it rains," he said. He tried to put a smile in his voice. "The tomatoes need it."

"All right." She always said that at these moments; anything else would just upset him.

Karen Kovac went with Terry Flynn to the Little Corporal Restaurant, an all-night place on Wacker Drive. It was nearly two miles across the Loop from central police headquarters but he told her that it was good to get out of the area when you worked around the clock.

They had breakfast together and returned by five A.M.

Sid Margolies was instructed to call Jack Donovan, but Donovan had removed the plug from the telephone receiver and there was no answer. They decided not to send a car for him.

The sun came up over the lake suddenly, as though it were not expected. The sun looked bright gold at first and then orange as it moved above the clear horizon. Because Lake Michigan is so wide, the horizon was a sea horizon, meeting water and sky. The sun splattered light on the dark purple-lit buildings of night. It was warm again. In the west clouds bunched, waiting to spring across the city.

Frank Bremenhoffer lived in a courtyard building, typical of a certain construction type in Chicago. There were twelve apartments on three floors arranged in a deep U shape around a central court which faced the street. These buildings were invariably made of brick, and most had been erected between 1918 and 1930.

They were comfortable places to live.

Matt Schmidt had arranged for two men from the district to wait in the alley behind the building and for two more men to wait on the street in front.

Terry Flynn and Sid Margolies were going in. Matt Schmidt and Karen Kovac waited on the sidewalk in the courtyard.

Flynn went into the building and rang the doorbell marked with Bremenhoffer's name. He waited and rang it again.

"Maybe they're on vacation," said Sid Margolies logically. He only made Terry Flynn sneer at him.

Flynn rang the bell again and then went downstairs to the locked door. It was a simple catch lock. Flynn took a heavy piece of plastic from his wallet and inserted it between the door and the jamb. The door opened.

"So which floor is it?" asked Margolies.

"It must be the second."

"But which door?"

"I don't know."

They went up the carpeted stairs quietly, but still the weight of their bodies made the stairs creak. On the second floor they paused.

"You want to flip for it?" asked Sid Margolies.

Flynn frowned again. Sid was making him mad.

There were two doors on the second landing. It was a fifty-fifty chance. Impulsively Flynn knocked at one door. He waited for a moment and then knocked again. He listened at the door. Suddenly he signaled to Sid.

Sid Margolies unbuttoned his coat and snapped the safety off his pistol which was in a shoulder holster. He waited at the side of the door.

Terry Flynn's coat was also unbuttoned. The .357-magnum revolver was visible in the clip on his belt.

"What is it?"

The voice sounded strange, lost in sleep.

"Police," said Flynn. "Is this the residence of Frank Bremenhoffer?"

Silence.

"Police."

Silence still.

Flynn knocked at the door again and tried to press himself against the side of the wall. It would not be usual for anyone to shoot through the door at him but, on the other hand, it was never unexpected.

"Who is this?"

"Police, ma'am. We want to talk to Frank Bremenhoffer."

"He's not here."

So it was the right door. Flynn glanced at Sid Margolies and then gave him the finger. They waited.

"Come back," the voice of the woman said.

"Where is he?"

"Work."

"We're police. Open the door."

Another pause. And then the door opened a crack, held by a strong chain. They saw an old, wrinkled face peering out. The eyes were young and shaped like almonds.

"Frank not here."

She said the English words with seeming difficulty but with directness.

"Where is he?"

"Work. I told you."

"Yes. Where?"

"He work at printing plant."

"Yes," said Sid Margolies, peering into the crack of the door. He could not see the inside.

"When will he be back?"

"He off work at seven A.M." The "A.M." sounded odd, memorized. "He back this morning."

"This is important, Mrs. Bremenhoffer. We have to talk to him. Where does he work?"

"Why?" She looked at the two of them.

"Mrs. Bremenhoffer." Flynn decided to tell her. "Your daughter, we think, Mathilde, is dead."

She stared at him.

"Your daughter is dead."

Her eyes looked vacant. "Frank will be home this morning. Guten tag." She shut the door.

"What the fuck," said Flynn softly. "What the fuck."

"Look, Terry." Sid touched him on the sleeve. "Get Matt up here to talk to her."

They went downstairs and talked to Matt Schmidt. It was decided that Matt alone would go upstairs.

He returned to the courtyard ten minutes later.

"She won't let anyone in. She's afraid. I told her again that Bonni was dead and showed her the picture in the papers, but she just shook her head. She told me her husband works at Halsted Graphics and Printing. He's on the eleven-to-seven shift. He ought to be here in a couple of hours."

"Should we go down and pick him up there?"

Schmidt shook his head. "Let's wait for him. And let's lay off the two uniforms in the front of the building." But he told them to keep the two men posted at the back of the building in case Frank Bremenhoffer had been in the apartment and would try to escape.

There was something else.

Schmidt went to the second unmarked car and looked in. Karen Kovac was sitting in the passenger seat. "You live near here," he said.

"Yes."

"Go home."

"I'm not tired."

"No," said Schmidt. "I'm the only one who's tired. It's clear

197

to me that you and Terry could go for days without sleep. But I want you to go home and rest up."

"I really want to be in on it at the end."

"This isn't the end," said Matt Schmidt. "I can feel it like I can feel the rain coming. Go home and see your kid and get some sleep."

"You're saying that because I'm a woman," she said sharply.

"Yes," he said. "That's right. But I still want you to go home. We'll call you in a couple of hours when we get him and interview him."

She was still angry, but she got out of the car and slammed the door. "Boys always want the girls to go home when they're planning to have fun."

"That's our homosexual need," said Matt Schmidt. He was trying to be funny. But she wouldn't smile.

"I'll go home, Lieutenant," she said.

"There's more to it," he said. "What if this isn't the end of it and we have to resume the decoys in the park?"

"You know he killed her. If he's the man in the film. Coming out of the movie theater."

"No," he said. "We don't know that. Terry is going to poop out soon. So am I. When we get Bremenhoffer into the area, I'm going to call you and Jack Donovan. And someone from the day shift. We're going to have to stay with him."

"All right," she said.

"Karen."

"What?"

"You might have broken this for us."

"I want to be in at the end."

"You will," he said. "I'm worried about you. You haven't slept for twenty-four hours. I know, that's nothing. But I like you. Unlike Terry Flynn whom I don't care about."

She shrugged. She felt deadly tired and still awake, too excited to sleep. She started to walk away.

Terry Flynn came up to Schmidt who was climbing into the squad.

"Why did you do that? Where the hell is she going?"

"Home."

"Why?"

"Because she looked tired to me."

"What the fuck kind of shit is this?"

"Lieutenant shit," said Schmidt. "Now leave me alone. I want to close my eyes."

"She practically broke this case."

"Yes," said Matt Schmidt. None of them would understand his premonitions so he did not try to explain them. They would just hate him, but that was all right.

Schmidt fell asleep dozing against the window. When he awoke, the sky was gloomy and rain clouds filled the horizon where there had been a sun. He reached under the seat and felt for his umbrella. His mouth was dry.

"What's going on?" He realized Terry Flynn had awakened him.

"Look."

Coming up the street was a man in gray clothes—gray work shirt and gray cotton work trousers—carrying a gray jacket under his arm. He walked with a barely noticeable limp. He had gray hair and thick eyebrows that nearly joined above his long, symmetrical nose.

"That's him, Matt. The one on the film."

They opened the doors of the squadrol and slammed them and walked across Kedvale Avenue toward the man. It was nearly eight thirty A.M., and they could hear the sounds of the rush-hour traffic from the Kennedy Expressway four blocks away.

"Frank Bremenhoffer?" Terry Flynn barked the name in the stillness of the street. He held up his hand as he crossed the street.

The gray man stopped and stared at Flynn.

"Bremenhoffer? Police."

The man had brilliant blue eyes and immense shoulders. He seemed to be taller than Terry Flynn though he was the same height. "What do you want?" He spoke with contempt. And without an accent.

"Frank Bremenhoffer." Flynn said it softly like repeating an incantation. "It's about your daughter, Bonni Brighton. We want to talk to you."

"I don't have a daughter. Excuse me."

Bremenhoffer started into the courtyard, but Flynn

blocked his way on the sidewalk. "Excuse me," the gray man said.

"Your daughter is dead."

"Is that so?" Bremenhoffer looked at Flynn and seemed to be on the verge of smiling.

"Your daughter was Bonni Brighton. She was murdered yesterday morning in a movie house in the Loop."

"Not my daughter. My daughter's name was Mathilde Bremenhoffer, and she ran away from home seven years ago to become a hippie in California. So it can't be that this person you mentioned is my daughter."

Flynn stared at him. He looked at the big man's shoulders and wonderd if he could take him. He wanted to have the chance.

"I'm very tired," Bremenhoffer said. "I worked all night. I would like to go to bed."

"We want to talk to you. We want to ask you some questions, that's all. About the murder of your daughter."

"Why?"

"Will you come with us?" It was Matt Schmidt's mild voice.

"So many policemen to ask questions," said Bremenhoffer. He turned and looked at them all. "It must be important."

"That's the thing about murder," said Terry Flynn.

Bremenhoffer sighed and looked at Flynn. "People get killed every day. You cannot catch the killers. I read about that old man who ran the grocery on the South Side, the one you had to let his killers go free. And they were *schwartzes*. You knew who killed him, and you could not keep the killers. What makes you so certain you want to catch the killer of this woman you name?"

"Because we have to," said Matt Schmidt softly. "Will you come with us for a little while? We need your help."

He smiled then. His teeth were strong and even, and the smile was like the snarl caught by the freeze frame.

"Okay, policeman. Maybe I am not that tired. I will help you catch the man who killed this woman you name."

"Your daughter," said Matt Schmidt.

"If you insist," said Frank Bremenhoffer. "We will call her that for now."

17. FRANK BREMENHOFFER SAT IN A STRAIGHT CHAIR NEXT TO THE TABLE IN THE WHITE-WALLED WINDOWLESS INTERVIEW room. The room was off the squad room at Area One Homicide in central police headquarters downtown. Bremenhoffer and Matthew Schmidt had waited there for Jack Donovan's arrival. At one point Matt Schmidt had offered Bremenhoffer coffee, but he had declined.

It was nearly ten A.M. before Donovan arrived at the building. By this time they had taken Frank Bremenhoffer to the morgue on the West Side, and he had identified Bonni Brighton as Mathilde Bremenhoffer. He had shown no emotion other than distaste for the corpse.

When Donovan and Flynn entered the interview room at ten thirty-five A.M., Flynn took a position against the back wall and stared at Bremenhoffer. Donovan sat down and began his questions: "Your daughter was killed shortly after eleven A.M. yesterday morning in the Ajax Theater in the Loop."

Bremenhoffer stared at him. His large hands rested

casually on the tabletop. He had hung his gray jacket behind the chair on which he sat. The jacket was damp; it had started to rain a little after nine A.M., when they returned from the morgue.

"Did you see who killed her?"

"How could I?"

Donovan looked at Flynn. Flynn stared at Bremenhoffer.

"We thought you might have seen who killed her."

"Really?" He began to smile.

"You were in the theater," said Flynn.

"Really?"

"Really," said Donovan. "We're setting up the film so you can see yourself. Coming out of the theater. You'll see yourself positively and clearly. You were the second man through the door at the back of the theater right after your daughter was stabbed to death."

"I wish you'd do something for me."

"What?"

"Stop calling that whore Bonni Brighton my daughter. My daughter was Mathilde Bremenhoffer and she ran away seven years ago and I just saw her body in the morgue."

Donovan stared at Flynn, but Flynn continued to look at Bremenhoffer.

Bremenhoffer smiled at Donovan. "I'm not crazy, you know. I realize that the woman who was killed in that theater—that whore—was once Mathilde but she chose to be Bonni Brighton and chose not to become my daughter anymore. So she is not my daughter. That is free choice, isn't it? It is her choice and it is mine."

Donovan waited.

"It is like this. I am sorry to hear this woman—this whore, even—got killed. I'm sorry about it the way I'm sorry when I read in the paper that a boat full of goddamn Pakistanis or Indians got drowned somewhere. It's too bad, but it won't give me indigestion."

"This happened a little closer to home. Your daughter was in the theater, and you saw her killed."

"I didn't know what happened."

Flynn moved from the wall to the table. He put his hands

on the table and leaned toward Bremenhoffer. "Why don't we cut the crap? You were in the movie house and you know goddamn well that your daughter was murdered there. You came out the same goddamn aisle where she was sitting. If you didn't see it, you need a guide dog."

"I didn't know what happened," Bremenhoffer said.

"Why did you run out?"

"I heard screaming. Why did anyone run out? I thought the theater was on fire."

"Bullshit," said Flynn.

"Really," said Bremenhoffer mildly.

"When your daughter was murdered, it was in all the papers all day yesterday and this morning. Why didn't you come forward?"

"I try not to read the newspapers. I'm a printer and I know what newspapers are."

"Or on television."

"I work the overnight shift, eleven to seven. When the hell do you think I would find the time or energy to watch television? Do you think all the people in this goddamn country have time to watch telelvision all day like zombies? Some of us are still alive. I did not know about this person who is dead. I know it now. And I told you I am sorry to hear about the death. It is too bad."

"Why were you in the theater?"

"I was invited."

Donovan glanced at Flynn. "What?"

"I was invited." Bremenhoffer looked at his large hands on the table. "Bonni Brighton sent me an invitation. So I went. I got off work and I went to the theater. I had breakfast first at the drugstore and then I went."

"She sent you an invitation?"

"Sure. It was probably her idea of a joke. She had very strange ideas. I think she might have been mentally ill. I thought that even when she was still my daughter."

"If you didn't want to see your daughter any more, why did you go to the theater?"

Bremenhoffer looked at Donovan steadily. "Curiosity."

"What does that mean?"

"I was curious to see what my former daughter had become. I knew she was a whore, of course. I wouldn't go across the street to see a whore. Besides, she had been a whore when she was at home. But I admit I was curious to see how you make money as a whore these days, so much money that you can get people to write about you."

"You knew your daughter was a film actress."

Bremenhoffer snorted and seemed to laugh. "Really, Mr. Donovan, are you so naïve? I told you. I knew she was a whore. She sent us money once. I tried to send it back."

Donovan did not speak. He stared across the table at the powerful man. He imagined Maj Kirsten's body. Her eyes had been open in death. He stared at Bremenhoffer's fingers. They rested silently on the table, almost contentedly.

"Who do you think could have killed her?"

"Who? Bonni Brighton? Anyone. She was a whore. Whores die. Who cares? Maybe it was one of her lovers. Or one of the women in the film. I suppose they were her lovers too."

"The ones she made love to?" asked Flynn.

"Love?" Bremenhoffer turned in his chair to look at Flynn. There was a trace of a smile on his thin lips. "You call that love? That dirty thing that they do? You are a sick man, Mr. Flynn, I can tell you. You should have more control of yourself."

"Do you think that someone she knew killed her?"

Bremenhoffer stared. He did not blink. "Sure. That's possible, isn't it? Most murders are like that, aren't they? Committed by someone who knows the person who is murdered?"

Was it time to warn him of his rights? Donovan sat for a moment in silence. Was Frank Bremenhoffer getting ready to confess? It was a tricky judgment. He had to be warned of his rights before the confession started. He glanced at Flynn who shrugged. The same thought was in both of their minds.

Donovan felt trapped because now he knew Frank Bremenhoffer was the killer.

Donovan got up from the table, went to the door, and entered the squad room. Flynn waited in the interview room with Bremenhoffer.

"Where's Karen?" Donovan asked Matt Schmidt.

"I sent her home."

"Why?"

"She looked tired."

"Come on, Matt."

"I didn't want her in on the interview. Not now. Maybe later. I don't think Frank Bremenhoffer is going to go all weepy on us and tell us he killed those women. I think we're going to have to interview him again. And maybe again. And I want to save Karen."

"Did you tell her that?"

"No. She wouldn't understand."

"I'm not sure I do."

"She looks like the murdered women. Maybe we can use her, one on one with him. Once we get a reading of him, what's likely to set him off."

Donovan shrugged. "It doesn't seem like anything will set him off."

"I know. I talked to him a while alone before you and Terry went after him."

"He's insane," said Jack Donovan.

Schmidt nodded.

Donovan reentered the room with Matt Schmidt.

Bremenhoffer looked up and smiled at them as though he were welcoming them into his home.

"Where do you usually go in the mornings?" Flynn asked.

"What?"

"After work. Where do you go?"

"I go home. I go to sleep."

"But not all the time."

Frank Bremenhoffer smiled. "Sure. All the time."

"Not yesterday," said Matt Schmidt.

"No, not yesterday." He seemed to like the new line of questions. He leaned back in his chair. "No, not yesterday and maybe not all the time. I do other things. Sometimes I go to the Art Institute."

He looked at them, but they did not react.

"Sometimes I go to the movies. I like movies."

"You don't take your wife?"

"No. She doesn't like movies."

"What kind of movies do you go to?"

"Every kind. I'm a printer. I get tired of reading, on the job and off the job. So I go to a movie. Germany had the best movies before the war. Remember the Clark Theater downtown? They would show the old movies. It was a good place. It's too bad they tore it down. Did you ever hear of Fritz Lang?"

"Yes," said Jack Donovan.

"Marvelous. And now I go to the Hitchcock movies when they appear. Also Bergman. He's a favorite of mine. Did you see Fritz Lang's great movie, *M*?"

"Yes," Donovan said.

"Really? You surprise me, Mr. Donovan. Maybe you are a student of film and not just a dumb cop."

Flynn bristled visibly, but Schmidt stared him back to a semblance of calm.

"Maybe you are a student of film," continued Bremenhoffer.

"Are you?"

"No. I don't think so. I enjoy movies and I remember them. In *M* you remember that Peter Lorre is finally caught and convicted by a jury of his criminal peers from the underworld?"

"Yes. For molesting and murdering children," said Donovan.

Bremenhoffer nodded. "Ja." It was the first German word he had spoken. "That is realistic and romantic at the same time. Fritz Lang is a master. Do you remember when the child's ball is seen, merely rolling away, and we know that Lorre has murdered the child we saw playing with the ball? Perhaps you don't remember that?"

"I remember," said Donovan.

"Tell me, do you think it is realistic that a killer like Lorre can be tried by his peers?"

Donovan looked at Bremenhoffer and tried to speak carefully. "You mean a man who is sick? Who essentially needs help, who commits murders that are the result of his fantasies? A psychological killer?"

Bremenhoffer shook his head. "That is nonsense, Mr.

Donovan. A man who kills is a killer. He must always have a good reason for murder. A man who kills a grocer like those niggers killed that man on the South Side had reasons. He was a white man and they hated him; or he wouldn't give them the money fast enough. Or some reason. We know it is a good enough reason for murder because we know they committed murder. All this nonsense about psychology bores me."

"What about a man who kills women?" asked Flynn.

Bremenhoffer turned to him. "What do you mean?"

"What are the good reasons for those murders in Grant Park, do you suppose?"

Donovan stared at Flynn; it was a dangerous line of questioning but he waited.

"I don't know. Maybe they were whores and their pimps killed them. Didn't it turn out that one of those women was a whore? She lived with this man who abused children?"

They waited.

"Well, that is one reason. But I am not qualified to speculate. You are the police. Tell me why whose women were killed."

"Maybe for the reasons you said," Flynn said.

"Maybe," said Bremenhoffer.

"Maybe you could help us find a reason?"

Bremenhoffer looked at Donovan with icy, lazy blue eyes. "Do you think I'm crazy?"

"What do you mean?"

"Nothing. Is there any more to talk about?" He started to rise.

"Siddown," said Flynn suddenly. "There's a lot to talk about."

Bremenhoffer stared at him and slowly sat down. "Certainly, Sergeant Flynn. What should we talk about?"

"Why did your daughter run away from home?"

Bremenhoffer shrugged. "I don't know. She had a good home. But I think she wanted to be a whore. You know what women are. They are really sex animals. If you cannot control them, they will go wild."

Schmidt looked at Donovan and signaled him. Donovan got up and followed Schmidt out the door.

"Well," said Donovan.

"Can we get a search warrant fast?"

"I'll call Judge Cummings in Holiday court."

"Fine. I'm sending Margolies over to his apartment. He's our best man when it comes to that kind of thing."

"And look in tbe basement," said Donovan. "He must have a storage shed there. And access to the rest of the basement."

Schmidt nodded. "He really is tough."

"Look in the furnace," Donovan said.

"Sid knows how to search."

"It wouldn't have made much of a bundle."

"Do you suppose the wife knew about it?"

Donovan shrugged. "I don't know."

Donovan returned to the interview room.

"Why do you think women are animals?" Flynn asked.

"Mr. Flynn—excuse me, Sergeant Flynn—if you had any background in history or philosophy, you would understand that it is the considered opinion of the great thinkers of mankind that women have always been less than men. That is to say, animals."

"Like who?"

"Plato. Aristotle. Thomas Aquinas. Shakespeare."

"Do you think those women killed in Grant Park were animals?"

"No, of course not. I am an American now, and I know that men and women are all equal. So perhaps we are all animals. Perhaps women were brought up a little and men brought down a little so that we should all be on the same footing. And below us, there are the niggers."

Flynn and Donovan stared at Bremenhoffer. He was smiling as though he had told a joke.

"I asked you a question before, Mr. Donovan."

"What?"

"Do you think it is realistic that a killer like the one in *M* can be tried by his peers?"

Donovan waited.

"Do you think such a man can be caught?"

"Yes."

"You're an optimist, Mr. Donovan. A romantic."

He shook his head. "I'm a realist."

Bremenhoffer raised his head. "Remember when the Grimes sisters were killed? Did you ever solve that crime? And what about that woman, Judith May Anderson, when they cut her body? You know you can't solve every crime. How many murders were there in Chicago last year. Was it eight hundred or nine hundred? And I will bet with you that the police only solved those crimes where the killers decided to give themselves up. Physically or emotionally, they let the police catch them. How can the police catch a killer who does not want to be caught? There are so many crimes and so many incompetent policemen who are caught up in their own petty lives. But even if they catch him, there is your office, Mr. Donovan. How many cases does the state's attorney handle in a year? Is it ten thousand or twenty thousand or fifty thousand? How do you make justice out of such a mess? No, it is all impossible and you should be smart enough to understand it. In *M* it is up to the criminals to do justice themselves. Because the police cannot do it."

"So who should judge the killer of Bonni Brighton? And the women in the park?" asked Donovan softly.

Frank Bremenhoffer smiled. "Why should that be necessary?"

"Because a killer must be caught."

"Let the killer judge himself. Perhaps he is not guilty of anything."

"Do you think that?" asked Flynn. "Do you think the killer is not guilty?"

"Perhaps," said Bremenhoffer.

"Do you know Maj Kirsten?"

"That is the name of the woman who was killed in the park. About two months ago, was it?"

"Yes. I thought you never read the newspapers."

"I don't. It is usually unnecessary because there are always busybodies down at the plant who are willing to tell you of every crime and every detail. She was a prostitute, I believe?"

"She was a schoolteacher from Sweden."

"Yes. That's what she did in the daytime. But she was a whore as well. One of them down at the plant said she lived with her boyfriend. Probably others. A whore."

"Like Bonni Brighton?"

"I told you all women are that if they are given the chance."

"Did you give Mathilde a chance to become a whore?"

Bremenhoffer stared at Donovan. "Of course not. That's why she had to run away. To become a whore full-time."

"Did she have any boyfriends?"

"I don't know."

"You hate whores, don't you?" asked Flynn.

"I have no use for them, if that's what you mean. Any more than you do or any decent man. Mr. Donovan, are you married?"

"We'll ask the questions," said Donovan.

"You look married, that's why I ask. So maybe you have a daughter? Is she going to be a whore someday. You don't worry about that? Don't tell me you don't worry. Is she in puberty? Have you seen how they revert to their nature? They are animals made for sex and procreation and nothing more."

Donovan looked down at his own hands. He was afraid they were trembling. "And Christina Kalinski was a whore because she lived with a Jew?" he asked.

"Make your own definition of a whore," said Bremenhoffer. "Not because she lived with a Jew. Weiss is a Jew but he is also a pervert. I have no quarrel with Jews. I was not a Nazi. I ran away from Germany before the war and my brother was killed in the underground during the war. I am not an anti-Semite."

"Weiss is a bad man" said Flynn. "But not as bad as the man who killed Christina Kalinski."

"Why. How do you figure that?" Bremenhoffer looked at him. "A man kills a whore but what does a whore do? She disgraces herself, her body, her God, and her parents. Can you compare the man who kills such a creature to scum like Weiss?"

"All whores should be killed?"

"Perhaps," said Bremenhoffer. "But that is impossible. That is like saying all wars should stop. All rats should be exterminated. All poverty ended. Perhaps all whores should be eliminated or taken away. Perhaps women should not have so much freedom to become whores, what do you think?

Have you read the Koran? It is very specific in placing women in society. Women are chattel in Arabic society. They belong to their masters."

"I think the man who killed Christina Kalinski and Bonni Brighton and Maj Kirsten was a sex fiend. An animal lower than a whore. A maniac and a leper to society." This was Donovan and he stared at Frank Bremenhoffer.

The gray man shook his massive head slowly from side to side. "What are we talking about anyway? What the hell are we talking about? Are we suppose to be talking about Bonni Brighton or what? I think you don't know what you're talking about anymore. I am talking about ideas and you are talking about mere reality."

"We're talking about murders. Three murders," said Flynn.

"Look, I'm not a goddamned immigrant, you know. I'm a citizen. You stop me in the street when I'm going home, you take me to that hideous place where you have the body of this woman who used to be my daughter. I try to help you as much as I can. Now you are talking about murders I know nothing about. I'm a citizen, Mr. Donovan, and you can't treat me like I just got off the goddamned boat."

"We appreciate your help," said Jack Donovan mildly.

"Why did you go to the Ajax Theater?" asked Flynn.

"I told you. I got an invitation."

"Do you have it? The invitation?"

"I don't think so. I turned it in at the theater. Or maybe I lost it."

"You didn't have an invitation."

"I told you my former daughter was a strange girl."

"How was she strange?"

"This is what was her sense of humor, if you can call it that."

"The same man killed Bonni Brighton and Maj Kirsten and Christina Kalinski," said Jack Donovan. He was trying to get the interview moving again; it was running around the same deep track.

"Is that right? I hope you catch him."

"We're puzzled by the clothes, though."

"What do you mean?"

"You know. What happened to the clothes?"

"Whose clothes?"

"You know."

"What clothes?"

"Her clothes."

"Bonni Brighton's clothes?"

"Christina Kalinski's. They're missing. He killed Maj Kirsten and left her dead, fully clothed. He killed Bonni Brighton and had to leave her fully clothed. But he took Christina Kalinski's clothing."

"So maybe it wasn't the same man."

Jack Donovan looked at Frank Bremenhoffer thoughtfully. "No. It was the same man. I hope you don't mind if we search your apartment."

Bremenhoffer finally reacted. He jumped up out of the chair, and Flynn grabbed his arm. "Siddown, siddown."

"You have no right to search my home," he shouted.

"Yes, we do, Mr. Bremenhoffer," said Jack Donovan. "Now, sit down."

"You can't do that. Ulla is there. She will be terrified."

"It can't be helped."

"You are worse than the storm troopers."

"Sit down," said Jack Donovan. "We have a search warrant, and our men are searching your house right now."

Bremenhoffer sat down suddenly and tried on another smile. "All right. Go ahead. I will talk to my lawyer. Do you think you're dealing with some goddamn Polack?"

"Judge Cummings signed a warrant. Probably twenty-five minutes ago. Our men are talking to your wife now about the clothes. About your daughter's death."

He continued to smile. "You can't talk to her. Ulla could never speak English well. She's a stupid woman, and she won't make any sense. And she's afraid of the police too. She was in a concentration camp."

Donovan did not return the smile. "We'll see what she has to say."

"This is harassment, Mr. Donovan," said Bremenhoffer. "I am the father of a murder victim, and you are harassing me for what reason I don't know. It's after noon already and I am still not asleep. I have to go to work tonight."

"Don't worry about that," said Donovan.

"This is harassment."

"You were in the theater when Bonni Brighton was killed. Why don't you tell us what happened?"

"Someone yelled. I thought there was a fire."

"Didn't you see your daughter in the theater?"

"No. It was dark. I was watching the film. It was not like Fritz Lang. My daughter was licking another woman. Between her legs."

"Did that make you angry? Did you want to do something then?"

"I wanted to throw up."

"Where were you sitting?"

"I'm not saying another word. You people are really clowns."

"Shuddup," said Flynn.

"Oh, the bully cop. Irish, aren't you? The Irish are very good at playing bullies. I saw the Irish in England during the war. They are good barroom bullies until the Englishman has had enough and then they are slapped down."

"That's too fucking bad you don't like the Irish because you're going to spend a lot of time with us," said Flynn. He grabbed Bremenhoffer by the shirt and pushed him against the wall. Donovan realized that Flynn was really angry.

"You don't frighten me, Mr. Flynn, Mr. Turkey Irishman," said Bremenhoffer. "Turkey" was a Chicago idiom for "Irish."

"Sit down, Terry," said Jack Donovan.

"Oh," said Bremenhoffer. "And you're the good cop, right? And this one is the bully. You're the one I'm supposed to be friendly with? Maybe confess to?"

"What do you want to confess?" Jack Donovan said.

"Nothing. If I felt that I wanted to confess, I would go to church and tell a priest. They would keep it a secret, all my sins. Would you keep it a secret, Mr. Donovan?"

Donovan waited.

"No, I don't think you would—if I had any sins to confess."

"What did you do with the clothing?"

"What clothing?"

"Christina's clothing. She wore a short-sleeved green dress when she left her apartment."

"Is that this man Weiss's apartment?"

"She wore panties. And pantyhose."

"Ach. I don't want to hear this stuff."

"She wore a brassiere. She had very large breasts, and she always wore a brassiere which unbuckled in the back."

"Why are you telling me this? I don't want to hear it."

"She wore black shoes."

"I don't want to hear this," said Bremenhoffer in a flat, deliberate voice.

"What did the killer do with those clothes?"

Bremenhoffer was silent. His fingers, Donovan noted, were bunched into a fist on the table.

"Do you think he took them home with him?" asked Donovan. "Did he hide them from his wife, or did she know he had them? That he had killed someone? Did he take them out from time to time? Did he like to feel them? Maybe he took them out and felt the material at night, when he thought he was alone. They were very soft and delicate—"

"You're a sick man, Mr. Donovan. Really sick. You are enjoying this. You must want to do these things yourself."

Donovan got up finally and went into the squad room next door.

"Well?" asked Matt Schmidt.

"Like you said. He isn't hard. If he was hard, then he would crack finally. But he plays with us when he talks."

"Yeah. That's the feeling I got."

"What now?"

"Well, we've finally got the showup set. We got a couple of guys from the traffic division who look sort of like him, and we got them some gray work clothes from Bailey's over on Van Buren. It'll be a good showup."

"Okay. You got the victims?"

"Got everyone," said Matt Schmidt. "We got three park victims and we got the copper who normally works traffic in front of the movie house and we got the creeps from the Ajax Theater. And speaking of creeps, we've got Fredericks, the movie critic."

"Any word from Sid?"

"No. I figure it'll take him a couple of hours at least to toss that apartment."

The two men opened the door of the interview room. "Get up, Frank," said Matt Schmidt wearily.

"Why?"

"You're going on stage," he said.

"I don't like this," said Bremenhoffer.

"We don't really give a flying fuck what you like," said Jack Donovan. The words were sudden and vicious and unexpected. They all stared at him.

It was the usual setup. The room was well lighted, and there were lines on the wall indicating height. Four policemen stood on the spots marked. They all wore gray shirts and gray trousers. They bore a rough resemblance to Bremenhoffer. He stood in the middle of them on a spot designated.

On the other side of a door, in a second room, waited the observers, including Angela Falicci, who had been attacked in the park on the day after Maj Kirsten's murder, and Tiny Preston and Gloria Miska, who operated the Ajax Theater. Motorcycle Officer Clarence Delancey was there as well, on his day off, and so was Traffic Officer James McGarrity who worked in front of the theater on Washington Street.

One by one each was led to the one-way window in the door and asked to study the men standing in the showup.

Each was given a reasonable amount of time to study the men. Each was asked if they could identify any of them.

Gloria Miska said she had never seen any of them before. Including Patrolman Ralph Curtiss who had been stationed in the lobby of the theater for four hours during the homicide investigation the day before.

Tiny Preston said he had positively seen one of the men regularly in the theater. He identified Desk Sergeant Michael O'Herlihy who had nine children and was president of the St. Agnes Holy Name Society. And who had never been in the theater in his life.

Angela Falicci said she was not certain.

"That's all right, honey," said Flynn. "Take a good look."

"I don't want to pick the wrong man," she said.

"It doesn't all depend on this, on you," said Flynn. "Just

take your time."

She picked a radio dispatcher.

Clarence Delancey picked a man he had spotted in the park twice in the past month.

Flynn was disgusted. "That's Jerry Mikolajczak from robbery, you goddamn idiot."

"I saw him in the park."

"So what? You're hopeless, Delancey. You oughta be selling apples. Go on welfare. Resign the department."

"I don't have to take this abuse—" Delancey began. He knew his rights.

In fact, the showup proved to be totally worthless; identifications were confused, and most of the potential witnesses were reluctant to make any identification at all.

When the farce was over, Bremenhoffer was led back to the interview room.

"Is that all?"

"We have some questions," Flynn said.

"You always have questions. But I am too tired to answer them now. Either let me go home or let me call my lawyer."

"You've got a lawyer lined up?" said Flynn.

"I know a lawyer."

He looked at Matt Schmidt then and at Donovan. The two men went into the squad room.

"What does Sid Margolies say?"

"There's nothing in the apartment. He's in the basement now. That'll take a couple of hours. The woman won't say boo. She's scared and Sid says he feels like a goon."

"We're going to have to let him go."

Matt Schmidt nodded. "I'm not surprised. I'd hoped Angela Falicci might have done better. But we've got the film. And Frank is definitely a little crazy on the subject of sex."

"But that's nothing. He was in the theater, which puts him at the scene. That's good. But what else do we have?"

"He hated his daughter."

"It's a shaky case, Matt."

Schmidt nodded. "But we know, don't we?"

"That he did it?" Donovan glanced back at the squad room. "Yes. There's no doubt about it."

18. SID MARGOLIES CALLED AREA ONE HOMICIDE AT FOUR TEN P.M. SATURDAY TO REPORT HE HAD FOUND NOTHING in the basement of the apartment building on Kedvale Avenue which would link Frank Bremenhoffer to any of the murders. Sid also said he was tired and wanted to go home. He was relieved at the building any another detective who had instructions to keep a tail on Bremenhoffer at all times.

The slow, painstaking police routine began.

Saturday slipped into Sunday and then Monday. It rained on the weekend and was bright and hot again on Monday. A week passed. They had managed to borrow, at one time or another, forty investigators who wearily questioned all the employees of the Halsted Graphics and Printing Company.

Karen Kovac theorized that Frank Bremenhoffer had killed Maj Kirsten because he thought she looked like a whore. He might have killed Christina because a co-worker informed him of her life-style.

None of them knew Christina Kalinski though.

In fact, none of them professed to know Frank Bremenhoffer very well. He kept to himself and was considered surly by some of them. When most of the printers played cards on their lunch hour in the back shop, Bremenhoffer read books. Alone.

The twenty-four-hour tail on Bremenhoffer began to give them a fuller picture of his life.

In the mornings, after work, he usually visited the Courtesy Tap, a little bar on Wells Street under the el tracks, which opened at seven A.M. for the functioning alcoholics who came in with their briefcases and three-piece suits and drank their breakfasts. Frank Bremenhoffer drank beer and sometimes ordered a shot of cheap brandy to go with the beer chaser.

On other mornings he went to the Art Institute and waited until it opened for the morning.

Other times, after visiting the tavern, he went to the movies.

To pornographic movie houses.

And he went home at noon. He apparently lunched with his wife and slept in the afternoon.

He took the El to work at night and did not own a car. On the El train he either read a book or stared out the window at the night city. Sometimes the book was a sensational paperback novel. The only periodical he ever was seen with was *Stern*, the German news magazine.

On Monday, while he was gone, they got a search warrant and permission from the printing company to search his locker at work. It was bare, except for a shop apron and a can of hand cleaner. The apron smelled of gasoline which a printer explained was used to clean off the type after pulling proof sheets.

Bremenhoffer was merely a lonely man like many others who led a solitary city life. He had his favorite tavern, he had his little peculiarities. He was a lover of art apparently; and he saw pornographic movies.

On Sundays Ulla Bremenhoffer went to early mass. Her husband did not accompany her.

Other aspects of the case continued while the investigators probed Bremenhoffer's life.

The body of Bonni Brighton was shipped to her brother, Bruno, in Van Nuys, California, twelve days after her murder.

Seymour Weiss, fifty-two, was indicted on charges of attempted rape, deviate sexual assault, kidnapping, resisting arrest, and contributing to the delinquency of a minor. At the same time Luther Jones, forty-three, was indicted on charges of pandering, kidnapping, deviate sexual assault, resisting arrest.

Seymour Weiss became convinced of the mob's disfavor and pleaded guilty to a reduced count of imprisonment and felonious assault. He was sentenced to four years in prison which would make him eligible for parole with a third of the time served. He was sent to the state correctional facility at Collinsville, a minimum-security prison.

Luther Jones pleaded not guilty and eventually stood trial and was convicted on all charges. He was sentenced to twenty-five to forty years in prison at the state maximum-security prison called Stateville, located near the city of Joliet.

The runaway girl found in Weiss's club was named Ramona Jefferson from Rochester, New York. After the child's maternal grandmother and guardian refused to assume custody of her, she was institutionalized by order of the family court judge. The court psychiatrist said tests indicated that Ramona Jefferson was probably an imbecile.

There was one further development. A traffic policeman named James McGarrity came to Lieutenant Schmidt one afternoon with a newspaper clipping showing the face of Maj Kirsten. McGarrity said he was certain he had seen Maj Kirsten around the time she was murdered. He had not remembered it before.

Schmidt questioned him, but McGarrity could give him no further information. He could not identify Bremenhoffer.

Jack Donovan kept a loose hold on the investigation but largely left Matt Schmidt alone. At the same time he fielded the weekly reports he had to make to both the state's attorney and the police superintendent.

The newspapers hounded them all about Bonni Brighton with a ferocity that exceeded that following the murders of Maj Kirsten and Christina Kalinski. *Chicago Today*, an afternoon paper, began to print a serialization of Bonni Brighton's unfinished autobiography.

Frank Bremenhoffer broke the camera of one photographer who came to interview him, and after that the reporters mostly left him alone. Besides, he was considered too dull to make good copy.

The police superintendent and the state's attorney questioned Donovan closely every time they held a session, but there was nothing to say and nothing left undone.

The case was dragging and they all knew it. And each day that passed made it more difficult to solve. After awhile even the newspapers seemed to grow tired of it. Which was fine with Jack Donovan and the rest of them.

Karen Kovac resumed her decoy role but nothing came of it, and she was eventually transferred back to the patrol division. They gave her a party on her last night in homicide and Terry Flynn kissed her. He explained the next day that he had been drunk and hadn't intended anything by the kiss, but Sid Margolies and Matt Schmidt razzed him about it all the same.

Karen Kovac applied for duty on homicide.

Leonard Ranallo was against the request and told the chief of detectives his opinion of women in homicide.

Matt Schmidt quietly told the chief of detectives that Karen Kovac was a damned good investigator and that if they could get a woman in his squad, he'd be very happy. Besides murders, the homicide division handled rapes, and he thought Karen Kovac would be invaluable in this area.

When Leonard Ranallo went on vacation in August, Karen Kovac was transferred back to homicide, to Matt Schmidt's squad.

19. THE SUMMER DRAGGED ON INTO THE DOG DAYS OF AUGUST AND THERE WAS NO BREAK IN THE CASE OR IN THE OPPRESsive heat or in the intolerable state of Jack Donovan's personal life.

They still had not heard from Rita.

Kathleen had returned to the South Side after living two weeks with her father in his small North Side apartment. She said she did not want to leave him, but he pointed out that she never saw her friends and his neighborhood was not as family oriented as it had been. He worried about her.

Even so, Donovan knew his daughter was not happy living back in her grandfather's house.

He would discuss it with Lily, but the discussions never went very far; Lily did not want to talk about Donovan's family or families in general.

"The kids are all right," she'd soothe him. And he let himself be soothed.

And every day passed without a word from Rita. When the telephone rang, he thought it might be her. But it never was.

He dreamed about her one night. She had come back home and they were all living in the first apartment they had rented, a long time ago. It was a stupid dream and it didn't go anywhere but when he awoke, he remembered the dream with regret that he was not still asleep. And that the dream could not be true.

One afternoon he sat in his old office in the Criminal Courts building and talked to Mario DeVito about his situation.

As usual he had taken a seat on the windowsill; Mario DeVito, who was using the office, sat on the couch with his feet up on a straight chair.

Mario had taken over the day-to-day running of the criminal division while Donovan was attached to the special murder investigation.

"I want to talk to you about Rita and the kids," said Jack Donovan. "I can't let the thing go on much longer."

Mario did not look sympathetic. "Why not? You've let it drag on for the last seven years."

"Rita hasn't been gone for the last seven years. My father-in-law is eighty years old. He can't take care of the kids."

"So?"

"So I got to figure out what to do."

"What do you think you should do?"

Donovan looked up. "Are you leading me?"

"You brought it up, Jack."

"I know what to do but I've lived alone for seven years. I'm in no shape to take on two teen-age kids. And the boy hates me."

"Who's in shape to take on teen-age kids? And boys always hate their fathers. Look at me. My Joey is fourteen. You know who he wants to be like when he grows up? You think he wants to be like his hardworking old man who goes out every day and catches the bad guys? No. He wants to be like his cousin, Sam Tosca. Tosca the hood. He wants to be a hood. Sam Tosca's got money, Sam's got good clothes, he drives an El Dorado. So I say, 'You show Sam respect when we gotta go to a wedding or something, because he's family. But you tell me you wanta be like Sam, I'll break your back.'"

"That's one approach, Mario."

"Hey, Jack. You don't know when your wife's gonna turn up again. You got those kids living out there with your father-in-law because you want them outta your sight. You just wanna send them money now and then and go out to visit once in a while, say, 'Hiya kids. It's Dad. Long time no see.' Well, fuck it. You know you gotta do the right thing."

"But Mario. I've been living alone for nearly seven years."

"So? I lived alone six years before I got married. So what? People do tend to be single before they're married."

Mario seemed impatient with the discussion. Or with Jack Donovan.

"How's the murder case? When you coming back? This job of yours is work, man. I don't give a shit for it. I want to get back to trial."

"You wanna get some food? I haven't been over to La Fontanella in weeks."

"No. I've got to go back downtown." Donovan stared at Mario's shoes on the chair. They were scuffed.

"I can't baby-sit every day," he said at last. "I don't think Kathleen would be the problem. She's really terrific. She was cleaning up the house, shopping, got me supper. Very independent." He said this somewhat proudly. "But it's August. What do we do about school? Do I move back to the South Side?"

"It ain't so bad," said Mario DeVito. He had known Donovan for a long time and, from time to time, they had depended on each other. He knew all about Rita and the kids and the problems. "Lotta people live on the South Side. Not everyone moved to the fuckin' North Side."

"I don't know."

"Jack, this is bullshit and you know it. I'm gonna take the opportunity to tell you right now what the hell's wrong, and wrong with you."

"I appreciate it," said Donovan. "I ask for advice, I'm getting the whole Ann Landers treatment."

"Hey, get fucked, buddy," said DeVito. He got up from the sofa, and went to the desk, and banged his fist on it. He stared at Donovan framed in the tall window. "Your fuckin' trouble is you're chicken. And you're chickenshit, while I'm at it."

He paused for breath. His face was red. "You wanna be a burned-out case, that's okay. You wanna just work and go home and get drunk or get laid with that bull-dike friend of yours, okay."

"Nobody asked you to talk about—"

"Shut your fuckin' mouth. You asked me. I don't say nothing to you and you came here and you asked me. So I'm tellin' you. You wanna be a private asshole, that's nobody's business but your own. You wanna go down to the South Side now and then and see Kathleen and do her that big fucking favor of your company, okay. But who the suffering fuck do you really think you are, Jesus H. Christ? You're just another bum like me and you got a crazy wife which is nobody's fault and you got two kids and everything is fucked up. Look at me. What am I? Is this the Sermon on the fuckin' Mount?"

Mario decided to hit the desk top again and did.

"You think life is neat? You think you're a submarine with watertight compartments? You put Rita here and the kids here and O'Connor here and Mario here and Lily here and you move from one to another like a zombie."

Mario threw up his hands. "So Rita ran away. Again. So forget it. No, don't forget it. Let it hurt you because it should. You loved Rita and you married her, so it should hurt you that she ran away. But cut the phony guilt trip. You figure you drove her crazy in the first place when you were a cop and she was trying to bang out kids every year like they were cookies. You know something? Maybe you did drive her fuckin' crazy. And maybe she just doesn't get enough salt in her diet. Who the fuck knows about anything?"

"You got to know," said Donovan.

"No. You got to keep trying to know. You didn't wanna be a cop no more because you couldn't get on top of it, because you couldn't understand what the hell was really going on. So you became a lawyer and you still don't understand what's going on. None of us do. Not a damned soul on the whole fuckin' planet understands what the hell is going on, and those who do are like Frank Bremenhoffer. They got it figured and they're crazy."

"Or like Rita."

"No. Rita doesn't know either," Mario said in a quieter voice.

"So what do I do, Dago?"

Mario, flushed, smiled. "You stop calling me names for one thing. And you gotta do the right thing. You know that."

"No."

"Yes, asshole. You know what the right thing is. You know you gotta get those kids and bring them up and make them eat their fuckin' spinach and when Rita comes home, you gotta help her just like you did the last time."

Donovan smiled. "Fuckin' spinach?"

"Sure. It makes your dick hard."

Donovan got up from the sill. "I don't remember you getting so mad before."

"I was waiting until you really needed it. I figured you needed it now."

"Dago bastard," said Donovan.

"Yeah." Mario patted his stomach. "Let's get the fuck outta this joint and get some lunch."

When Jack Donovan went home that night, he told Lily what he was going to do.

She said it was his funeral.

20. FRANK BREMENHOFFER DID NOT VARY HIS ROUTINE UNTIL SEPTEMBER 1, WHEN SID MARGOLIES ANNOUNCED that the suspect was going on vacation.

"Where?"

"Northern Wisconsin. Two weeks in a cabin near a place called Minocqua is the way I got it," said Margolies. He looked at his notebook and then closed it with a snap. None of them would think of asking Margolies how he got his information.

It was their weekly meeting at Area One offices. Jack Donovan, who was seated on Terry Flynn's desk top, scratched his nose.

Enthusiasm for the murder investigation had waned among the politicians involved. The stories about the three murders had dropped from the newspapers and media notice. Halligan and the police superintendent were both on vacation, and the weekly report Donovan was required to make to them had quietly been dropped. Everyone was losing interest, and now Frank Bremenhoffer was going on vacation.

227

A second psychological profile prepared by their man from the University of Chicago stated that it was quite possible that the killer would suddenly commit several murders and then return to a quiescent state and never kill again. On the other hand he might strike again very soon.

"Sid. I want you to keep on him."

"I don't like Wisconsin."

Everyone was startled by this, even Matt Schmidt. No one had ever heard Sid Margolies express resentment over an assignment.

"Why?" asked Schmidt.

"Flies. Big as horses. This guy is going up by Canada. That's where all the flies come from."

"They come from the tropics," said Flynn.

"You don't know a damned thing about flies," said Sid Margolies. "They breed in those lakes up north, and they come down here. Only they're much bigger up there."

"Not in August," said Matt Schmidt.

"It's September," said Sid. "I was there in June once. They ate me alive. Fifteen years ago and I never went back. I was a fly's smorgasbord."

"There aren't any flies now," said Donovan. "You're the best shadow we got. You'll like it."

Margolies shrugged back into character. "Okay. I'll tell my wife. She won't like it. But it'll be okay."

"You'll get per diem," said Schmidt.

"Sure. It'll be okay. I hope you're right about the flies. They ate me alive last time."

Jack Donovan moved on September 2.

The apartment was on the Northwest Side, not far from Irving Park Road and Pulaski.

Donovan did not like the neighborhood, which was largely Polish and German and was strongly family centered. But the apartment, large and light, provided separate bedrooms for Kathleen and Brian.

The boy seemed resentful. In the end Donovan had tried to have a long talk with him, but it did not work. He moved in with his father reluctantly.

All the O'Connors were angry, and Arthur O'Connor said that now he would be all alone in the world.

They still had no word from Rita. The first time she had run away, she had disappeared for a year. It was nearly two months now.

There was a certain heaviness of spirit in all of them. Even Kathleen, who seemed best able to adapt, was subdued the first night in the new apartment.

They sat around the new kitchen table and ate hamburgers which Jack purchased from the McDonald's down the street.

"This isn't the easiest thing for any of us," Donovan said that night. He had a can of beer. He had given Brian a can of beer as well. The little gesture toward comradeship with his son had been taken as a matter of course. Donovan looked at Brian. He was as tall as his father, but he looked like Rita. There was a darker cast to him, and his eyes were deep.

"No, it isn't," said Brian Donovan.

"It'll be all right," said Kathleen.

"Brian, this has to be done," Donovan said.

"No, it doesn't. I could have stayed with my grandfather. That's where my pals are."

"Well, sometimes you got to make new pals."

"Because you want to live on the North Side, and you don't want us to stay where we lived."

"Yes," said Jack Donovan.

Kathleen didn't say anything. She bit into her Big Mac.

"I just think it stinks."

"So you've said," said Jack.

It went like that for the first few weeks. He hired a housekeeper recommended by Karen Kovac's housekeeper. Her name was Mrs. Woljczek. One day Brian said something unkind to her. She smacked him in the face.

Mrs. Woljczek prepared dinner; for the first two weeks Jack Donovan made it a point to go home to dinner every night. Brian was usually late. Once, on a Saturday, he went back down to the South Side on the bus and didn't come home until four in the morning. He was high and smelled of beer.

After two weeks in Wisconsin Frank Bremenhoffer and his wife, Ulla, came back to the city.

Sid Margolies filed a long report. There had not been any flies.

Frank Bremenhoffer ran two miles every morning and swam vigorously in the small cold lake near the cottage. He rarely spoke to his wife. The temperature of the lake was forty-nine degrees.

"How do you know?" Terry Flynn had to ask.

"It was so cold when I went in that I was curious, so I bought a thermometer from the hardware store. I took sample readings in shore, out two hundred yards, and in the middle of the lake. That's the average. I have it broken down if you want."

They declined.

Margolies reported that Bremenhoffer went fishing in the late mornings and did not have much luck. He played cards in the afternoon with the man who owned the resort or read books. He drank beer in the Bowery, a bar on Highway 51 in Woodruff, or at the cabin. They had rented a new Ford for the two-week vacation trip. It was blue in color and had 4,218 miles on the odometer at the end of the trip.

"Are you interested in buying it?" asked Flynn sarcastically.

"No," said Sid Margolies.

Margolies filed for his expenses later in the week and because he was very meticulous and carried a receipt for every expense—including the thermometer—he did not have any trouble with the accounting section. Which amazed everyone else.

The case had taken on a kind of torpor, and while the special investigation existed in theory and on paper, it was beginning to disintegrate. Karen Kovac started classes in police school to fill her in on the areas of evidence and investigation where she was lacking; she was considered a curiosity at the police school because it quickly became known that she had transferred to homicide.

Kathleen Donovan started classes as a freshman at Maria High School, a Catholic girl's school on the Northwest Side. Suddenly she began to look very grown-up, and the sudden change in her makeup and demeanor startled and annoyed

Jack Donovan. Until Karen Kovac told him it was very normal.

Kathleen said she liked school.

Brian did not. He went to the public school nearby after St. Ignatius High School refused to accept him as a transfer student; his grades were too low.

Donovan, after a flurry of activity in his private life, resumed his old depression. The case depressed him and so did his son. He did not know what to do with the investigation and he did not know what to do about Brian. He tried threatening him one night when the boy came home from a party, obviously drunk. The threats only drove Brian further into his shell.

Because of these things, Donovan almost accepted the offer when Lee Horowitz said he could drop the murder investigation and go back to his old duties at the Criminal Courts.

Instead he was amazed to find himself lying to Horowitz.

"I think we're getting onto something," he said. "We need a little more time." They sat in Lee Horowitz's large office on the fifth floor of the Civic Center. Lee sat behind his large oiled-walnut desk. It was September 21, the first cold day. The back of the breathless summer had been broken.

"Getting, schmetting," said Horowitz. "You know as well as I do that anything this old gets moldly. It's been three months...no, four months...since What's-her-name was killed. The first one."

"Maj Kirsten."

"We got other fish to scramble," said Lee Horowitz. "The mayor's man indicated this morning you could drop the whole thing. Everyone go back to what they were doing."

"Fine. But I think we ought to keep in touch on this investigation."

"That's for the cops to do," said Horowitz. "We've got to sharpen up on the West Side. I looked at the figures for last month. The conviction rate is way down and you know Bud ran last time saying he maintained the highest conviction rate of anyone."

"Yeah." Politics bored him. He yawned. Despite his

depression he felt better these days; his stomach didn't bother him. It was probably Mrs. Woljczek's evening meal.

"Well, Mario DeVito may be good at trial work, but he couldn't administer his way out of a briefcase."

"So what do we do about the murders?"

"Nothing. That's the police's business."

The mayor said he wanted—"

"The mayor wants when the heat's on. Like everyone else. This is politics, Donovan, not tiddledy winks. When the heat ain't on, he don't want so bad."

"Lee. We're going to get him."

"What's the matter with you, Jack? You running for something?"

"No. But we know who he is. And we're tailing him. I talked to him, Lee. Like this. Like I'm talking to you. He's a bad man."

Lee shrugged. "There's lots of bad guys. You think this guy is bad? Good. Lock him up. Indict. Who cares three months from now?"

"I do." He couldn't believe he was saying these things. "We're going to get him. We all feel it. It's going to end up okay. That bastard killed three women and he doesn't care about it and we're going to get him."

Lee shrugged.

"Don't shrug, Lee. Don't gimme that shit." Jack Donovan stood up. "It's worth more than a shrug."

"What do you want to do, Jack?"

"I want to keep it alive. For a while longer. Hell. For a long while longer."

"Jack, in seven years I never knew you to get so passionate." It was how long Donovan had been in the office.

He waited.

"Good, Jack." Lee Horowitz stood up. "Get the prick."

21. WHEN THEY FINALLY DEVISED A PLAN, IT SEEMED SO LOGICAL TO ALL OF THEM THAT THEY THOUGHT THEY HAD decided on it at the same time. Actually it was Sid Margolies who had provided them with the information that eventually led to the scheme.

On September 23, the leaves were already beginning to fall from the trees. For two days it had been raining, and strong winds had whipped the elm and oak leaves from the trees and flung them into clogged gutters. Several streets were flooded at the places where they passed under railroad bridges— hundreds of such bridges crisscrossed the city. Police on the South Side arrested a gang of juveniles who attacked motorists stranded by the little street floods in the under-passes. The weather was miserable, and there was every indication that once again fall would be short and ugly.

There had been five hundred sixteen murders in the city so far in the year. There was still a good chance that they might break a record.

This time they all met in Jack Donovan's temporary office

in the Civic Center building downtown. It was after six P.M., and the building was nearly empty. Bright lights still illuminated each of the wide halls. In the broad plaza in front of the building rain dashed against the rusting hulk of the Picasso statue. There was no one in the plaza.

They had chosen to meet here because the room was so large. The heating system continued with its omnipresent hum. There were chairs enough for all of them, but they chose their usual places to stand or lean or sit.

Because the windows in the Civic Center went from floor to ceiling and had no ledge, Jack Donovan sat on top of a two-drawer steel file cabinet on one white wall. Karen Kovac sat at the table with Matt Schmidt. Terry Flynn sat on the edge of Jack Donovan's desk with his feet propped on the wooden chair next to it. And Sid Margolies leaned his elbow against the four-drawer file cabinet on the opposite side of the room. Margolies was the only one who had his ball-point out, poised over a clean page of his notebook.

Margolies had just delivered his report on the routine movements in the dull life of Frank Bremenhoffer.

With fall, Bremenhoffer had altered that routine somewhat.

He slept earlier. After work he went directly home. Presumably he slept then because at four or five P.M. he appeared on the street again and walked three blocks to Irving Park Road, to a tavern called the Lucky Aces. It was an ordinary neighborhood tavern, like a thousand others scattered throughout the city.

They had wanted to see what went on in the tavern where Bremenhoffer spent at least two hours each night before returning home. But that was the tricky part.

As Terry Flynn interjected, "A policeman in plainclothes looks exactly like a policeman in plainclothes." If Margolies went into the tavern, there was the fear that he would be recognized.

They had chewed on that problem for nearly a week. They wanted to see if Bremenhoffer was meeting someone in the bar. Perhaps a woman.

The plan, haphazardly but logically, had developed from the problem.

Karen Kovac came up with the solution on her day off and without telling anyone.

She was off on Thursday. At three P.M. she walked down her block to Irving Park Road, then walked three blocks east to the Lucky Aces. She wore a white blouse, black shirt, and nylons. She wore lipstick and had powdered her face and put eye shadow on. She looked altogether different.

She ordered Scotch and soda at the bar in her husky voice and drank it slowly.

She had had three drinks when Frank Bremenhoffer entered the tavern a little after four o'clock.

Karen Kovac did not look at him at first, but she was aware he was in the taproom. She saw his reflection in the mirror behind the bar. By now she was engaged in conversation with a man who appeared to be a construction worker: he had mud on the cuffs of his jeans and wore several sweatshirts in layers instead of a jacket. He was drunk.

"Heya, Frank," said the bartender. He was a slight man and wore a plastic bow tie on his white shirt in the old-fashioned style. His name was Jerry, and he didn't own the place.

Bremenhoffer chose to sit down across the bar from Karen Kovac.

The bar was U shaped. Karen Kovac, the construction worker, and four other patrons sat on the west side of the bar, near the bowling machine and cigarette machine. Bremenhoffer sat alone on the east side, near the silent jukebox.

Above the bar, on the south wall, a television set flickered multiple ghost images of a Chicago Cubs baseball player at bat. It was the end of the season, and the game had been delayed twice by rain. No one was watching the game, and the sound was turned off.

There were two fat women on the other side of Karen Kovac. They seemed to know Bremenhoffer, and one of them said "Hiya" to him. He didn't answer except for a slight nod.

It was four-twelve P.M. Jerry the bartender brought Frank Bremenhoffer a glass of tap beer and a shot of Christian Brothers brandy.

The construction worker suddenly decided to kiss her. His breath smelled of cigarettes and beer. She let him kiss her but then pulled back as he touched her breast. She wore a brassiere. For a moment she let his hand linger there and then straightened up. "Too rough," she said pleasantly. He lurched at her and nearly fell off the barstool.

"Hey, baby," he said.

"C'mon," she said. "Finish your drink."

She looked across at Bremenhoffer who was staring at her. She looked into his eyes. It was the first time they had seen each other. For a moment she thought of Bonni Brighton.

"You're cute," she said to the construction worker.

Bremenhoffer stared at her.

"Hi," she said across the bar to him.

She looked at his face, a smile frozen on hers. He was impassive. His eyes were wide open. Cold. Drowning blue eyes. She forced herself to continue smiling. She was not sure of what she was doing; she was acting on instinct. He finished his beer quickly and then got up.

"Heya, Frank," said Jerry.

But Bremenhoffer was out the door. Jerry went to his place at the bar and felt for change. There was none.

After a fourth drink Karen Kovac disentangled herself from the affections of the construction worker. He wanted to take her to his place. He lived in Argo.

She told him she wouldn't go with him.

He asked her for a kiss.

She got up and left the bar, leaving a fifty-cent tip. The bartender said, "Seeya" as she pushed open the door.

All of which—except for a graphic description of the embrace—she related as part of Sid Margolies's report. They sat transfixed during the narrative.

"I think he would have killed me," she said.

Matt Schmidt glanced at her. "You're right. Why the hell did you do that? Why did you talk to him?"

"It seemed exactly right at the time."

Schmidt looked angry. He broke a pencil in half and rummaged on the table for another.

"Look, Matt," she said. "He never saw me. Remember? You sent me home when you arrested him."

He stared at her. "It's a helluva time to get back at me through women's lib."

Terry Flynn laughed out loud. "For Christ's sake, Matt. It was a terrific idea. If I worked an idea like that—on my day off, no less—you'd get me the Lambert Tree Award." The award was given annually to the policeman who had commited the most heroic act of the year.

Donovan smiled. "If you did it, Flynn, I don't think the construction worker would have tried to kiss you," said Schmidt. That loosened it up for all of them.

"I think it's the way to get him."

Karen Kovac said it softly after they had finished razzing Flynn. They looked at her, and she saw Flynn nod. He understood.

Jack Donovan put his hands behind his head and leaned back against the wall, one foot propped on the low filing cabinet. "Karen is right."

Sid Margolies said pedantically, "You mean you figure you can get him to attack her?"

"Something like that," said Donovan.

"Isn't that entrapment?"

"No," said Donovan. "If we do nothing illegal and suggest nothing illegal to Bremenhoffer, it isn't entrapment. Any more than Karen's decoy operation in Grant Park would have been. And it's either do it this way or wait until he decides to kill someone else ten years from now."

"I don't like it," said Matt Schmidt.

"Why not, for Christ's sake?" asked Flynn.

"It's a risk," he said.

"So's everything else," said Karen Kovac.

"You understand the purpose of the plan, do you?" asked Matt. "You want Frank Bremenhoffer to attack you with a knife and try to kill you. You understand that?"

"Yes," said Karen Kovac quietly.

"All right." He sighed and reached into his shirt pocket for a cigarette. But, of course, there were none. "What's the risk?"

Sid Margolies said, "I'm on him every day, from morning until late afternoon. We can put a bug in Karen's purse—"

"Stop talking like we were feds," said Matt Schmidt. "Where the hell are we going to get devices that small? We don't have all the money in the world, you know. If you want to play G-man, go join Drug Enforcement Administration or something."

"All right." Sid Margolies sounded hurt. He shut his notebook. "I'll keep her in sight." He said it with some confidence. In fact, Sid Margolies had never lost a tail.

"What if he wants to go home with her?" asked Matt Schmidt.

Donovan said, "I live not far from there, but I've got the kids living with me. And Karen's got her boy."

"Well, that shoots it," said Schmidt.

"Not necessarily," said Terry Flynn. "I don't think Bremenhoffer's gonna want to walk her home." Donovan looked at him. "I think he's gonna want to follow her home."

"What's the difference?"

"Well, for starters, we get a key from someone to walk through an apartment building. All she needs is a downstairs key, for the vestibule door. In case he follows her just to see if she's on the square. If he's suspicious, that is."

"He'll check the names on the mailboxes," said Schmidt.

"Matt, when's the last time you knew the last name of someone you picked up in a bar?"

Margolies guffawed and Donovan smiled. Matt Schmidt blushed.

"All right. But I don't want Karen using her own building. Or Donovan's. I don't want their kids involved in this mess," said Schmidt.

"We get another building," said Terry Flynn.

"That's an awful lot of easy getting."

"Remember Artie Shay?"

"The real-estate man?" asked Donovan. "Yeah."

"Well, Artie manages or owns a helluva lot of buildings up in that area. About two years ago there was this homicide in a whorehouse on the North Side and I was sitting in for the sergeant at Area Six and we got Shay's tit out of the wringer. He wasn't mixed up in the killing, but he was in the whorehouse. Anyway he's married and got ninety kids, so we did him a favor. Now he can do us a favor. And get us a building key."

Schmidt nodded. Then said, "But what is Karen going to do exactly?"

"In the bar?"

"Yeah."

"What comes naturally," Flynn said.

Karen Kovac did not smile. "I think it's the only thing that might work."

"Well," Jack Donovan said, leaning forward and putting his feet on the floor, "Yes." He stood up and stretched. "This case is nearly four months old. Lee Horowitz has talked to me and so has Halligan. Leonard Ranallo is running interference for Matt with the police superintendent. They're tired of the case. And they don't want all this manpower tied up on it."

They waited.

"Ranallo thinks he can buy us another month. Of course, he doesn't even know that Karen Kovac is on Matt's squad now. That would really drive him crazy."

They smiled at this. All except Karen Kovac.

"We've got to flush Bremenhoffer," said Donovan. "I can't think of any other way. We don't have any hard evidence except that he was at the movie house the moment his daughter was killed. That's good if it would stand with something else. But there's nothing. Nothing to link him with Maj Kirsten and Christina Kalinski either. Except possibly Karen's theory is right, that he killed Christina because he heard about her. We've checked his acquaintances at the Loop bars he hangs out in and at the Halsted Graphics place. But we didn't know about the Lucky Aces until this past week. So maybe Karen can find the link to Christina there. Or maybe Bremenhoffer will go after her. And if she wants to do it, we've got to give it a chance. It's our only chance, I think."

The little boy had dark hair, but he looked like his mother. Terry Flynn guessed he was about nine years old. Karen had told him the age but he had forgotten. Like his mother, he had a quiet demeanor and large eyes that seemed to absorb more than mere patterns of light and shape.

"This is Mr. Flynn," she said, taking off her raincoat. He

unbuttoned his trench coat and shrugged himself out of it and then extended his large, freckled hand to the boy. The boy took it and shook it gravely.

"I'm happy to meet you," he said. "Are you a policeman?"

"Yes," he said.

An old woman came out of the kitchen. She had a thick body and dark hair that was pulled back fiercely into a tight knot.

Karen Kovac said something to her in Polish and the woman smiled. She had a gold tooth in the front of her wide mouth. She wiped her hands on her apron and extended her hand. "Hullo, Mister."

"Hiya," said Terry Flynn, and he took the woman's grasp. Her hand was surprisingly soft and small.

Karen Kovac made Terry Flynn a drink—Scotch and water—and he sat down in the living room. The apartment was small and the living room narrow. It was deep inside the U of the courtyard apartment building—a building constructed like Frank Bremenhoffer's—and he could look out the front windows and see the rest of the three-story brick building extended out in two wings to the street beyond. It was raining.

She had invited him to supper two weeks ago. This was supposed to be her day off. Of course, she and Terry had been at the conference in Jack Donovan's office downtown and now it was nearly nine P.M. They had stopped to have a drink before going home.

Mrs. Krabowski, the woman who sat with Tim and prepared his evening meal, was at the door with her black coat on and a babushka tied around her head. She smiled at Terry Flynn and her eyes sparkled darkly; he thought she must once have been a beautiful woman. He got up from the couch to say good-bye.

And then Tim appeared at the doorway as well, dressed in a fall coat.

He carried a little bag.

"Where you going?" Flynn said.

"Tommy Kubliczek's house. I'm staying overnight. It's Friday night and we're going to watch monster movies.

Tommy Kubliczek's got his own TV set right in his room. How about that?"

"How about that?" said Terry Flynn, who did not know what to say. He had expected only supper. With Karen. And with Tim, her boy. And dull talk. And the chance to look at her again, to study the angles of her face and to remember what her eyes looked like.

The door closed on them after motherly admonitions about brushing his teeth and not making her ashamed of him. He held firmly to Mrs. Krabowski's hand.

They heard the vestibule door close downstairs and then Karen Kovac went to the window and watched the boy and the old woman hurry along the wet walkway to the street.

"I didn't know Tim wasn't going to be here," said Terry Flynn.

"Neither did I." She went to the kitchen and returned with a drink. "He makes his own arrangements. He's a sensible boy and I know the Kubliczeks. So I told him it was all right."

"He's a good-looking kid," said Terry Flynn. He was not very good at talking at the moment. He looked at the drink in his hand and tried it.

"Why don't you sit down, Terry?"

"Sure." He sat on the couch and she sat on the chair opposite him. The apartment was spectacularly clean. A large black-and-white television set was on the window wall, and it was plain that the couch and chairs had been arranged to watch television. On the wall above the two upholstered chairs was a picture of Tim in shirt and tie and white trousers and blue coat—his first communion picture, no doubt, thought Terry Flynn. And there was a good print of Picasso's guitar player.

"I'm afraid to put my drink down," he said. "This place is so clean I feel dirty just being here."

"That's Mrs. Krabowski. Don't be intimidated. She likes to clean the way some people like to play cards. It passes the time." She smiled. "Believe me, I'm not so neat."

To prove it, she placed her drink down on the coffee table between them. A damp spot formed on the wood.

"Good. That makes me feel better."

241

"She made stew."

"Good. I'm Irish, you know."

"No, I didn't," she said. She felt at ease with him. It seemed like a long time since she had felt at ease with anyone. Especially a man.

"It's warming up."

"I like to be with you, Karen."

She didn't say anything.

"You see, no subtlety. Just knock down the door and start bashing heads in."

"Yes. It's obviously a good thing you decided not to become a diplomat or a politician. You would have been very unsuccessful."

They were quiet. They were both aware of the moment and neither of them had been prepared for it, for the emptiness of the apartment, for their being together alone.

"Terry, I appreciate you standing up for me on this tavern thing. I don't know why Lieutenant Schmidt was so opposed to it."

"Oh," he said. "That's easy." He started to reach for a cigarette and then glanced at the clean astray beside him. It was too clean. He withdrew his hand. "I think I got Matt figured on that."

"What is it?"

"He likes you."

She stared at him.

"No. Not like that," he said. "He really likes you. He got you into the squad you know, after you went back on patrol."

"How?"

"He dropped a word to the chief of detectives. While Ranallo was on furlough. So they moved you back in. Matt's got a lot of clout in the department in a quiet way. Which is the only way to have clout, I suppose. He's a good dick. One of the best I've seen. You work with him, you really begin to understand what this work is supposed to be about."

"But why didn't he want me to work that decoy? He let me work it in the park."

"Because when you went into the park the first time, with me, he didn't know you from Adam. He was just trying to catch a killer. And then the second time he let you work in the park, he was convinced that Bremenhoffer was the killer and that he wasn't going to go after you."

"So it was all wasted, all those days in the park. And you knew."

"Hell no, I didn't know anything. I just figured it out eventually. By that time, he liked you. Enough to get you into homicide. But that's why he really didn't want you on this decoy operation in the tavern. He's afraid you'll get hurt."

"So why did he get me in homicide?"

Terry Flynn thought, what the hell. He pulled out his package of cigarettes and then discovered he was out of them. He crumpled the package and threw it in the ashtray.

"I told you. He likes you and he thinks you're smart. If he didn't think you were smart, he wouldn't have stuck his neck out for you. Because one of these days, Leonard Ranallo is going to find out he's got a broad in homicide, and he'll chew Matt Schmidt out a new asshole."

She waited.

"Homicide isn't dangerous mostly. You just go around and talk to people who tell you lies. But in this case it is dangerous, and Matt just didn't want anything to happen to you. He knew it was a good plan and a good idea. I think he was probing at it to find some flaw in it. So you wouldn't have to do it."

"He wouldn't worry about you."

"Sure he would. He's a nice guy. One of the genuine sort. He's got a nice wife and he's got a nice kid who is a nice certified public accountant and does my taxes for me for nix. Even before I came into Matt's squad. There are nice people in the world."

"How would you know?" she said smiling.

He sometimes thought her smile would make him choke or say something odd or just hurt.

"Listen, there's nobody's got an eye for nice people like a guy who ain't nice."

"So you think it's dangerous?"

"The operation? Sure, there's some danger. At the minute he makes his move—if he makes his move. On the other hand, Sid Margolies may talk like a zombie, but he's a good man.

He'll be behind you all the way. So there's risk, but what the hell. You only live once."

"So you don't care if I risk my neck?" she asked. She was still smiling and Terry Flynn felt warm, even safe, in this cocoon of an apartment on the Northwest Side with the rain beading the windowpanes.

"Sure," he said. "But you want to do it, you should get a chance."

"You sound like a women's libber."

"Fuck that shit," he said. "I hate all that talk."

"Don't you see how hard it is though?" she asked earnestly. Her voice was very husky now. She had caught a cold in the middle of the week that gave timbre to the natural depth of it. "Matt Schmidt is afraid for me because I'm a woman, not just because I'm a cop in a bad position. You see? He's a nice guy but if you were the decoy, he wouldn't have said anything. Don't you see that it's always like that, even when someone means well, they're putting you aside, on the shelf, out of the way?"

"No." Flynn looked at her. "Yes. Yeah. Sure I see it. Everyone does. But it turns out, you are a woman, you know."

"I know."

"I like you. As much as Matt Schmidt does. And I didn't stand in your way."

"No. That's why I said—"

"Don't say it again. I hate all that radical stuff. It gives me a pain in the ass."

"It's not radical," she said.

They ate the stew which was a good deal more Polish than Irish and when they had finished, they brought the bottle of wine she had bought for the meal into the living room. He sat on the couch again, and this time she sat beside him. It was still raining.

"I really like this wine. I never drink wine. Except Dago red when I go out to the West Side. What the hell is it?"

"Zinfandel. It's a kind of California wine."

"You know about wines, right?"

"A little, I think. I read a book from the library. I try out wines."

"Yeah. I happen to know all about beer." He paused like a comic. "It's wet and when you drink it, it makes you feel very good. And the next day, after you drank about fifty or sixty beers, you don't feel quite as good."

She laughed. Out loud. "You're the most natural man I've ever met."

"Yeah?" His face reddened. But not with anger. He felt warm again. "Well, all us South Side boys got that quality. When we're swinging through the trees like natural men."

"Please kiss me."

Of course, he had kissed her before. There had been that time at the party when she had been sent back to patrol. And one other time.

She led him back into the dark part of the apartment, to the bedroom. They did not turn on the lights. For a moment they lingered and kissed, and then they moved toward the bed. He was afraid of her at first, as though she were fragile.

But that didn't last.

22. SHE BECAME A REGULAR IN THE LUCKY ACES TAVERN ON IRVING PARK ROAD ON THE NORTHWEST SIDE OF THE CITY.

She stopped in four times the first week and, at Donovan's suggestion, took four days off.

They called her Karen. She said she had moved into the neighborhood a few months before and that she hardly knew anyone. She played the bowling machine with the construction worker she had met on her first visit. He had four children and showed her their pictures in his wallet.

The two fat women who had been in the bar the first day also developed personalities. They were called Alice and Lou, and they came to the bar to drink. Lou was a widow and Alice was her friend. They usuallly got their load on by 6 P.M. and staggered out of the tavern into the fading autumn twilight, holding each other's arms.

The bartender on days was Jerry. The owner was Homer, and he worked nights. He said he preferred to work nights. He would come in after five P.M. to handle whatever rush-hour after-work business there was.

Karen usually arrived at four P.M. and usually left by seven P.M. She tried to arrive before Bremenhoffer and to leave after he left.

The owner, Homer, lived in Arlington Heights and commuted in a new Buick Electra 225. One night he offered to visit Karen at home, but she declined.

It was not very long before Karen Kovac went to the Lucky Aces tavern six nights a week, and if she missed a night, they asked her the next night what had happened. Or they said they had missed her.

At first Frank Bremenhoffer came only two or three times a week. And then something seemed to impel him to come every night. When he arrived at the tavern, he drank two or three beers (as Karen related in her report) and sometimes had a single shot of brandy. Afterward he went directly home (according to Sid Margolies who followed him), and he never missed a night of work.

It was a routine assignment, deadly dull.

All these things happened every day, week after week; which is to say, nothing happened at all.

But they accumulated details. More and more.

Frank Bremenhoffer went to his doctor three times in the period of their observation. A fellow worker at Halsted Graphics said he suffered from angina pectoris or chest pains caused by heart problems. But the doctor apparently could not discover a physical cause for the pains. When the police interviewed him, he refused to tell them what was wrong with Frank Bremenhoffer.

They learned that Bremenhoffer sometimes visited Post Office News, an old magazine store on Monroe Street downtown, and bought the *Abendpost*, a German-language paper published in the city. He also picked up his copies of *Stern* there.

The details seemed to mean nothing and the days went on. All the details were recorded on sheets of report paper and filed in a gray metal cabinet in Matt Schmidt's office. Details and details and nothing happened.

Gradually the investigation team set up by the politicians became nonexistent. On October 14, Jack Donovan closed up his temporary office downtown and returned to the Criminal Courts building on the West Side.

Gratefully Mario DeVito slipped back into trial work. The people who worked in the various departments of Criminal Courts rarely mentioned the Grant Park murders or the murder of Bonni Brighton in a movie house in the Loop. Too many other crimes, current crimes, intruded on their consciousnesses.

Terry Flynn was assigned to a particularly grisly homicide on the South Side involving the deaths of three young black children found butchered in an apartment.

Flynn cleared the case in a week. They had been killed by the boyfriend of the mother. It wasn't very difficult.

Leonard Ranallo asked Matt Schmidt what he was doing besides the Grant Park case. Matt Schmidt showed him a file drawer full of new cases which had come into Area One Homicide in the past six weeks. He said he was very busy on the murder of a dentist on the twenty-third floor of a downtown medical building.

Ranallo was satisfied.

In fact, Matt Schmidt did not have the slightest idea of how to proceed in the case of the dentist. No one had seen the murder, and robbery had not been the motive.

Maurice Goldberg was transferred to Criminal Courts in September at the insistence of Jack Donovan. He began to work for Mario DeVito and wished he wasn't.

And nothing happened.

One afternoon Leonard Ranallo asked whatever had happened to Sid Margolies, and Matt Schmidt said that Sid Margolies was working on a couple of cases which kept him out of the office. One involved the murder of the dentist. And the other involved the murder of a white female.

"Not that goddamn Bonni Brighton case?" asked Ranallo.

"Yes," said Matt Schmidt.

"Okay. It's your funeral." Whatever that meant.

Each afternoon Sid Margolies parked outside the Lucky Aces tavern on Irving Park Road and watched Karen Kovac walk inside a few minutes later. And then watched—on most days—Frank Bremenhoffer come down his side street and walk across the street at the traffic light near the expressway and continue to the same tavern.

Jack Donovan continued to check each morning with two calls to his friends at police headquarters.

The first was to Matt Schmidt, because the murders were still on his mind and, technically, he was still in charge of the investigation. The order from the mayor's office had never been rescinded.

The second call was for word of his wife.

There was no information to be gathered from either daily call. Rita O'Connor Donovan had completely disappeared. As a courtesy to Donovan her picture had been reprinted on the daily bulletin distributed to the thirteen thousand men of the department each morning. Still they had not spotted her. There were so many runaways. So many people who had to escape.

Each day that passed, the tension seemed to go out of the park murders case. It was like rubber which had been stretched too far and too long; each time it was returned to its original shape, it was a little more slack. The case was slack and they all knew it.

And still, doggedly, Karen Kovac returned in the afternoons to the Lucky Ace tavern. She became a champ on the bowling machine and some of the men liked her.

When the construction worker stopped coming (he had completed his job on the Northwest Side), she became even more popular.

One afternoon Lou came into the tavern alone. Alice had fallen at home and broken her arm.

In October Terry Flynn took Karen Kovac and Timmy to a resort called the Red Lantern in Indiana, on the shore of Lake Michigan. For the sake of propriety, or to avoid making Tim uncomfortable, he took a separate bedroom. The three of them walked the cold, pounding beaches, and felt the spray from the chill lake waters. There wasn't much to do, but they seemed to have a good time. When Tim asked Terry Flynn if he was in love with his mother, Terry Flynn didn't know what to say. So he said nothing.

On October 29, two days before Halloween, it snowed for the first time in the season.

The snow began early in the morning, falling majestically in large, wet flakes which quickly covered the pavement and then the rooftops.

Traffic was treacherous. Residents in the upper apartments of the one hundred-story John Hancock Building complained that clouds obscured the street below. On the other hand, the sun was shining into their apartments. Generally people cheated of their autumn felt the snow was unfair.

Karen Kovac caught cold again, from her son, who had brought the virus home from school. She missed two days at the tavern. Timothy was supposed to have been the Great Pumpkin at the school Halloween tableau and felt keenly disappointed by his illness.

Karen watched television with him at home.

When his father came to see him on Saturday, Timothy told him about Terry Flynn.

Karen's ex-husband asked her later if she intended to get serious with this man. She said, quietly, that it was none of his business, and he left angrily two hours early.

On October 31, police in Johnson City, Tennessee, near the North Carolina border, arrested a suspect in an armed robbery of a gasoline station. A routine check revealed he was Norman Frank, wanted in Chicago, Illinois, for the murder of Albert C. (Shorty) Rogers.

Norman Frank did not fight the extradition proceedings. In fact, the Johnson City detective who turned him over to Sergeant Terrence Flynn of the Chicago police department said, "This here boy seems like he just gave up and quit on himself." Flynn noted that in his report.

They flew back to Chicago, and Norman Frank asked him if they had caught the killer of Maj Kirsten.

"We know who it is," said Terry Flynn. "We're going to get him." As it turned out, neither Flynn nor Norman Frank really believed that.

23. AN UNUSUAL THING HAPPEND ON NOVEMBER 2, NEARLY FIVE MONTHS AFTER MAJ KIRSTEN WAS MURDERED.

Frank Bremenhoffer bought Karen Kovac a drink in the Lucky Aces tavern. It was nearly 5 P.M.

The third snowfall of the season had started at noon, and by five o'clock the tavern was empty and the jukebox silent. Jerry the bartender stood at the end of the bar, near the television set, talking quietly to a liquor salesman.

"It's goddamn lousy weather," said Frank Bremenhoffer. She sat two stools away from him.

"Typical Chicago," she said. "Snow in July and one hundred degrees at Christmas. All screwed up."

"I hate it," he said. He spoke so suddenly that she did not really know what he referred to.

Frank Bremenhoffer drained his glass and looked at her. "You wanta drink?"

"Sure," she said. She finished her Scotch too quickly and it hit her. "You're Frank, right? I know nearly everyone's name and I seen you plenty of times but I never talked to you."

"Yes," he said. Very quietly. He looked at her oddly for a moment and then turned to the bartender at the end of the U-shaped bar. "Jerry." He signaled. "A drink for both of us."

Jerry came down the creaky wooden slats slowly. He poured Karen a Scotch and soda in a six-ounce glass and gave Frank Bremenhoffer a beer from the tap.

"Gimme a shooter too," said Bremenhoffer.

Jerry carefully measured a shot of Christian Brothers brandy into a shot glass. He picked up the money lying in front of Bremenhoffer on the bar and went to the cash register.

"Here's to ya," said Karen Kovac. She saluted him with her raised glass. "Good health."

"Yes." He sipped his brandy. "Do you live with your husband?"

"What kind of a question is that?"

She wore a wedding band. It was part of the story she had worked out. Actually, when she had been married to Timothy's father, she had never worn the band. He had given her a handsome ring which she still had in her jewelry box. The wedding band she wore belonged to her grandmother and was made of delicately wrought gold.

"'Live.' That's a good word," she continued. "You might say that."

"What does that mean?" asked Frank Bremenhoffer. His eyes were deep and cold despite his smile.

"It means what it means." She slurred her words. Not on purpose. "Hey. You buy a girl a drink and you wanna go home with her right away. Am I right, Frankie?"

Her voice was hoarse now from the intervening weeks of heavy drinking. And somehow she could not shake her cold.

He turned away from her.

She knew she had gone too far. She eased back; it was a delicate situation.

"Hey, come on, Frankie. I'm just kiddin'." She turned to look at her drink and picked it up and slid over one stool closer to him. "Just a joke." It was hard to say that; the words slurred again. She wondered if she were getting drunk. "Listen, Frank. I'll tell you. I gotta make a joke about it sometimes because it makes me wanna cry."

Actually Karen Kovac never cried. Except for the time when the final divorce decree came through. And when her father died a long time ago.

"Y'see, Frankie, my husband's a paraplegic. You know what that is."

Bremenhoffer turned to look at her.

"He got this muscle disease about eight years ago. Sure he still gets around. But what the hell am I supposed to do? I'm twenty-five years old. Look at me, I even look older. But I got my whole life. What do you figure I oughta do, Frank?"

He regarded her.

She rattled on. She hoped it sounded all right. "I don't mind telling you. You look like a sensitive guy, not like some of these bums. What the hell am I gonna do? I'm still a woman, you know? Don't you think so? I got my needs. I'm healthy, you know? He's just this... I don't even figure he misses it anymore, with his medication. It isn't like I was messin' around before, but you figure I ought to sit around all day and watch him work his stamp collection? Drives me crazy, that godamn stamp collection. You know he's got a part-time job still and he can drive himself around with one of those cars with handles. But what about me?"

He inspected her as though she were an insect impaled on a pin. The summer before, she remembered, Tim had bottled a lightning bug. And let it die. Frank Bremenhoffer's eyes were large now and they appeared nonjudgmental. Just curious.

She turned toward the bar and let her nyloned leg brush against his gray work pants. For a moment there was pressure and then nothing.

She leaned back on the stool and she knew her breasts strained against the material of the dress.

"Got an eyeful?"

Bremenhoffer was staring at her. He finally said, "The poor bastard."

She looked at him. "Who? You mean him? You mean my husband, my own private vegetable in a wheelchair? What about me? Don't I get a chance for someone to feel sorry for me, Frank?"

Alice and Lou entered the bar, arm in arm. Their dark coats were covered with snowflakes. Alice's arm was still in a cast, and she leaned on her friend. They wore rubber boots and appeared to be drunk.

"Oh, ho," cried Alice. "Little Miss Karen. And Frank. Hiya, Frank." The old women giggled and staggered to their customary stools on the west side of the bar, near the end. Jerry the bartender moved down to them to get them beers.

Frank Bremenhoffer drained the last of his beer.

"Let's have another, Frank," said Karen Kovac.

He got up from the stool. "That is your husband's money," he said. He pushed the stool neatly against the brass rail which encircled the bar.

"So what?" she said. "It's mine now. You wanna drink?"

"*Schwein*." He said it almost to himself.

Pig. She stared at him. She remembered the voice on the tape now, the voice recorded at the moment Bonni Brighton was killed in the movie house. The special recording laboratory could only pick out two meaningless sounds: shhhhhh. And vvvve. Not *schwein*. But she knew now it must be his voice.

He brushed past her.

"Siddown, Frank." She had the sensation of being very high in the air and of almost falling.

He buttoned his coat at the door and looked back at her.

"See ya, Frankie," she said.

His eyes were deep and full of hatred.

"Shut the door, Frank," said Lou. "It's cold. In or out."

"Yeah," said Alice. "In or out." They laughed. "Or in and out," said Lou. They laughed again.

"You wanna 'nother?" asked Jerry the bartender. He had already removed Frank Bremenhoffer's glass and shot glass.

"Sure, Jerry," she said. What did it mean, this first contact with Bremenhoffer?

Probably nothing.

She thought to call Matt Schmidt but decided against it. Why bother him? It probably didn't mean anything. They had waited so long. It would take time to lure Bremenhoffer to the bait. He had been so careful since he killed his daughter.

She got up after she finished the final Scotch and soda and buttoned her coat slowly. Then she started for the door, saying her goodnights. She felt drunk.

Tomorrow she would be off. She and Terry Flynn were going to dinner together.

She wondered about him now. He was so undemanding, so relaxed in her company. She wondered how long it would last until they would have to resolve something. She was afraid that resolution of their little happiness would have to mean it would end badly.

Karen Kovac pushed open the door of the tavern and looked down the street. As usual, Sid Margolies was parked at the curb in the brown Dodge. In a no-parking zone halfway up the block. She didn't look at him.

They had a usual route.

She would walk to Keeler Avenue on Irving Park Road and then turn south for two blocks to the apartment building managed by Art Shay. She would let herself into the vestibule, open the downstairs door with a key, and then wait in the hallway. When she heard two blasts on the auto horn from Sid Margolies, she would know it was clear again, and he would give her a ride home.

It was the same routine every night.

It would be good to be home tonight, she thought. She was tired and more than a little drunk and the cold weather depressed her.

She turned down Keeler Avenue.

She did not even look for Sid Margolies behind her. He was always there.

It was absurd.

Sid Margolies, that most careful of men, would always regret it, but it was absurd all the same. Especially because it had not been his fault.

As usual he had watched Frank Bremenhoffer leave the bar at five-fifteen P.M. He noted the time—he had two notebooks full of Frank Bremenhoffer's times in and out of the Lucky Aces tavern. Then Margolies turned on the ignition and carefully pulled into the stream of traffic on Irving Park Road.

When he was struck by a bus.

The CTA bus, which was westbound, had suddenly swerved to avoid a pedestrian darting into the street from the north side, and the bus skidded on the fresh snow in the middle of the roadway. The large green bus then plowed into the front of Sid Margolies's eastbound car just as he pulled wide into the slick street.

In a moment the auto engine was torn from its mountings by the force of the collision and hurled into the firewall, which collapsed, and on into the dashboard, while Sid Margolies strained forward to meet the engine.

Margolies's face registered surprise as his head slammed into the windshield, shattering it. The glass cracked severely and parts of it sprayed across his startled face.

As he fell back, unconscious, his hands twisted the steering wheel into an odd shape.

A few moments later the fire ambulance screamed past the Lucky Aces tavern and Jerry the bartender, who had been watching the accident from the window, looked at Lou and Alice and said, "These goddamn buses. They act like kings of the road."

Terry Flynn took the case report and returned it to the file cabinet next to Matt Schmidt's desk.

"That's it, Supremo," he said. "All the paper work on Norman Frank is now complete."

"Fine," said Matt Schmidt. "Poor little bastard."

"Yeah, that's funny," said Terry Flynn. "I feel the same way about him. I rode with him on that plane and I almost liked the little creep. Not that I want to go on a hunting trip with him, but he wasn't . . . well, that's not it either. He was a bad guy. He killed his buddy. But he wasn't a bad guy."

"The park murders have been weird," said Matt Schmidt. "We cleared one homicide accidentally, and got two other bad guys in prison for molesting kids. And found one runaway."

"A lot of good we did for that runaway," said Terry Flynn. "They put her in one of the state nuthouses so she can grow up to be a vegetable."

Schmidt couldn't disagree.

"But we got Brother Luther off the streets for at least eight years and we got Brother Seymour in so much hot water with the outfit that they'll probably give him a job licking the inside out of garbage cans when he comes out."

Schmidt smiled. "You've got a way with words, Terry."

"I know. It's my good education. Good Catholic education does it every time. I spent four years in a boys high school thinking about nothing but cunts and tits."

"Without ever seeing one."

"No, the librarian was a woman. She was about fifty and weighed three hundred pounds and she had tits like watermelons. I thought I'd go crazy thinking about her during study period."

"You've outgrown that, I hope?"

"Sure. But I still can't go in a library without getting a hard-on."

Schmidt smiled. He had decided a few weeks before that Terry Flynn would make a good detective, and when Ranallo routinely decided to move him to another area—Area Five on the Northwest Side—Schmidt blocked the transfer after a long talk with the homicide chief. He wanted to show Flynn all the things about the job he could show him.

When Terry Flynn heard about it, he smiled. "So you want to be my Chinaman, Matt?" 'Chinaman' was Chicago slang for sponsor.

"Something like that. Despite your obvious vulgarity and the fact that you still wear polyester sports coats, I think you have possibilities."

Terry Flynn looked at the clock on the wall next to the calendar from the Federation of Police.

It read five o'nine P.M.

"I'm supposed to meet Jack Donovan over at Ladner Brothers for a drink. You wanna come around? I can arrange it so they give you milk."

"No thanks. I got a little work here, and then Gert is going to make me supper early. We're going to a film festival."

"On the South Side?"

"At the university." Matt Schmidt had lived in Hyde Park for forty years; it was the home neighborhood of the University of Chicago and was a cultural island in the South Side sea.

259

"Oh. Yeah. Well, I guess I'll go."

"Terry?"

"Yeah?"

"You still seeing Karen?"

"Sure. Once in a while."

"She's a good kid," said Matt Schmidt.

"Yeah."

"I like her a lot."

"Yeah."

"I wish you'd come out to the house sometime. The both of you. For dinner."

"Sure," said Terry Flynn. "That'd be nice. But I don't think your wife likes me too much."

"Why do you say that?" Matt Schmidt was surprised.

"I don't know. When I talk to her on the phone. When I gotta call you. And the night I sent out the squad when we thought we got Bonni Brighton's killer sewed up."

Schmidt looked at the report on his desk. He looked at the word "Urgent" and then pushed the report aside with a sigh. "No, don't worry about that. That's just Gert's professional jealousy. She doesn't want me to spend too much time with cops."

Terry Flynn grinned. "Yeah. I understand. They're a bad bunch." He gave Matt a gentle slap on his back. "Okay. You ask Karen sometime."

"I just asked you. Why don't you set it up."

"Okay." He paused. "If she wants to. She's kind of funny, Matt, and I don't want to crowd her about it. Or anything. I like her the way it is. You know, she really wants to be something in the department, I think. She really wants to be a cop."

"She is a cop."

"Yeah. But you know. She ain't just serving her time." Schmidt smiled. "See you tomorrow."

"No. Sunday. I got Friday and Saturday off this week."

"And Karen?"

"She's got Friday and then three days next week."

"Okay. Say hello to Karen. Have a nice weekend."

"I will."

Dominic Lestrada pulled over to the curb on Franklin Street. It was five-fourteen P.M.

Since Jack Donovan had moved to the Northwest Side, he rarely took Dominic Lestrada's standing offer of a ride downtown. But tonight he was going to meet Terry Flynn at Ladner Brothers saloon, and after they had finished a few drinks, they were going on the town together.

Kathleen had suggested it to him.

"You come home every night and you don't have to," she had told him.

"I want to," he said.

"No," she said. "A man needs some time off with his friends. Why don't you go out one night."

He had said he did not need any time off from her and then he had asked Kathleen where she had picked up her sociology.

"It's not sociology. It's psychology. And we study that now," she said in a very grown-up voice. Kathleen continued to astonish him. She managed the house now with a grown-up dexterity. She even did the shopping and, on some nights, relieved the housekeeper of the chore of the evening meal.

When he had mentioned her startling suggestion to Terry Flynn one afternoon early in the week, he had said, "Yeah. Kid's right. Take time off. If you don't have any friends any more on the West Side, I'll take you out and get you loaded."

He agreed. Mario DeVito had also been invited but begged off at the last minute.

Jack was looking forward to it.

It was not snowing in the Loop and he walked the wet, rain-swept street a block down Madison to Ladner Brothers old saloon in the shadow of the El tracks. He pushed his way in and found a place at the bar.

It was five-nineteen P.M.

"Vodka and tonic," he said. "No lime."

At five twenty-one P.M. the telephone rang on Matt Schmidt's desk. He picked up the receiver.

"Hiya, Matt?"

261

"Yeah."

"This is Haggerty over by Area Five."

"Hiya, Jim," said Matt Schmidt.

"I got some bad news for you."

He waited. His hand was on the desk, flat on the report he had set aside.

"Your man Margolies was in an accident with a bus."

"What time?"

"About eight minutes ago. We got it so fast because the fireman on the scene knew it was an unmarked car, and he pulled Margolies out. Sid said something about homicide and he called us right away."

"How's Sid?"

"Oh, I don't know. Fucked up, I guess."

"What about Karen Kovac?"

"Who the hell is that?"

"Where did they take Sid?"

"Swedish Covenant—"

"Listen, Jim, Sid was on a tail for us. We had a woman working the Lucky Aces tavern. A policewoman named Karen Kovac. Can you get someone over there to see if she's in the place?"

"What if she is?"

Yes, he thought. What then?

"Nothing. Just go out. See if you can get one of the district men in there fast. Just in and out. Look for a blond, blue eyes, short haircut. I can't believe there will be two in there."

"A looker, huh?"

"Yes," said Matt Schmidt.

"And what if she ain't?"

"In there? Go to 3787 North Keeler Avenue. That's a three-story apartment building. If she's not in the tavern, she'll be waiting in the vestibule of the building. Just have your man signal her by honking on his auto horn twice. She'll come out, and then you can tell her what happened to Sid."

"Okay."

"Listen. I'd appreciate it if you handle the second part with one of your guys. Just tell the district man to take a look around the tavern and walk out and call you. But tell him not to blow the operation. That's why I want you to handle the second part. In case. I don't want it all over the district that we're running an operation there. Word gets around."

"Yeah, Matt. Don't worry. I'll take care of it."

"I know. I'm coming up there now. Myself."

"Sure, Matt."

They broke the connection simultaneously.

Frank Bremenhoffer watched Karen Kovac leave the tavern at five-fifteen P.M. He stood in the window of Alger's Drugstore on the corner away from the tavern.

He felt in the jacket of his coat for the knife. The blade felt flat and wide in the pocket. He placed his thumb against its razor edge.

Pain encircled his chest again. He found it difficult to breathe. He waited at the telephone booth next to the window and watched Karen Kovac look to her left and then start down the street in the opposite direction. She turned the corner at Keeler.

"Can I use the phone or what?"

It was a kid with a stocking cap. He couldn't guess if it was a boy or a girl. The kid had long hair and a thin, pale face. There were traces of snowflakes on the stocking cap.

"Sure," said Frank Bremenhoffer. He smiled. "I was leaving anyway."

He opened the door of the drugstore and looked down the street, in the direction Karen Kovac had glanced. He saw a large car pull out from the curb and watched the CTA bus collide with it in the middle of the street. The crash startled everyone for a moment; even the kid who had asked to use the telephone ran out the door. "Jesus, someone's been killed I bet."

Bremenhoffer shrugged and started away.

Toward Keeler Avenue.

He saw her in the ghostly light of the lamppost scarcely two hundred feet ahead. In the soft snow his footsteps scarcely made a sound.

She was a whore, he had decided.

Donovan pushed his way out the door of Ladner's just as Terry Flynn pulled the car up on the corner of Wells Street. "Get in," said Donovan, and Terry slid back into the driver's side. He leaned over and opened the lock for Donovan. The car was dirty and old and wrappings of fast-food sandwiches littered the floor.

"Matt Schmidt just called over to the tavern," Donovan said. His face was white. "Sid Margolies got hit by a bus."

"Jesus Christ. Is he dead?"

"No one knows. But Matt got the word and they're looking for Karen."

"Oh." He seemed very calm. "I don't suppose anything will happen tonight."

Donovan stared at him. "But what if it does."

"When did this happen?"

"Twenty minutes ago."

"And Karen left the tavern?"

Donovan shrugged.

"It's rush hour. It'll take us a half hour to get up there."

Donovan said, "Fuck the car. We'll grab the El. Go over to Dearborn. If we're lucky, we can be there in twenty minutes."

Flynn gunned the car into life and backed wildly away from the curb. He turned on the hazardous flashers and began hitting his horn. He swung wide into Wells Street, shot down an alley, and turned into Monroe Street a moment later. In two minutes he had pulled up at the Milwaukee Avenue—Kennedy Line subway station on Dearborn Street. They fell out of the car and ran down the steps.

As luck would have it, they caught the train just pulling into the station.

It was five thirty-one P.M.

24. KAREN KOVAC SAW THE APARTMENT BUILDING JUST AHEAD, THROUGH THE THICK CURTAIN OF FAT SNOW-flakes falling rapidly on the side street. She had done this nearly every working night for six weeks now; it was almost like coming home.

Just like coming home, she thought and smiled to herself. Coming home drunk. She fumbled in her purse for the key to the downstairs door. Her head felt thick, and the afternoon Scotches had dulled her perception. Drinking on duty, she thought. They'll court martial me. She couldn't find the key.

She staggered across the cross street.

Sid will be scandalized, she thought. Drunk again. She giggled to herself.

Then she had the key in her hand. And dropped it into the snow.

She did not see him.

It was five thirty-one P.M.

Her throat. She felt a tearing at her throat.

She staggered in the snow. Then she felt the hand on her

neck. She was being pulled back, down, into the snow.

She kicked out her right leg and struck the leg of her attacker. But she fell anyway, tumbling helplessly into the wall of the gangway between two apartment buildings.

There was a snap, like the sound of a twig breaking. And then the incredible white streak of pain blinded her for a moment as she tumbled down three steps into the deep gangway.

I've broken my arm, she thought calmly, and then was nearly overcome with a wave of nausea.

There was warmth on her cheek.

It was her own blood.

He pushed her back then and she turned and fell onto the damp concrete. The snow eddied into the well between the two buildings. She threw up suddenly and violently onto her arm and at the same time, through some instinct, she pushed against him with the soles of her shoes. One shoe struck him in the groin.

"*Schwein!*"

He cried a deeply rumbling curse and seemed to explode backward into the steps and the snow bunching at the top of the steps.

Gone. The pressure was gone. She felt warm. She could sleep.

She kicked again, ripping her nyloned legs against the rough pebbles imbedded into the gangway sidewalk. She twisted to one side and began to crawl away. This was madness. She could only crawl and he was behind her and he could—

Her useless left arm brushed against the pebble-grained walls of the gangway and she screamed hideously in fright and pain.

She tried to turn to face him. The gangway was so narrow. She could not see him any more in the swirling snow. And then she saw his grayness coming out of the snowstorm. He was speaking to her in angry, methodical, vile words.

Karen turned again in the narrow trap of the gangway and pushed herself backward into the darkness. But Frank Bremenhoffer was coming for her, limping, deliberate, his arm raised.

"Whore," he said.

She saw the knife then. In the lamp from the street. The blade glittered along its ten-inch length. She thought she could see his eyes clearly through the haze of the stinging pellets of snow that blew into the gangway as though they were lost.

His eyes were cold and drowning.

She kicked him in the leg.

It would be easier to fall back, she thought. She was so tired. She wondered if death came like this, as tiredness. He was speaking again, but he was far away.

It didn't matter.

He kicked her very hard in the right leg and then again, inside her leg, in the thick part of her thigh. Her skirt was torn and the pain sickened her. She wanted to retch, but she had nothing more. She smelled her own vomit on her coat.

Then she saw her purse on the wet concrete floor of the gangway. It was open. She remembered now. She had opened it to remove the keys. Where was Sid Margolies?

"Spread your legs, you whore," he said. He knelt down on the pavement. He reached for her leg and held the knife in the other hand.

"Tell me, whore, how much—"

She couldn't hear him. She reached out her right arm for the pistol. He was over her. She felt his legs crowd between her legs.

Poor Tim, she thought. No mother, no father. Well, his father would be there, she supposed. And no more visits from Terry Flynn. Was that bad? Sid Margolies was sitting in the car, and they would never accept her into homicide.

No, she thought.

The pistol was in her purse and the purse was open but it was two feet beyond her grasp, and she would be dead in a moment. This is the way it was for all of them, she thought. Maj Kirsten. And Christina Kalinski. And Bonni. And now poor Karen Kovac.

She hit him again, above his penis, in the bladder. The blow was not delivered with much power because he was between her legs, on his knees, and she could not get leverage.

He cried out and the knife fell, ripping into the fabric of her coat. She felt warmth again, on her arm. Had he stabbed her?

She struggled to remain sitting. She hit him again, in his throat.

He grunted and fell back just for a moment.

She rolled onto the gangway floor and reached for her purse.

She felt the pistol. Pushed at the safety with frozen, frightened fingers.

"You whore." He struck her in the mouth with his hand. Once and again. Her vision blacked out for a moment. Blood oozed from between her lips.

He raised the knife above him.

She looked at him, over her, blotting out the snow and the light, all the grayness looming over her vision.

The sound of the shot in the narrow gangway between the two buildings deafened them both for an instant.

The .25-caliber bullet exploded upward from the short barrel of the pistol and entered the underside of his jaw, hurling up into the softness of his mouth, splitting his tongue. Then the bullet exploded off a perfectly formed upper back molar. A chip from the bullet drove up through the palate into the bottom of the brain. The rest of the bullet angled sharply off the molar through the soft tissues in the nasal cavity and out the right eye.

Frank Bremenhoffer's eyes were wide open, surprised.

He seemed to rise for a second, as though to reposition himself over the woman on the floor of the gangway. He scraped his hand against the pebbled wall as he rose. He held the knife tightly. After a moment he ceased his upward rise and fell forward.

She opened her eyes, and he was still beside her. But someone had thrown a piece of cloth over his face. There was blood on the white cloth.

Who was talking to her? She tried to move, but someone held her.

She opened her eyes.

It was Jack Donovan. And Terry Flynn held her. She stared at Jack Donovan's white face. She thought she heard his voice. Terry was brushing at her face, keeping the snow away.

"I killed him," she said flatly. She thought her own voice sounded odd.

"Yes," said Terry Flynn.

"Where's Sid?"

"He was hit by a bus. Don't talk, Karen. We're waiting for the firemen."

"He wanted to kill me," she said. She was crying but there were no tears in her eyes.

"Don't worry. He's dead."

"I killed him."

"Easy, Karen, honey," said Terry Flynn. He looked as though he would cry. His face was white.

"My arm hurts. He hit me."

She felt so cold. And wet. The snow was lighted by the orange streetlamps. There were people crowding around the gangway entrance. She heard sirens.

"My God, my God," she said. "I didn't know I would shoot him. I'm so sorry. I'm so sorry." Now there were tears. "I didn't know."

"You did all right," said Terry Flynn.

"He's dead," she said.

"It's over," said Flynn. "Over, Karen."

"No, no, no," she said. Her voice was weak. "He hit me. He hit me. He broke my arm. Is my arm broken? Oh, I got the gun. I kicked him and I got the gun and I shot him and I thought he was going to kill me with the knife. Oh, God, I really hurt, oh God. I killed him."

Jack Donovan looked at Karen's face. It was very pale, and he thought she was in shock. The blood from her mouth had dried on her chin. There was vomit on her coat and now it was on his and Terry's coats as well.

"Take it easy," he said. He realized then that he was always trying to comfort someone and that it never worked.

"I want to go home."

"It's all right, Karen," said Terry Flynn. "Honey. Honey." He repeated it like an incantation.

Please, she thought. Tell them I'm sorry. And then she closed her eyes.

The firemen crowded down into the narrow gangway behind Jack Donovan. It was firemen who came to the scene because in Chicago, firemen handle the living; police, the dead.

He heard them but he could not see them. "She broke her arm," he said. "I think she's gone into shock."

"Just get outta the way, buddy. We'll take care of her." Jack thought the fireman had a gentle voice. "Just put her down, buddy," the fireman said to Terry Flynn. He looked up at him as though he didn't understand.

Jack Donovan stood up. "Put her head down," said Jack. Terry did as he was told. He stood up and moved back, further into the gangway.

She was stretched out beside the body of Frank Bremenhoffer.

The firemen were quick. They maneuvered the stretcher between the two forms and bent down and picked up Karen Kovac as though she were as light as a child. They put her on the wooden-framed stretcher and threw a blanket over her.

"There's two dead people," a woman on the sidewalk cried. She was answered by a wave from a neighbor across the quiet street. The squares of windows on the block were all lighted. The white-and-red fire department ambulance lights whirled lazily and menacingly, mingling in the shadows of night with the blue circling Mars lights on the squad cars.

They carried her into the ambulance.

Two policemen moved down the gangway steps and threw down a rubber body bag next to the corpse of Frank Bremenhoffer.

Terry Flynn followed her to the door of the ambulance where Matt Schmidt stood with the watch sergeant from Area Five Homicide in which the death had occurred. Almost shyly Schmidt came to look at her. She opened her eyes.

"Everything is all right," he said. "You did fine, Karen. Better than fine."

"But Sid."

"Sid is okay. He has some broken ribs and a concussion. He can sue the CTA and become a rich man."

The firemen slid her into the ambulance.

Terry Flynn impulsively climbed into the ambulance beside her.

"I'm so sorry," she told him.

He nodded. "I know." He took her hand. "Don't worry any more."

The ambulance began to crawl away.
Schmidt looked at Donovan. "If Karen had been killed—"
Jack Donovan shrugged.
Neither of them said it again.

25. NINE DAYS AFTER THE DEATH OF FRANK BREMENHOFFER IN A GANGWAY ON THE NORTHWEST SIDE, THE COOK County coroners jury returned a routine verdict of justifiable homicide.

Ulla Bremenhoffer had told police that she had witnessed her husband burning bits of clothing in the old incinerator in the back of the building one afternoon. She had never questioned him about it. Police concluded that her report cleared the mystery of what happened to Christina Kalinski's clothing.

A day later they at last understood about Christina Kalinski.

The man's name was Ivan Yurokovich. He was a short man with a bald head and the circles around his eyes suggested he had not been sleeping well.

Outside, November assaulted the windows of Area One Homicide. The temperature was twenty-five degrees and it had snowed again during the night. The city was covered by dirty, piled-up snow, and the streets were breaking up under their burden of ice and rock salt.

When Ivan Yurokovich entered the office, only Terrence Flynn was available to talk to him.

It was not the first time he had spoken with police. Two months before, an investigator from general assignment briefly assigned to the Kalinski investigation had interrogated him, but he had asked Ivan Yurokovich all the wrong questions.

"Siddown," said Flynn. He felt friendly. It was Wednesday and he would be off for three days after five P.M.

Karen Kovac was at home, recuperating, and he had promised to take her and Tim to dinner on the West Side. To a restaurant he knew that was owned secretly by another policeman and a former lawyer.

"I see this in papers. This man Frank Bremenhoffer. You kill him. It was good. He was bad man."

"You bet," said Terry Flynn. "We always get the bad guys."

"You say he kill Christina."

"Who?"

"Christina. You say he kill Christina."

"Yeah. Christina Kalinski. Sure."

"Are you sure?"

"Fuck yes. You think the cops would kill someone unless he was a bad guy?"

"Then I was bad man too."

Flynn did not speak.

"You know this man Michael Kalinski."

"Yeah," said Flynn. "Christina's father."

"He is my friend. I do bad thing to him."

"Why?"

"I kill his daughter."

Flynn sucked his cigarette and didn't make any further move. Yurokovich had his head bent down. The bare light in the room illuminated his scalp. When he looked up again, there were tears in his eyes.

"Michael Kalinski and me, we are friends. I go with him to Susy-Q place. We find Christina. She is doing bad things. Her father yell, but she no come home with her father. I feel for him. Michael is old country like me."

Flynn nodded.

"I am just janitor. You know. Downtown. Some days, you know, I go to have beer in morning down to this place."

"Yeah."

"Some day, I talk in tavern. This place, workers go. I see janitors there like me, other men. Also printer man. We talk. I tell him about this woman. 'Christina bad girl,' I tell him. This man is Mr. Bremenhoffer, German man. I tell him about Christina. Now I see he kill Christina."

So Karen had been right. And they had missed him. They had questioned all those people and they had missed this man who put Bremenhoffer onto Christina Kalinski.

"He kill girl because I tell him. Is that right?"

Flynn shrugged.

"No. Probably not. Just let me type up a statement and you sign it, okay?"

"But I am guilty."

Flynn looked at him, at the tears at the corner of the old eyes.

"No." He pulled a piece of paper into the typewriter. "Not really." He began to write the man's name.